Show Stopper

Also by Mary Monica Pulver

Ashes to Ashes
Murder at the War
The Unforgiving Minutes
Original Sin

Show Stopper

Mary Monica Pulver

Walker and Company
New York

For you, Mom

Copyright © 1992 by Mary Monica Pulver

All rights reserved. No part of this book may be reproduced or
transmitted in any form or by any means, electronic or mechanical,
including photocopying, recording, or by any information storage and
retrieval system, without permission in writing from the Publisher.

All the characters and events portrayed in this work are fictitious.

First published in the United States of America in 1992
by Walker Publishing Company, Inc.

Published simultaneously in Canada by Thomas Allen & Son
Canada, Limited, Markham, Ontario

Library of Congress Cataloging-in-Publication Data
Pulver, Mary Monica.
Show stopper / Mary Monica Pulver.
p.   cm.
ISBN 0-8027-3210-0
I. Title.
PS3566.U47S55   1992
813'.54—dc20   91-40397
CIP

Printed in the United States of America
2 4 6 8 10 9 7 5 3 1

▽

Acknowledgments

A lot of people, some unknowingly, helped me with this book. Of the ones who did it on purpose, I especially would like to thank Investigator Stephany Good of the Minnesota Bureau of Criminal Investigation for answering questions and reading the original manuscript for procedural errors. For training techniques and other good hints, I thank both Anne Fitches of Seranna Farm. Several people in the Hennepin County Medical Examiner's Office have on more than this occasion helped me with critical details. Kurt Jordi, my erstwhile dressage instructor, was very patient with me. Mention would also be made of someone in the Arabian horse show business, but she asked me not to, on the grounds that she was a little too frank and is in enough trouble as it is.

▽

1

Kori's lips were pursed; she was whistling Bach's "Little" fugue, but so softly it could not be heard over the pickup's monstrous engine. She was a slender woman with long hair pinned up in old-fashioned braids, a pale complexion, and steady gray eyes; at twenty-six not as beautiful as she would be at thirty-five. She was wearing jeans, a dark red turtleneck sweater, and a heavy sheepskin jacket. Her hair was frizzy-curly, so dark it looked black in any but the strongest sunlight, of which there was none right now; and even this close to the start of her day it was working its way out of its braids.

She cast a little glance into the side mirrors. Was the Bronco still behind them? She moved the steering wheel just a little to the right, glanced in the mirror, and way, way back, behind the horse trailer, caught a glimpse of familiar head-lights. Very good.

She heard a scattered thump of raindrops on the truck's roof, and then there were eggwhite spots on the windshield. The pavement was shiny from a previous shower. The rain was seldom heavy, but never quite over. It had come mixed with a thin fog that frustrated any hope of hurry. The wipers

1

leaped up and settled back on intermittent, and Kori pressed the accelerator down just a little. They were half an hour behind schedule.

There was a dazzle of oncoming headlights, then the bellow of a truck and semitrailer churning up a hurricane in the other lane. Its passing was felt down the length of the six-horse trailer, an unwelcome complication even with the heavy engine. But then the soft, weighty sway faded and her hands loosened their grip on the steering wheel. She hadn't met many of the behemoths, but they made for a scary meeting, with only a broken yellow line between them and her. She consulted her watch: almost eight o'clock.

They were nearly half an hour behind schedule. Worse, this was a revised schedule; they had planned on arriving at the show site yesterday afternoon, giving them ample time to set up and get Blue Wind ready for the dressage competition this morning. But the day before yesterday the farrier had called to say he'd been in a car accident, nothing too serious, but he was laid up for at least a week. Three of the horses going to the show were scheduled to be reshod, and it took five phone calls to find another farrier who could fit them into his schedule—late yesterday. And so time that should have been spent on the road was spent waiting. The substitute farrier called twice to say he was running late, and finally showed up at 11:00 P.M. to wake them from their doze in the barn office. It had been well after 2:00 A.M. before he finished.

Her thoughts went to the five horses in the trailer. Copper Wind, her stallion, was an experienced traveler, as were the three mares; no doubt they were standing well braced, aware that the noise and bouncing were not life-threatening and would end. Coppy would even be pleased to be on the road; for all he was a gentle soul at home, he loved the excitement and applause of a horse show.

Lazy, clever Storm Wind would be hoping the door latch on her box stall at the show was one she could unfasten, so she could get out and go find a meadow with a mud hole in it, perfect for alternately snacking and rolling—Kori sometimes thought Stormy was as much pig as horse. Except that she was also dainty and exquisitely pretty as only the Arabian can be.

Hurricane's name described her: large (too large, thought Kori, who refused to breed her), energetic, and determined. She also was beautiful, but performed unevenly at halter, sometimes "setting up"— going into the official pose—almost without guidance, and other times discovering someone in the crowd or another horse so interesting she would ignore her trainer's cues. Last year she had gotten a fourth, a sixth, a championship, and no ribbon at all.

Even more of an unknown quantity was the yearling, Leaves You Breathless. Kori didn't like bringing babies to shows; too often they reacted poorly to the stress of travel, to the strange smells and unfamiliar box stalls. But not only was Breathless particularly lovely and elegant, she had seemed from birth to consider everything a well-meaning attempt to amuse her.

The road abruptly widened into four lanes; they were coming into a town. Cars appeared as if from nowhere, most headed the same way she was; a few passed them with a high spray of road water. She lifted her foot a little from the accelerator as the traffic suddenly thickened, a small town's version of rush hour. Whether they'd arrive in time for that first competition was going to be a close call.

Red taillights glowed ahead; she downshifted, slowing. In an effort at patience, she sent her thoughts drifting again to the yearling riding in the trailer.

Leaves You Breathless had been named at birth, when her character and beauty were scarcely promises, but it was as if she had learned the name's meaning early on and done her best to live up to it. Kori was almost afraid to show her, afraid that the beauty was an illusion that would vanish under the cruel gaze of a show judge.

Or that the filly would hate the stress of being shown and come home with her sweet disposition soured forever.

Or catch some disease from another horse at the show and, after prolonged, painful, and expensive treatment, die.

Snap out of it, my girl, thought Kori. This morbidity is not because you are afraid for the filly, it's because you are entered in the dressage competition. If she had only to arrive, unpack, set up, and prepare to show at halter and in Country English Pleasure, as usual, she wouldn't be fretting like this.

She shifted into first, pulled forward, stopped again. It started when she was at an all-breed show in Chicago two years ago. Someone had given her a ticket as a gift, then turned up and insisted she come along to the Dressage-to-Music event. Kori had grown up on horseback and thought she was pretty good at it, but dressage was a revelation. The riders were young, some of them barely in their teens, but they addressed their horses in a subtle, almost invisible way. And their horses moved differently, using their haunches for impulsion, and reaching so far forward in the extended trots that they seemed to float over the ground. The horses angled cross-legged across the arena, made small circles to show how flexible their necks and spines were, stopped, backed, and changed leads during tiny, collected canters, sometimes so frequently they looked as if they were skipping. And during the whole demonstration, the riders appeared to sit perfectly still, erect and calm, no heels poking flanks, no visible rein pulling. It was incredible, fascinating.

Then a month later that same friend remarked that it was peculiar that someone who was as good a rider as Kori was, with a horse as obviously talented as Blue Wind was, wasn't competing in something more advanced than English Country Pleasure classes—and did Kori know there was a very talented dressage instructor in her neighborhood?

Kori took the hint and signed up for an evaluation. A week later a car drove up to Tretower and from it emerged a Prussian, complete with accent.

He watched her ride Blue Wind in her indoor arena for half an hour, then conceded that she wasn't so bad. It did appear, however, that she didn't know how to sit on a horse, nor did she use her legs properly, or realize that the reason she had a tailbone was to address her horse with it through the saddle. She had signed up for lessons at once, ashamed of her many failures.

Then began a song with endless verses. One verse went, "No, no!"—all the verses began No, no!—"You go from a rising trot to a sitting trot just three steps before a halt. Not two, not four. Now, so, tilt the pelvis"—this always demonstrated with a graphic pelvic thrust—"squeeze with the thighs, drop the hands, and she will halt. Again please."

This was generally followed by the verse, "No, no! Do it again; she must stop with all four feet right under her. And always, keep eyes forward, elbows bent, heels down. And sit up straight; you look like a dying flower."

The song always ended, "As much as you practice, as better you get," which he said at the end of every lesson.

So she would go home and much practice. The exercises to deepen her seat left her sore, the long hours made her dependent on Danny for the training of the other horses, and she had less time to spend with her son, who at twenty-one months was turning into a strong-willed charmer.

But Blue Wind became ever more of a joy to ride, soft in the mouth, flexible, generous, athletic. And her ability to master the combinations of foot positions, leg pressures, shifts of posture in the saddle, and subtle rein signals seemed bottomless.

Kori was brought back to the present as the car ahead of her stopped abruptly. She braked, frowning. Had she remembered to pack her hairnet? Her new gloves? Yes and yes. The smile bloomed again. Dressage competition had her scared, but she would use what they had learned in dressage in the Country English Pleasure class, and there Kori was sure she and Blue would finish in the ribbons.

But first they had to arrive at the fairgrounds.

She glanced over at the young man crumpled against the passenger door, fast asleep. Danny could sleep anywhere, through anything. She had volunteered to make this morning drive; he was not a morning person and had a hard day ahead of him. Not that she didn't as well, but she was a lark, the unfortunate sort of person who could not sleep in, particularly when there was important business at hand.

The traffic crawled forward, and the headlights picked up a sign: Lafite, Pop. 73,650. Kori began looking for another sign. A quarter mile later, there it was: Fairgrounds. An arrow pointed right. Kori, signaling, pulled into the right turn lane, then swung the truck and its trailer onto a narrow road, careful not to cut the corner, because the trailer followed its nose in a straight line and would fall into the ditch if she did.

"Danny."

"Hm?"

"Danny, wake up, we're here."

"Um. What timezit?"

"Twenty after eight. We've got fifty minutes until I'm due in the arena with Blue Wind."

Danny pushed himself upright, groaning, then yawned prodigiously, stretching until he realized he was about to thrust a fist into the face of his boss. "Ah. So this is it, huh?" He peered through the windshield. "Shit, what is that?"

"Fog mixed with rain. It rained most of the way, or we'd have been here forty minutes ago."

"And you drove the whole way? Why didn't you wake me up? Is Brit still with us?"

Kori checked the mirror again. "Yes. And I'm fine."

"Well, still—fifty minutes? Good thing Brit's got show experience."

"We need more than experience, we need jet-propelled skill. I hope she's got that, too. Get the map out."

Brit was new, a temporary groom hired just for this show. Tretower's groom had left to have a baby, and might not be back, so Kori had Brit come to Tretower a week ago, both to find out how good she was and to let the horses get used to her.

Danny punched open the glove box, took out a thrice-folded sheet of paper, and smoothed it flat on the dash. He was the Tretower horse trainer, a thin man of twenty-three with straight mud-brown hair and narrow eyes. He was wearing a thick brown sweater strewn with hay stems, a consequence of loading the empty space in the trailer with hay. He reached up and turned on a map light.

On one side of the paper was a simplified map of the fairgrounds, with the horse barn circled in red. It was located diagonally from a big rectangle marked Arena. The map was standard issue; other barns, uncircled, were labeled Sheep, Swine, and Fowl; and there were areas marked Midway, Racetrack, Office, Concessions.

"What street are we on?"

"Illinois Avenue."

Danny located it on the map, then peered ahead into the wet murk. "Turn left on Livestock Lane, which will run us right by the horse barn."

He turned the paper over. On its reverse was a line drawing labeled Horse Barn. The barn was a long rectangle cut into sixths by five aisles and thirds lengthwise by two aisles. The main entrance was at the east end of the center aisle, a very broad affair, though there were doors on all four sides of the barn. The box stalls were in sets of eight, four each back to back. Inside the main entrance, a row of four had been set aside as the show office, and other sets of two had become wash stations, straw storage, and rest rooms.

Two facing sections of four stalls were circled in green and marked Tretower.

"The southeast and southwest doors are equally close to our stalls," said Danny. "But there's a sharp curve in the middle of that alley on that side, so let's just go in the main door on the east side." He left the sheet and checked the forms stapled to it, their confirmation of entry and receipt for fees paid. "Where's our papers?" he asked, meaning the entry forms, horse registration, membership cards, and veterinary certificates necessary to make them official entrants in the show.

"Big brown envelope behind your seat." Danny squirmed

around and found it. "You go straight in and get us registered and come right to us with Blue's number," Kori said. "Let's see . . ." She slowed, ducking to look for a street sign, couldn't find it but saw instead a small white board with hand lettering and an arrow pointing right: Lafite All-Arab Horse Show. "Here we are." She did a hand-over-hand turn, engine whining, checking her mirrors to ensure the heavy trailer wasn't going to climb the corner and crush the fireplug that also marked the corner. The new road was curbed like a street, and in the next block there was even a crumbling blacktop sidewalk, lined with hot dog emporiums, cotton candy stands, Fresh Lemonade Fresh kiosks, all boarded up and sad-faced in the rain, some in need of paint. The fair wasn't until July; meanwhile the county earned fix-up money by renting to horse shows, antique fairs, classic car conventions, traveling rodeos, even big family reunions.

Kori rolled her window down a little to test the air. A chill, moisture-laden breeze immediately flowed in across her hands and face. "Blue won't like this," she said. "And I won't have time to warm her up. Darn, we're going to make a real mess of this."

"Aw, it's only Training Level; they can't expect much, can they?"

Kori made a wry face. "With Loretta judging? She'll expect perfection at the least. I hope there isn't a line at check-in."

"Shouldn't be; the only thing going on today is dressage and we're cutting it so close, everyone else riding in it should be already here. You want me to come and clap?"

"You don't clap at dressage; the audience sits in ghastly silence. Anyway, you'll be busy unloading and getting set up."

Kori caught a whiff of horse mixed with the odor of fresh-baked sweet rolls. Fresh-baked anything was Kori's weakness; ordinarily her stomach would have spoken up to remind her she had sent down only half a hasty muffin so far today, and that was some hours ago. But the dressage competition to come overawed her stomach, pulling it into a silent knot. She checked her watch; Blue Wind liked at least fifteen minutes of warm-up before she performed, and she wasn't going to get it; they were going to be lucky to make it to the arena on time. Perhaps Kori should scratch her entry and try again when she was better organized?

But Loretta only rarely condescended to judge Training Level performances; even if Kori did poorly, Loretta's comments on the marking sheet might prove very helpful. Besides, Kori didn't like backing out just because she wouldn't be at her best.

The street opened to four lanes, but was mostly blocked at that point by sawhorses with signs on them: Lafite County/All-Arabian Horse Show/Competitors Only. Beyond the sawhorses were the big cement-block show arena and the livestock barns, low and white, with red roofs. She maneuvered the truck and its trailer around the blockade, and stopped halfway along the white barn marked Horses. She was still reaching to shut the engine off when Danny opened the door on his side and popped out, envelope in hand.

She set the brake and spent a few seconds being grateful for having arrived safely and shifting mental gears from truck driver to horseback rider. Right, she thought, and bailed out on her side.

$\bigtriangledown$

2

IT WAS SURPRISINGLY CHILLY for so late in April, and the thin mizzle blowing in the piercing breeze didn't help. Kori went to the rear of the pickup and, standing on the broad bumper, pulled the blue plastic tarp off the gear, then reached into the bin and grasped the thick leather handle of a gray plywood chest.

Suddenly the truck dipped a little and a tall, muscular young woman in jeans and windbreaker was standing on the bumper beside her. Brit, wearing that silly baseball cap with the clapping hands on it. She reached for the handle and asked in a voice oddly gentle for her size, "Your costume and Blue's tack in here?"

"Yes."

"It's heavy; how about I take it and you get the horse?"

"Right." Kori jumped down, hurried along the long maroon trailer, and wrenched the back doors open. The warm scent of horses enveloped her, and she heard them shifting up the double row, anxious to be unloaded. From up front she could hear the high-pitched call of the yearling.

Brit, struggling to get the chest out of the truck, immediately responded, "In a minute, Breathless. Well, maybe a couple of minutes." Brit had a special fondness for the yearling.

Kori backed Blue expertly out of the trailer into the street. The mare, muffled to the jaw in her long quilted blanket, looked all body; her lower legs, what could be seen of them, were thick with leg wraps. Her blanket was a dull green with three chesslike towers outlined in maroon on is rump, the emblem of Tretower Farm.

"Um, hey! Where are we in the barn?" called Brit. She was standing in the big open doorway, the chest braced against her denimed thigh, blushing at her need to shout. For a big, strong, capable girl, Brit had a surprisingly diffident manner.

"South end, middle section, Aisle B, both sides!"

Kori tied Blue to the back of the trailer and went in to check on the rest of the horses. They had come through the journey with no obvious problems, so she came out, untied the mare, who was ducking her head to stretch a kink out of her neck, and led her across the sidewalk into the barn. She counted down the rows, found their place, and saw Brit had already pulled items out of the gray chest: tall black boots, white stretch pants, white blouse with choker collar. She was hanging a black riding jacket, still in its dry-cleaning plastic, on the heavy metal mesh that marked the top half of one of the stalls.

"How's the baby?" asked Brit.

"Fine." Kori tied Blue Wind to a stall across from Brit, unbuckled the mare's blanket, and pulled it off. Blue was not, in fact, blue, but white, with a silver rump and black hairs in her mane, tail, and around her eyes. Because of the blanket, her coat was smooth and shiny and would not need to be brushed.

Kori undid the wrapping on Blue's tail, went to the chest, handed out her black saddle blanket and her beautiful new Ainsley dressage saddle to Brit, then reached for the wooden carpenter's tool carrier. Instead of nails and hammers, it carried brushes, a sponge, cloths, baby oil, baby powder, sheen spray, curry comb, a package of tiny rubber bands, and other necessary items for fancying up a horse before it was taken into the ring.

Whenever anyone thought to object to all the artificiality, he or she was told that to bring a horse into the ring with no effort to pretty it up was to insult the judge. Kori did not often say what she thought—that to assume a horse "blooming" with baby powder and shiny with Vaseline was prettier than a horse in its natural state insulted the horse. Still, she took the carrier over to the mare, squatted beside a foreleg, and dug out the bottle of hoof black. A potent-smelling liquid, it was applied with a fuzzy dauber. Its purpose was to turn the mare's dark and somewhat streaky hooves a uniform shiny black. Since she was in a hurry, Kori applied generously, and the excess ran up the dauber onto her fingers, and down the hoof onto the floor, leaving a new U-shaped mark among the countless others already there. She duck-walked around to the other front hoof. Blue bent her head as far as the tie would allow and watched, but this was a familiar experience, so she was only mildly curious.

Finishing the fourth hoof, Kori straightened to find Brit already tightening the cinch. "You better go change," she said. "I can braid the mane. You want all little ones on top or a French along the side?"

"French, it's faster. Thanks."

Kori took the clothing, checked the jacket pocket for the de rigueur gold pin, then hurried off to the ladies' room to change.

By the time she got back, Brit was nearly finished with Blue's mane. A French braid is supposed to be a quick way to turn a horse's mane into a neat, decorative line along the crest. Despite her best efforts, the braid had grown from immediately below the crest at the top to about three inches long near the bottom. But Kori had never been able to do even that well, and Brit's product was otherwise neat. As Kori watched she was carefully weaving the long end back into the braid so it didn't need a rubber band to hold it in place.

Danny walked up with five white cardboard squares numbered 21 through 25 in fat black numerals. "Blue is twenty-three," he said, handing her the card and a wire holder that looked like a giant paper clip. "Which hat?"

"Hunter's. In the chest." She checked her watch and felt a twinge of anxiety.

He went for it, and got her gloves as well. "What else?"

Kori took the black velvet hunter's hat and put it on. "That's all, I hope. I'd better get over there. Start unloading the horses or the show authorities will be after us for holding up space at the curb."

Brit asked, "You want me to read? I know how." It was permitted to have a reader stand in the arena and call out the pattern to be ridden.

"No, Peter complains I recite the first Training Level exercise in my sleep. But walk me over and help me mount. Bring a sponge and rag with you."

She took Blue under her chin by the reins and started up the aisle, Brit following behind, sponge and polishing cloth in hand. They paused at the big double doors leading outside. The mizzle had almost stopped, but the wind was as chill as ever. Blue balked, unwilling to go out without her blanket, but Brit administered a friendly push, so she dropped her head and plodded forth.

The arena was on a diagonal from the barn; they went across and up the broad, paved street, whose curb was blocked at intervals with horse trailers, ranging from a shabby little two-horse carrier to an immense RV complete with TV and telephone antennae. People of all sizes and ages were unloading horses, saddles, suitcases, and potted plants. More horses, some blanketed, some saddled, clattered up and down the street. A long white trailer across the street was not a horse carrier, but a mobile store dealing in saddles, bridles, whips and crops, halters, blankets, liniment and horse beauty products, neck sweats and leg wrappings, cowboy hats, hunter's hats, jodhpur and Western boots, toy horses, and souvenir T-shirts. The owner and his wife were propping up the covers over the windows, preparing for business.

Blue looked around, but not with any interest. "Seems like she's kind of tired from the trip," said Brit. "Will she be up enough for this dressage business?"

"Well, the horse is supposed to be naturally quiet, or under strict control, or so bored by the whole thing it looks like one or the other. So long as the patterns are done correctly, it doesn't matter how you get the effect, so morning pokiness can only help. No, the problem is going to be lack of flexibility; Blue's really stiff when she's cold." She checked her watch and lengthened her stride.

The event had, in fact, begun nearly an hour ago, but Kori's place in the order of performance was third from the end. She knew how long it took a horse to do the pattern, and calculated she wasn't actually due in the arena for another five minutes, if the competitors were running on time, which seldom happened. There might be time for some warm-up after all.

The horse entrance to the arena was marked with an open space covered with coarse sand, where competitors gathered. Two horses were already there, their riders dressed, like Kori, in tight white riding pants, tall boots, and those velvety black hats that identify the English rider as cowboy hats identify the Western. Jackets varied in color from buff to black, and all had big black numbers pinned to their backs. Brit held Blue while Kori fastened the cardboard number card to her jacket collar with the giant paper clip, and mounted. Brit then used the cloth to wipe Kori's boots, and the sponge to wipe the mare's nostrils. "Good luck," she said with a smile.

Kori, now very tense, did not smile back. "Check what number goes in before me and the one before him," she said, gathering up her reins and pushing the mare into a walk.

Brit hurried up the broad, gentle ramp that led into the arena and checked a big diagram with names and numbers on it. She came back to report, "Number eleven, and before that three." Pointing toward the street, "And that's three walking away right now, all finished."

"Rats, they're right on schedule! Never rains but it pours. . . . Oh, well, you get back to the barn and help Danny." This last was said over her shoulder as she nudged Blue into a trot. When she turned at the end of the sandy area to come back again, she grimaced; the mare was stiff as a board.

Kori pulled back into a walk, reached over her shoulder to make sure her number was securely hooked, and winced. She was as stiff as the mare; she wished she'd had time to do her own warm-up exercises after that drive.

She stopped by the entrance, leaned sideways, and peered in, trying to see what was going on. A pretty chestnut mare was coming toward the exit down the right side at a relaxed, end-of-the-workout jog. The rider, a slim man in a sky-blue jacket, was rising rather high to the trot, his booted feet held well away from the horse's flanks.

Kori frowned. The horse had a nice white star and three white stockings, one almost to the knee on the near front. And with that natural way of picking up her feet, sure, thought Kori; that has to be Wellaway.

But Wellaway's rider wasn't her owner, Amelia Haydock— not that Amelia would be riding in Training Level dressage; Wellaway was doing very well at Third Level, thank you, with Amelia on board.

Kori practiced backing by pulling Blue Wind back three steps to give the rider exit room. As he started down the gentle ramp, he lifted his hunter's hat to adjust it, and Kori got a glimpse of bright curls before it was replaced. Could it be? Ye gods and little catfishes, it *was* Keith Bulward! While a brilliant showman of horses at halter, Keith had never been seen at any show actually sitting on a horse, much less riding in a performance competition.

She watched him come out onto the sandy waiting area. He appeared unhappy, sitting slumped, head down. He pulled Wellaway to a halt, dismounted, and with no warning, slammed the mare in the face with his clenched fist. The mare screamed in pain, throwing her head up and backing, half rearing. Bulward yanked on the reins and stepped forward, arm coming back to strike again.

"No!" shouted Kori, startling an already alarmed Blue. She pressed her heels in, urging the mare forward. "That's enough, Keith!" she added when the man still appeared about to strike his horse.

Bulward, looking over his shoulder at her, said, "Not that it's any of your goddam business, *Ms.* Brichter, but she asked for it." Nevertheless, he lowered his fist, and Wellaway immediately came forward, eyes showing white all around, ears going in every direction. The other two riders were approaching, making alarmed sounds of inquiry.

"Wellaway never asks for anything but a pat on the nose," said Kori, shifting in the saddle as Blue Wind, now very alert, danced and sidled to the left.

Keith turned to lead the mare away. "If I were you, *Ms.* Brichter, I'd be starting up that ramp, not poking my nose where it didn't belong."

Which was good advice, however snottily given, and Kori turned her horse away. Keith wouldn't strike Wellaway again, not with two other witnesses alerted and watching.

She started up the ramp, trying to think what got into Amelia. Because she, Kori, wouldn't leave Keith Bulward alone with any Tretower horse for thirty seconds, much less let him borrow a favorite to use at a show. Keith's horses performed flawlessly when shown at halter, which some people took as proof that the rumors about his maltreatment of them were false—while others considered it proof they were true.

At the top of the ramp, she turned Blue to one side and began to ride along the wall between the dirt floor of the arena and the bleacher seats rising up behind it.

Because dressage competitors ride one at a time, it is a slow-moving competition; and it's a subtle art, not much fun for the uninitiated to watch, particularly at the beginner level, when there are none of the every-other-stride changes of lead that even repetition can't pall. That's why it is scheduled at the front end or in a separate arena from a show, where the uninterested can skip it.

So even the small, widely scattered audience that dotted the rising tiers was a surprise to Kori. Moreover, someone whooped as she started her sedate walk around the wall, as if this were a regular competition and she, or the horse, or their entrance, were something spectacular. She did not look around to see who was offering support, but concentrated on keeping her back hollow, elbows bent, thumbs up, heels down, toes slightly in, face front. Blue was still very alert, and she, realizing this was Blue's reaction to her own adrenaline rush, tried to shift her concentration to the task at hand.

Obliquely, she studied the area marked off by thin white rope set in posts only a foot high. It was a large oval, forty-four by twenty-two yards. At intervals around its periphery were white sheets of paper stapled to tall slats, each marked with a big capital letter. The slat at the entrance to the oval was marked with an *A; C* was at the opposite end. *E* and *B* marked the midpoints down the sides, *K* and *F, H* and *M* the spaces between.

At the far end, behind the *C*, was a raised dais, and on it a table covered with a white cloth, on which rested a small brass bell, an antique silver coffee service, and a single porcelain coffee cup—though behind the table were two women. The plumper one wore a silver fox jacket over a plaid flannel shirt, and a large, dead-black wig. Or a wig and several switches, it being difficult to imagine just one wig containing that much hair. Loretta loved to startle the eye. She was an excellent dressage judge but an unforgiving one, and while her comments were often helpful, they were given in the most cutting terms. Her pen was busy, and Kori wondered what she was writing on the bottom of Keith Bulward's test sheet.

Beside Loretta sat a bullied-looking young woman, Loretta's secretary, who, if she wanted coffee, had to buy it herself and keep the cup hidden on the floor between her feet, never mind that Loretta never drank more than a cup or two from the eight-cup pot on the tray. Loretta's secretaries rarely lasted more than a year.

As Kori and Blue approached the dais, the secretary flipped over a sheet of paper. Blue shied, snorting, then froze.

Loretta's attention shifted from her writing to this incorrect behavior.

Kori nudged Blue in the ribs, but the sharpness of her nudge only confirmed Blue's suspicion that she should prepare for flight in a direction yet to be determined. So she stood fast, communicating her fears with switching ears and rigid pose.

Loretta stared, waiting, and Kori, blushing, at last resorted to broad and bold commands with hand and heel to turn left. Blue, receiving her direction, whirled and would have fled had not Kori brought her immediately back down into a trot.

As she did there came the genteel tinkle of the brass bell. The test was about to start.

As they neared the entrance to the oval, Kori began rising to the trot, and the pattern they were about to ride began unrolling in her head. "Enter Point A, working trot rising, to Point X (an imaginary point, the very center of the ring). Halt and salute." She began to turn Blue in at Point A—and the horse lunged the other way, making a break for the exit. Kori turned her just in time, making the bolt into a crooked sort of circle, and began to realize just how spooked her mount was.

But the bell had rung, and there was no time to soothe the terror out of Blue. They entered the arena at too fast a trot, and Kori barely had time before Point X to squeeze her legs inward, thrust her pelvis very slightly forward, and drop her hands, closing them just a little. Blue started to halt, but Kori's aids were still too strong, so she sidled to the left, then stopped, feet all anyhow, her head too high on a neck unarched, angry tail twirling like a windmill. Kori felt the blood rush to her face as she touched the narrow bill of her hat, then her thigh, her salute.

Loretta nodded grimly, pen already poised to write, and Kori cued Blue to start forward. The horse lurched into a trot. Kori was approaching Point C and thinking: Track right to B, circle right in a twenty-meter circle, sitting trot. The secretary took a sheet of paper off a stack and flipped it over.

This was the second time Blue had been threatened by the Crackling White Thing, and again she shied, then froze. They were still a few yards from Point C.

Loretta watched coldly.

Kori tried a subtle nudge in the ribs, but Blue ignored the hint. Kori tried again, this time to tell her mount that they didn't have to come any closer, but should trot to the right. Blue shifted her feet but didn't move, and when the command came again, she backed up, sending her own message that if her rider was frightened, then she, Blue, was likewise afraid.

But Kori wanted obedience. She surrendered to the exigencies of the moment and thumped Blue with both heels in a hard and all-too-visible movement. Blue leaped sideways awkwardly, but kept moving.

Once started, Kori relaxed a little and Blue promptly unwound her spine a little. Kori, understanding at last that she was the one at fault, concentrated on lightening her hand and relaxing. Blue made her circles correctly, if stiffly, but the "collected canter, left lead" helped warm her up, and when the circles were repeated in the other direction, she bent into them willingly.

Training Level tests are only a few minutes long, through they seem longer. Long before Blue had recovered all the ground she had lost at the start, it was over. The last movement, like the first, consisted of coming at a rising trot from Point A to Point X. Blue halted exactly on the spot, her neck flexed beautifully, all four feet squarely under her, steady as a rock. Kori almost smiled with relief, repeated the touching of her hat and then her thigh in a final salute. Loretta nodded and the test was over.

Kori walked Blue forward a little, turned right, and came

back down along the low border at a relaxed walk, reins long. No one whooped. She rode out through the entrance, not even nodding to the next contestant on her way in. At the bottom of the ramp, she dismounted. Blue, as always, lowered her head for the expected pat on the nose—which Kori gave her. "You must never blame the horse; it is never the horse's fault," the Prussian had told her. And it was certainly true in this case.

She took Blue back to the barn, removed her saddle and bridle, wiped her down a little, gave her a bucket of water. She must find some time to take the horse out for a proper warm-up and some schooling, because they were scheduled for Test Two in about an hour and a half. This was good, because it gave her a reason not to go find Keith Bulward and shout at him.

There seemed to be no one in the Tretower area of the barn. She went down the row, looking. The stall fronts were thick, smooth planks halfway up, then heavy wire mesh to a height of eleven feet. All the Tretower horses were knee-deep in straw, munching on hay. Kori could see big yellow plastic buckets of water in each horse's stall. Copper Wind grunted a greeting but did not stop eating; the horses had not been fed before setting out on the road, and he was hungry. The yearling Breathless, on the other hand, was very glad to see a familiar face. Kori spent a couple of minutes communing with her, telling her that not only was everything fine, things could only get better.

Next to Breathless was an empty stall with gray canvas privacy drapes over the mesh. Inside, grass-green indoor-outdoor carpet was laid on the floor. The portable tack hooks were hung ready for bridles, and boxes of brushes, coat sheen, hoof polish, scrapers, splint boots, and so on had been put along the back wall. Two powerful lamps had been clipped to the top of the side walls and plugged in overhead. This was the prep stall. But no one was in there.

Next door, another empty stall was set up as a tack room. Here were piles of blankets, three saddles and saddle pads waiting to be hung on their stainless steel hooks, chests and suitcases waiting to be properly stored or their contents unpacked, bulky feed sacks on top of hay bales. A folding cot leaned against the hay. But no one was in there, either.

At the inside aisle end of the double row of stalls was the gear that would decorate and define the Tretower area. A banner to hang across the end of the aisle was draped carelessly over pots of plastic geraniums; a long piecrust table, rather battered, was half draped with its dull green felt pad on which lay some of the trophies the horses had won at previous shows and the videotape player on which would be played the endless-loop tape advertising Tretower. Though not set up, it looked as if everything had been unloaded.

She looked up and down the broad aisle outside the area, where other contestants were setting up. There was a squeal of metal on concrete as a fairgrounds employee pushed a wooden cart with two enormous metal wheels down a cross aisle, delivering straw bales. But no Danny or Brit. She went out to see if she had been mistaken and they were still unloading the trailer.

But the trailer waited, empty and locked, for someone to come and move it away from the entrance. Anxious now, as well as angry, Kori strode toward the parking lot.

And there she found them. Brit was standing beside the open door of the Tretower Bronco, her battered suitcase beside her. Danny was shouting into her face, his arms spread high and wide, a sign of extreme exasperation.

"Dammit to hell, you *can't* just cut out on us!" he was saying.

"But I just can't stay," Brit replied, her voice more firm than Kori had ever heard it.

"Well, so what if he's here? He won't do anything, will he?"

"He may." Brit turned away and climbed up into the Bronco. "Hand me my suitcase."

"Wait a minute, Brit!" called Kori. "If you're taking a hike, you better do it on foot. That vehicle belongs to Tretower."

Danny, who had picked up the suitcase, dropped it. "Boy,

am I glad to see you!" he said. "She says she can't stay because Keith Bulward's here."

"That's right," said Brit.

Kori came up, saying, "So he's here, so what? I know he fired you, but that's no reason to run from him. You've shown him up by getting another job right away."

Brit flared, "He didn't fire me, I quit!" Then the flare died. "But it doesn't matter; I have to get away from here, right now." Brit climbed down, stood with shoulders hunched, turned partly away from them. "Can one of you run me in to the bus station?"

"Not without an explanation," said Kori. "And it better be good. There's only the three of us, barely enough to manage. If you quit, we'll have to pack up and go home, too. I don't want to do that without an extremely good reason."

"I know that. And I'm sorry. I'd stay if I could, believe me."

"Then why don't you?" asked Danny. "Just stay out of Bulward's way!"

"I can't hide the whole time! Not and work. It's impossible; he'll see me." She rubbed viciously at her nose and sniffed.

"So what if he does?" said Kori, exasperated.

"He said people like me shouldn't be allowed to handle show horses, who needed to always be reminded who was boss. He said I wasn't any good with them because I was making pets out of them. But I never had to get a horse scared to death of me before he'd do what I want, like he does. And I know people who are doing pretty good with 'pet' horses!"

Kori said, "From what we've heard from other people, and the little we've seen of you ourselves, you're good with horses yourself."

"So he told you to get out of the business. Who died and left him in charge?" Danny said.

"But he knows all kinds of people, judges and owners, doesn't he? He can make it stick, if he wants to."

Kori said, "Not with me, he can't. Look, I called Bulward before I hired you, and he said some bad things about you.

But I know him, and I remembered you said you've been working with other people's horses since you were about eleven. So I called around, and couldn't find anyone else who would give you a bad reference. If you're as bad as he says, none of them would've hired you, not even him. I asked you to work at the ranch for a week before the show so Danny and I could get a look, and he agrees that you're reliable and competent. Forget about Bulward, you've got nothing to worry about."

"But he's such a miserable rat—you don't know the trouble he can cause. He's terrible. He—well, it's a long story."

"Tell us, we've got some time now."

Brit turned completely away and stood, head down, mumbling to the side of the driver's seat as if it were a confessional. "It—it started kind of like flirting. You know, like goes on all the time in the barns." Brit gestured and Danny made a noise that meant we know. "I thought he wasn't any more serious than everyone else. Only he made it serious. Always—touching, and grabbing. Finally I told him to stay away from me, but that made him worse." Her voice became even softer. "He—he tried to—force me. That's the real reason I left. He said—oh, all sorts of bad things. He said I was a tease, that I was asking for it."

Kori made a sound that boded ill for Bulward, and Brit turned around. She said unhappily, "Keith told me that if I ever got within his reach again, he'd finish what he started."

"Aww!" scoffed Danny.

"No, you don't understand," said Brit. "I think he meant it—just like I meant it when I said that if he tried it, I'd kill him."

$\triangledown$

3

CLOVERLAND FARMS, HAVING TAKEN first, third, and fourth in dressage, decided to throw a party. The invitation went out via grapevine: everyone welcome, come at seven.

The party setup was typical of a spontaneous horse show affair. Set in the broad aisle of the horse barn, it featured two borrowed, rain-softened picnic tables covered with plastic sheets topped with white paper tablecloths. For food, there was a five-gallon yellow plastic water bucket filled with potato chips, two cartons each of three different kinds of grocery store dip, a cutting board with one knife and two kinds of cheese, paper plates heaped with Ritz crackers and Wheat Thins, a jar of cheese spread with a butter knife stuck in it, and two big jars of green olives with a single spoon between them. For drinks, there was an ice chest of canned soft drinks, another of beer, and a gallon of the kind of wine that comes in a box. There was a tall-to-tilting stack of paper napkins. A garbage can lined with a brown plastic bag stood at one end of the tables, ready to receive trash. A boom box was under one table; in it, a tape was playing "Itsy-Bitsy, Teeny-Weeny, Yellow Polka-Dot Bikini."

Close to forty people were there, wearing anything from jeans and sweatshirts to spring dresses draped with fringed shawls. Kori wore a long skirt, boots, and her favorite Irish fisherman sweater. She hesitated on the edge of the crowd, looking for Danny or Brit.

"Well, here's the second-place winner!" Mr. Cloverland cheered, and came to shake her hand. "That was quite a comeback from your first ride," he said, smiling. He was a medium-size man with light brown hair and blue eyes both pleased and tired. He and his wife worked at other jobs to earn enough money to keep their horses.

"Yes, wasn't it?" said Kori. "Blue really outdid herself after that first mess. Loretta was positively encouraging."

"You'd have taken first if it wasn't for that first ride. What was it, nerves?"

"Partly. And something we saw just before going in."

Cloverland's smile turned pained. "I heard about that. Amelia's here, and she's mad. Bulward is going to be one sorry sucker. How's your son?"

"Jeep's fine, thanks. Walking and talking and trying hard to get potty trained. And he won't be two until the fourth of July."

"That's right, he's a Yankee Doodle baby, isn't he? Is he here with you?"

"No, he's home. He has a cold so I didn't bring him this time." Jeep, like other children of horsey parents, had come to his first show wrapped in a receiving blanket.

"You had him up yet?"

"Oh, yes, he rides in front of me all the time."

"Then maybe you should enter him in the lead rein class in Springfield next month."

"No, no, I'm going to wait until his feet hang over the edges," laughed Kori. A lead rein class offered a chance for very small children to wear riding clothes and sit tall in the saddle while a doting parent led their horses into the show ring. Each tot was presented with a blue ribbon to be proudly shown off for the rest of the day. Kori had thought it a cheap trick and a waste of valuable time until a few weeks ago, when she saw Jeep hanging on the rail, watching a lead rein class in Indianapolis.

"Hey, Kori, glad you came!" said a new voice, and a woman Kori's age came up to exchange cheek pecks. Cloverland drifted politely away.

"Hi, Valerie," said Kori. "I didn't think you were coming to the Lafite show."

"Oh, I wasn't, but Mark said he just had to get a look at Amelia judging the mares. Miss Liberty goes as far as the regionals this year, we hope. But Amelia's no Billy Harris, and Mark wants to get a look at what she likes. It'll be interesting to see who she picks for a blue now that Keith Bulward's out of the running."

This led to a discussion of Amelia's embarrassing weakness for handsome young trainers, then to a critique of other judges. They came to a friendly agreement that while Billy Harris was incredibly objective, Peter Cameron was probably the best Arabian horse judge in the country. "So okay, who's the worst?" asked Valerie.

"That I can't tell you," said Kori. "I know it's not Amelia. She's got a real eye."

Valerie nodded. "You ever suspect they give classes on how to be the worst? I mean there's always that little handful right at the bottom."

Kori laughed, and said, "Come and have coffee with us tomorrow. You know where we are?"

"Yes, we're right behind you, Aisle A. I'll come and clap for that yearling I've been hearing about, if you'll come and clap for Salim ben Salim."

"Agreed. Will you excuse me? My throat is just parched."

"If you didn't bring your own cup, you'll have to drink out of a can," warned Valerie. "Whoever went out for supplies forgot cups."

Danny stood by the picnic tables, waiting his turn at the cheese tray. He and another trainer passed the time arguing methods. "Yeah, well I went to a John Lyons symposium last year and learned a lot," said Danny.

"Yeah, but have you read *The Problem Horse*?"

"We don't have any problem horses."

"Hey, her stuff you can use on a horse even if he isn't a problem. I tell you, Tellington-Jones knows what she's doing."

Danny snorted. "Come on, horse phrenology?"

"No, reading a stiff upper lip and a loose lower lip isn't whatever-you-said, it's common sense. Like giving your horse a massage is common sense." Danny snorted again, but the other insisted, "I tell you, it works. You go up your horse's neck like this." He demonstrated a kind of rolling motion with his fingertips. "You can do it all over, neck, flank, back, to relax a horse. I can get a horse so relaxed he starts drooling."

"Must look great to bring him to the ring that way."

"Seriously. You got a horse that gets so tense he can't pay attention to your aids? Do this"—He made a circular motion with his fingers—"and all of a sudden he's reading your mind. You work for Kori Price Brichter, right? I know her, and I bet you get a book or tape by Tellington-Jones before the year is out."

"Aw—!" started Danny, but just then a place opened up and he moved in to begin cutting himself a fat slice of cheese. He was glad to be interrupted; he didn't want to admit it, but he suspected Kori had several of Linda Tellington-Jones's books already.

"Evening, Kori," said a deepish voice behind her. She turned and saw Amelia Haydock, wearing her gold wool suit and a blood-red silk blouse, the power outfit she wore while judging. But the colors went poorly with Amelia's short hair, which was dyed a peculiar dark maroon.

"Good evening, Amelia."

"Did better second time, I hope," said Amelia, and it was a moment before Kori realized what she was talking about.

"Oh. Yes, thank you. Much better. In fact, we ended up

taking second." Kori made an amused grimace. "Loretta thinks I ought to continue my dressage lessons after all."

Amelia didn't even smile. "You saw Keith," she said.

Kori looked around. "You mean here at the party?"

"This morning. With Wellaway." Normally terse, Amelia became positively telegraphic when upset.

"Ah. Yes. Um, is she all right?"

"Don't know yet. Blood in her nose. Shipped her home this afternoon."

"But you're staying here?"

"Have to. Judging."

Kori, aware she would be bringing Hurricane into one of Amelia's classes tomorrow, said, "Um, Amelia—"

"My fault. Misjudged him. You saw."

"I didn't know he was going to do that. He just dismounted and—"

"I saw him!" Amelia barked to stop her. "Followed him out. Piss-poor ride. His fault, entirely."

"I told him to stop."

"I know." She sighed, and looked suddenly older. "Never struck with the hand, never."

Kori couldn't think what to say. Amelia was like a mother to all her horses, but especially Wellaway. It was wicked of Bulward to hit the mare, and stupid to do it where Amelia might catch him. And doubtless Amelia was right, the poor ride was his fault entirely. He must be able to turn on the charm, if Amelia, who was practically born on horseback, never realized earlier the sort of person he was.

Not that there weren't rumors about Amelia as well. Some said she was a lesbian, others that she was a sex change gone awry. Some held her up as a classic example of what could become of a spinster with a thwarted maternal instinct. Amelia, they said, should have had children; then she wouldn't be so stuck on her animals, and might cease adopting ambitious young people who took advantage of her. Like Keith Bulward, who now had fallen desperately far from grace. "What are you going to do?" asked Kori.

Amelia glanced away, her expression sly. "Dunno yet."
But it came back with a smirk that as much as told Kori to
keep her eyes on Mr. Bulward, to see just how unhappy she,
Amelia Haydock, could make him.

Kori excused herself and began again working her way into
the crowd. Fragments of conversation drifted over her.

". . . didn't know a pastern from a forelock last year and
was reserve in Western Pleasure last week . . . ," laughed a
woman.

A mother to her child, "No, darling, Marcie doesn't rise
to the trot nearly as well as you do."

". . . one of those goddam movie star colts here, looks like
goddam Trigger," someone was grumbling. She paused to
hear more. Gossip about horses shown or to be shown could
be valuable.

"Yeah, but Zumbrowski likes 'em light-colored and
flashy," replied his companion, equally glum. "Probably give
him a first tomorrow."

Kori's ears grew interested points. Gossip about judges
was even more valuable, and Bob Zumbrowski was judging
the yearling fillies tomorrow, too.

"Shouldn't've let Barty register that goddam colt," said
the grumbler. "Color's all wrong for an Arab. He calls it a
golden chestnut, but it's a goddam palomino. Bet if you
check, you'll find a half-Arab in that line not three genera-
tions back."

The grumbler's companion, a ruddy-cheeked man in a
loud houndstooth sport coat, saw her listening, and said,
"What do you think, Kori; Barty's pulling a fast one?"

Kori, blushing to find herself discovered, said, "Baron
Barty breeds for extremes in color, but his line, so far as I
know, is pure."

"Yeah, but his line is strictly Polish, and those goddam
Poles aren't pure Arab, they can't be!" objected the grumbler.
"Look at the goddam size of 'em! Christ Almighty, I saw a
mare—a *mare*—sixteen goddam hands at Sahara Sands last
spring!"

"Now I hear," said his friend, "that the reason Polish horses are so big is that every spring they run the foals across this big river, see, and they keep only the ones who make it across."

Kori thought of Hurricane, but didn't want to get into the argument about breeding for size. "Is Barty here?" she asked.

"Naw, Stoddard's showing for him," said the houndstooth.

"Is Stoddard his new trainer then?"

"I suppose. But the only Barty horse here is that colt."

"Yearling?" asked Kori, and held her breath.

"Two-year-old. Why?"

Kori exhaled. "I've got a yearling filly with me. Very pretty, very light gray, but not very snorty." She already knew Zumbrowski liked fiery temperaments. Kori hoped to end up near the top of the Best Arabian Yearling class, hard enough to do with a filly, and wasn't anxious to find a spectacular colt competing with her.

"He's not so keen on snorty fillies as he is on colts. Good luck."

"Thanks." Kori pushed her way on.

". . . slugged her, right in front of witnesses. I hear Amelia about skinned him alive when she came to get Wellaway."

Not anxious to be asked about that, either, Kori kept moving.

". . . can't find one that'll fit me, and the new rules say I can't ride with my old hunter's hat . . ."

". . . Fred's gelding got his tail caught in the wheel, came to a dead halt. Doesn't he know that when your horse's tail is that long you should tie a cord across the front of the buggy and tuck the horse's tail behind it? So he sits there popping his whip while his horse tries to figure out what to do. That dumb ring steward finally comes over, but he just pulls it loose and waves him back into traffic, instead of sending him out of the ring . . ."

Kori went around the angry driver and his amused friends and found herself at the picnic tables. In front of her were the cheese and crackers. She began building an hors d'oeuvre from a Ritz, a slice of cheddar, a dab of horseradish dip, and a fragment of Swiss. She was looking around to see if there were ripe olives when someone jostled her elbow reaching to push a potato chip deep into the French onion.

A gob of what was more dip than chip went into Danny's mouth, and he grinned around it at her. He was wearing old jodhpurs and a green flannel shirt. "Uh uhn, ah?" he tried, then chewed, swallowed, and tried again. "Some fun, what?"

Kori nibbled her cracker critically, then gestured with it at the guests and said, "It's the gossip at these things, not the food, that makes them fun."

"Something wrong with the food?" Danny grabbed a careless handful of potato chips and asked, "What have you heard so far?"

"Well, Stoddard's showing a Barty colt—look, there he is." Taking another delicate bite of her cracker, she directed Danny's attention with a glance at a tall man not far away. He had rather a lot of graying brown hair and an aristocrat's bearing. His tweeds were as authentically shabby as they were impeccably cut, but his well-polished shoes were cheap imitations. He was leaning a little, as if the beer can in his hand was very heavy.

Danny tongued a chip into his mouth and said, "Drunk. I guess he's having a hard time with the fact that he's washed up as a trainer."

"Aha, but maybe he isn't. Didn't you hear what I said? He's got Barty's two-year-old colt with him."

"Are you sure?"

"Reed told me about it." Kori nibbled her cracker. For months there had been all kinds of speculation on who Barty would hire for his new trainer.

Danny dredged another chip through the dip. "So Stoddard Eckiherne's got the tryout."

"Tryout?"

"What I heard is, there was someone here with a Barty horse he trained, on trial, to see how he does."

"Oh. Well, he should do okay. I hear the colt is a movie star, and with Zumbrowski judging he's got a good chance for a first from him."

Danny made a face. "Now, maybe not. See, Keith Bulward brought Aaron Greenspan's two-year-old colt along. Have you seen it?"

"No, why?"

"He's the palest chestnut I've ever seen, shimmers like he's made of twenty-four-karat gold. Not a white hair on him. That's serious competition for Zumbrowski's vote. And guess what else about Zumbrowski?"

"What?"

"He likes the trainer to hootchie kootchie to catch his eye. Queer as a three-dollar bill, I used to think, till I realized he's as quick to watch a girl hootchie as a guy kootchie. Stoddard knows how to set up a horse, but Keith's the one who dances and wiggles and pops his whip till you can't help but look at him." He tongued a potato chip into his mouth. "Stoddard had better be fresher in the ring tomorrow than he's ever been, hangover or no hangover, or Zumbrowski won't know that movie star is there."

Kori lowered the hand with the cracker in it. She wasn't particularly fond of Stoddard, but she hated to see him lose to Keith Bulward.

"Too bad this had to happen," said Danny. "I was hoping Stoddard could make a comeback; he's a lot of talent going to waste." Danny squatted over the ice chest to fish for a soft drink. "Want one?"

"Yes, please, a ginger ale. Maybe Stoddard can bring it off even with a hangover."

"Look at him, you can see he knows better. Too bad, he really, really needed this job with Barty." He handed her a can of Canada Dry and lifted the tab on his RC. "I remember the first time I met Stoddard; it was at the regional where he showed reserve stallion, reserve mare, most classic, and won English Pleasure on Pasha's Magic. It was my first regional, and when he talked with me over his hot dog at lunch, it was like getting advice from God. He was on his way down then, though I didn't know it. Scary how once it started it was like the chute was smeared with Vaseline."

Kori idly picked the Swiss off her cracker. "The two-year-olds won't go in till nine tomorrow. I bet if he left now and went right to bed—maybe I should suggest that to him."

"Don't bother. Can't you see what happened? Stoddard figured he could come here and just walk out with at least a reserve championship for that colt. But with Keith bringing a flashy two-year-old colt to compete against him, he might not even win the class. The deal's out the window; Stoddard won't get the trainer's job."

Kori stopped in the act of biting into her cheese. "You don't think Keith showed up here on purpose with a colt just to spoil Stoddard's win? Why would he do that?"

Danny laughed. "You're beginning to think like Stoddard, like it's some kind of plot. Everywhere he goes, here comes Bulward to mess things up for him. No, this time it's pure chance. That colt Keith's showing is Aaron Greenspan's. Aaron's got financial problems and wants to sell some horses, but he needs a good price for them. So he has to maintain or even boost the reputation of his farm. That's why he hired Bulward. And it's working. Bulward's taken the colt to two shows and finished in the ribbons both times. But to get in the regionals, he needs a first or reserve at a Class A. That's why Bulward brought the colt here, for the same reason Stoddard brought Barty's colt here: It's a Class A show, but a small one. There's probably gonna be seven two-year-olds in that class. Those two have the looks, but only Keith's got the style. So far as Keith's concerned, the fix is in; Stoddard might as well go home."

"Well, a reserve win—"

"Call it what you like, reserve is second. Coming in reserve would work for Keith, because Aaron's colt would qualify with a reserve win; but it won't work for Stoddard. A reserve ribbon at a big show would be okay, but here, he needs a nice, clean, bright first, a high-ribbon finish in the Junior

Championship, or Barty will decide Stoddard's not right for his barn. And unless Keith really messes up, Stoddard isn't going to place first."

"Maybe one of the other horses—"

"Will take reserve, giving Stoddard a third. Worse and worse."

Kori couldn't think what to say. Danny, an experienced showman, didn't make flat statements about a horse's prospects unless he was very sure. She glanced over at Stoddard, who was upending the last of his beer into his mouth, swaying dangerously. There was nothing celebratory about what he was doing; he looked like a loser drowning his sorrows.

Kori took her can of pop and drifted away. Danny grabbed another handful of chips and followed. Neither looked at Stoddard.

They found Brit in a group of fellow grooms giggling over some bit of gossip. Brit was in jeans, a pair of cowboy boots gaudy with red leather inserts, and a green billed cap with "Nothing Runs Like A Deere" in yellow on it. Their arrival broke up the pack of gigglers, who melted away, leaving Brit behind.

"I've been thinking," said Danny. "It's kind of a surprise that Keith turned up here after all. I mean, there are other small shows, and he's got Positiw to get ready for the Ann Arbor show next weekend."

"No, he pretty much stopped training Positiw right about the time I quit," said Brit. "He has to knock off the training far enough ahead of time to give the welts time to fade."

"Welts?" Danny repeated doubtfully, not sure if she were joking.

"Like I told Miss Haydock, Keith uses the whip pretty heavy when he's training, especially on the stallions. Makes them nice and snorty in the ring."

"Brit," said Kori quietly, looking around for eavesdroppers, "you mustn't say things like that, especially to someone like Amelia. She's mad enough at him already and she might think you're serious."

"What makes you think I'm not serious?" Brit tilted the bottom of her can of RC to drain it.

"Look," said Danny, "there's always been rumors about that bastard, but—"

"I am speaking as an eyewitness!" said Brit, bristling at their doubts. "Amelia said she heard I used to work for him, and I said yes, and told her all about him. She asked me if I'd ever seen him hit a horse, and I told her what I saw myself, which is, he whips them hard enough to raise welts. If a horse misbehaves and it's close to a show, he blankets him up good and goes at it; you can hear the horse screaming all over the barn, but it doesn't leave a mark. He's always real nice to us for a day or so after he wales on a horse; it's like doing that cheers him up somehow."

Danny breathed, "Holy shit! How come you never told us about this before?"

"Because he's not the only one, and I didn't want to find myself badmouthing him to someone else just as bad. Because talking about it makes me so mad I almost want to take a horsewhip and show him how it feels!"

"Danny," said Kori, "I saw Keith hit Wellaway in the face this morning. He used his fist and he hit her hard."

Danny turned. "I heard—you *saw* it? What was it about? Did the horse bite him or something?"

"He rode Wellaway in dressage, and they didn't do very well. I saw him come out, dismount, and swing, all in one motion. Apparently Amelia saw him, too. When I saw her a little while ago, she was talking about Keith in two-word sentences."

"I hear when she came to get Wellaway she called Keith names nobody knew she knew," Brit said.

Danny grimaced as if in pain. "Of all the stupid"—then his surprise swerved in a new direction. "Wait a second! Dressage? Keith? I thought he didn't know people could ride horses."

"He always could ride," said Brit. "People in his barn said so. Not real well, they said, but he could. And then he signed

up for dressage lessons a couple of months ago. They said
Amelia Haydock talked him into it. She likes—liked—him
and was always telling him ways to improve his image."

"I've seen them together at other shows, Keith and Amelia," mused Kori. "I can't imagine what she sees in him."

"He's young and pretty," said Danny. "And she's a frustrated old maid."

"She is not! She's, well . . . more like a frustrated mother.
If she was of a younger generation, she'd have arranged to
have a child without marrying the father."

"Not a chance," said Danny. "She's funny about men."

"Keith's a man," said Brit.

"No, Keith's a boy," said Kori, reluctantly, because she
wasn't sure Amelia fit into the mold they were making for
her.

"Actually, she would have made a terrific mother," grinned
Danny. "Once she killed and ate the father."

"Knock it off, Danny," said Kori, frowning.

"She sure stuck up for Keith up till now," said Brit. "I
heard her last fall saying she was angry at all those false
rumors about him beating up on his horses. I almost told
her then, but she's not easy to just walk up to and talk
with."

"You got that right," said Danny. "But now she knows the
rumors were true. I wonder what she's gonna do about it?"

Keith Bulward was wearing the outrageous lemon-yellow
sport coat that was his trademark in the show arena. It was
so bright that it toned down the false brightness of his hair,
which fell in artless tumbles over his forehead and down the
nape of his neck. He was not tall, but proportionately narrow
and youthfully slender, so his lack of inches was not apparent until one came up to him. He didn't mind being short;
it made the horses he showed look bigger, and it allowed him
to get away with a lot of reaching up, jiggling, and dancing
under their noses that would have looked ridiculous if they
had been done by a big man.

And fed the triumph of putting one over on someone bigger than himself.

"You may have seen him in Chicago last year," he was saying in his deceptively gentle voice, sure the words were carrying several rows beyond the circle of people around him. "Big fellow, got a twenty-inch neck and a sixty-inch waist. Shifty blue eyes, smokes a pipe like he's still learning how." He goggled his own blue eyes a bit, looked left, right, left, mimed puffing on a pipe. "Came up to me and said, 'Mr. Bulwark' "—Bulward stopped to let the audience snigger. " 'Mr. Bulwark, I unner*stan*' you got a lady horse for sale.' " More sniggers. " 'An' I been studying horses for a whole six months now. My daughter, she's always been nuts about horses, y'see, an' she thinks these here *A*-rabs is about the prettiest kind of horses there is. Now I can tell a honest man when I see one' "—someone sniggered again, but Bulward ignored it—" 'so I think I'd like to have a look at this here lady horse you got for sale.' Whoo-*eeee*," continued Bulward, "this ol' boy took one look at Bellisima and that pretty foal by her side and reached for his checkbook! Thought he got the bargain of the year."

"Don't you think you should have warned him, Keith?" asked a man.

"Well, there two answers to that one, Hank. One is, if I'd known the fellow had in mind a breeding program centered around Bellisima, I might've mentioned it. And the other is, *cave canem*, let the buyer beware!" Bulward laughed, and most of the people joined in.

"You mean *caveat emptor*, Keith," said a woman's voice, by the chill in it not one of the laughers. "*Cave canem* means beware of the dog. Though, come to think of it, that also describes how people should approach any business deal with you."

"Whoooo!" said someone, and there was more laughter.

Keith turned around and saw Kori. "Woof!" he said, leaning past the grinning people to get near her face, showing beautiful white teeth in a snarl. "Woof, woof, woof!" And he laughed, delighted with his quelling wit, as she turned and walked away.

Brit was filling a water bucket at the horse shower—Hurricane had knocked hers over an unknown while ago, long enough to have gotten thirsty, anyway. Brit was going to sit sharing gossip with some friends, now the party had broken up, and then seek the narrow canvas cot and the few hours' respite it offered. Tomorrow was going to come awful early. The place wasn't quieted down yet, not that it ever got completely quiet, filled as it was with antsy horses rattling buckets and calling to stablemates, and young, healthy people who met mostly at these shows.

Dumb stalls, with their uneven floors. She thought she'd found a flat spot to put Hurricane's bucket on, but evidently not; it was apparent from the size of the puddle that Hurricane had knocked over the bucket when it was almost full, which meant she'd gone without a drink for some while. Her mind's eye could see the animal taking long, grateful pulls at the water, slaking her thirst, washing away the dust, grateful for one less reason to be unhappy in this strange place. . . . I should have checked sooner, she thought.

The shower looked not too different from the kind you might find in a gym, except it was horse size and without a curtain at its open end. The shower head was at the end of a hose, which made it possible to wash a horse and not get yourself entirely soaked.

There was no spigot in there for filling water buckets— those were located near the main entrance—but the shower was closer to the Tretower stalls. Brit unhooked the shower head and turned the dial on the wall all the way to Cold. A lever on the shower head released the flow of water and she let it run briefly, then began to fill the big yellow bucket.

It made a lot of noise, so when she released the lever she was startled by the sound of footsteps very close by. She straightened, and there was Keith Bulward in his lemon-yellow coat, face tight, looking at her with narrowed eyes.

"Don't you touch me!" she warned.

"Bitch!" he replied without slowing.

"I'm not afraid of you!" she said, but not loudly and only after she was sure he was going to pass the shower. He turned at her voice, and the hatred on his face sent such a chill through her that she held up the shower head like a weapon and said, "If you come anywhere near me, I'll really hurt you!" but her voice had an unconvincing quaver, and when he took a threatening step toward her she backed to the wall. He gave a harsh, triumphant laugh, turned on his heel, and strode away, still laughing.

$\triangledown$

4

KEITH WAS GRABBING HER, he had her from behind, holding her arm against her chest with terrifying strength, and whispering in her ear. The horses were trying to help, but they were tied to the fence; they were screaming in helpless rage. His other hand came around, and he had a knife, and there was blood coming out of her abdomen, and the horses were screaming—and she was fighting her way awake, and the horses were screaming.

Breathless was having a fit, and the other horses were calling for someone to come and help.

Brit struggled out of her sleeping bag, which had twisted itself across her shoulder and around her hand, and sat up.

It was dark; the line of low-watt bulbs down the length of the barn did not disperse the shadows in the tack stall where she was sleeping. She felt with her toes for the Wellington rubber boots beside her cot, found them, and fumbled her feet into them. She stood and groped for the ratty chenille robe draped over a saddle and pulled it like a blanket around her shoulders.

She slid the stall door back and stood a moment, trying to remember where everything was. The yearling was ricocheting off the walls of her stall, shrilling in panic. Copper Wind's deep voice came from the other side of the row of stalls, and the mares were stamping and calling.

"Hey, hey!" called Brit. "Settle down, I'm awake now. Settle down." She stretched her arm up to work out the kinks from the weird position she'd been sleeping in, and started toward the yearling's stall, only to halt and frown sleepily at the metal-wheeled hay cart, which was pulled up close to the prep stall door, blocking her way. Who had left that there? She kept frowning as she slipped around it.

"Here, now, sweetheart, here now," she began to croon as she reached for the yearling's stall door. She heard the animal brushing against the far wall as if to escape from her. She leaned sideways, letting her weight slide the door open, and saw the ghostly outline of Breathless wavering in the corner. "Settle down, sweetheart, it's only me. Are you hurt? What's wrong?"

Breathless fell silent, then went "huh-huh-huh-huh" as if in inquiry.

"I'm here, I'm here; what's the matter?" Brit was still struggling out of her own nightmare, and leaned back against the wall of the stall for support while reaching for Breathless. "Come to Brit, baby," she murmured. "Come here."

The yearling's nose brushed her hand, then the whole creature was suddenly close against her, and Brit felt her violent trembling. "Hey, something's got you really spooked, hasn't it? What, did you wake up and not know where you were?"

The other horses were moving restlessly, but their calling was becoming sporadic now that Breathless had shut up and a trusted human was here and taking charge.

Brit reached for Breathless, stroking and crooning, feeling the bunched muscles slowly relax as the trembling went away. Silence fell outside the stall with an almost audible sigh of relief.

Brit yawned. What time was it? She lifted her wrist, but the light was too dim to see. She slid down the wall to sit in the hay. "Whew, I'm tired," she murmured.

"Huh-huh-huh," replied Breathless, nuzzling her knee.

"Yeah, yeah, it's okay now, right?"

The yearling snorted and mock-shied away, then lifted her nose toward the prep stall next door.

"No, it's not time to get started. I hope." Brit, feeling herself falling back to sleep, struggled to her feet. "You all right now? Good." She walked around the stall, but found nothing that might have hurt or frightened the yearling. "I'm gonna look at the other horses, and if they're all right, I'm going back to bed. No more nonsense from you, hear?"

Breathless snorted lengthily, and Brit took that as a promise of compliance. She left, trudged tiredly up and down the Tretower segment of stalls, finding nothing except still-nervous horses. She spoke gently to each, went back to the tack stall and felt her way into the cot, and was asleep almost before she could pull her sleeping bag over her head.

It was like a buzzing insect burrowing heartlessly into her eardrum. She tried to squirm away, and that woke her up. She was in a tack stall, on a narrow, fold-up cot. Which tack stall? Lafite, the Fourth Annual. Right.

It was still dark, not a trace of dawn's earliest light. Surely she must have more sleep coming. But the insect was still there, and she recognized it as her new little travel alarm, which she had very cleverly put clear across the stall, tucked behind one of the chests.

"Kur-rap." She threw off the sleeping bag, gasped at the chill of the air, and snatched it back again. But she had to do something about that alarm before she woke up her neighbors.

Again.

She remembered the earlier waking. What a strange thing that had been. Did Tretower Arabians make a habit of waking up in the middle of the night at shows? She sure hoped not.

Hugging the bag's warmth around her, she stumbled across the uneven floor—hoof-stamped earth under a thin carpet laid yesterday during setup—found the chest by sound and touch, groped behind it for the clock, and pressed the right button. The noise stopped like a pain going away, but by then she was fully awake.

She went back and sat down on the narrow canvas cot, still huddled in the sleeping bag. She curled one rapidly chilling bare foot over the other. You'd think all the horses in this barn would have brought the temperature up higher. Must be close to freezing outside.

What time was it, anyway? She stood, reaching high, found the switch on the lamp clamped to the top board of the stall, and snapped it on.

Too bright, too bright! She sat down, squinting, shading her eyes until they adjusted.

When she checked again, it was 5:34, time to get going.

Okay, what's first? Today was AOTS, Amateur Owner to Show. An amateur owner is a person who owns the horse being shown, but doesn't take money for riding, showing, or training, and doesn't compete in classes that offer cash prizes. Kori was an amateur; Danny wasn't. The weanlings went into the ring at seven, but Tretower wasn't showing any weanlings. Hardly anyone was, which meant that the yearlings, shown next, would probably get their first call about a quarter past seven. And that meant Breathless had better be washed, dried, combed, brushed, warmed up, and ready to go by the time Kori arrived, which would be at seven, if not before.

And the other horses would need feeding and watering— and then Hurricane had to be gotten ready for the three-year-old filly halter class, and Blue Wind readied for the Country English Pleasure class—busy, busy day ahead.

Brit stood, pushed her bare feet into rubber Wellingtons, shoved her arms into the chenille bathrobe, gathered her clothing, toothbrush, comb, and other necessaries, and went down to the ladies' room. There she met other sleepy grooms, several of whom made cutting remarks about being wakened last night by a spooked horse. Brit ignored them, joining instead in the complaints about trainers and owners who lolled in comfortable motel beds while their grooms struggled with lazy, recalcitrant, even vicious horses for little pay and less gratitude. Because misery shared is misery halved, Brit came back to the Tretower row smiling and ready to face the day.

The barn lights came on, but almost everyone who had slept in the barn was now up and moving. She dug in her suitcase and came up with her most lucky hat, the one with the little teddy bear seated on the bill, and tugged it on.

She took a nylon lead down from its hook and went to get Breathless and got her first surprise of the day. The filly, instead of her usually friendly self, was almost as panicked as she had been last night, rolling her eyes and dancing all over the stall, afraid of Brit, afraid to go out the door. Persuaded at last to do so, she jumped rather than walked out, and naturally skidded and nearly fell on the concrete walk.

"Is this any way to behave?" scolded Brit, waiting to be sure the filly had her feet under her before pulling the nylon lead to start her up the aisle. "Last night you woke up the whole barn with your nightmare, and this morning you act like everyone's out to get you. Steady, now, whoa girl, whoa." Brit spent a few precious moments soothing the filly, then led her away.

At the shower, Brit cross-tied Breathless, then lifted down the shower head, setting the dial so the water was just warm. She had to let her smell it, then smell it again after she turned on the water, before the filly would allow Brit to wet her down. Which was strange, as the setup was not unlike the one back at Tretower, where Breathless had taken baths with pleasure any number of times. But the filly calmed down once they got started, turning her face into the stream when it came close enough, and standing still while neck, back, flanks, and legs were soaped and rinsed.

There was an electronic pop, and a cheerful man's voice was broadcast. *"Attention in the barn. First call for weanlings, first call. We aim to start on time, so let's bring them to the arena. First call for weanlings, AOTS, Amateur Owner to Show."* The electronic pop was repeated as the speaker cut out.

Brit turned the water off, and pulled a narrow, flexible metal blade from a back pocket. Working from the top, and quickly, because an impatient line was forming, she scraped water from the filly's coat. Breathless snorted and shook her head, sending a shower from her mane in every direction, setting off a chorus of complaints from the waiting grooms.

"Aw, whyn'tcha try the shower at the other end of the barn and see if the water's any drier up there?" Brit said, but not angrily. "There, all done," she added, and came to unhook the cross-ties.

"Who's the filly?" asked the groom next in line, a plump redhead named Hilary.

"Leaves You Breathless, out of Blue Wind by Copper Wind. Owned by Tretower Farm." Breathless, now her usual friendly and curious self, pushed her nose forward to inhale the scent of the speckled gray gelding Hilary was with, thus displaying her delicate head and the flawless curves of her neck.

"Holy cow," breathed Hilary, and there was a murmur of agreement.

"Thanks," said Brit. "Marvin's looking pretty good." Marvin was the speckled gelding, a reliable performer in English Hunter classes. His registered name was Buckley's Chance; he was nearly twenty and had come by the barn name of Marvin so long ago no one remembered anymore how it had happened.

Brit started back down the passageway, Breathless following tamely until they neared the turnoff to the Tretower aisle, where she slewed around, snorting.

"Again? Come on, we haven't got time for games right now!" Brit coaxed with tugs at the lead, but Breathless's head came up and she braced herself, hind feet well under her, ready to stand up. Without warning, Brit reached around and smacked the filly on her rump, cupping her palm to make a nice, loud crack. Startled, Breathless leaped forward, and once she was under way, Brit hurried her down toward the prep stall.

But all the way, the horse pranced, tail up, eyes rolling, so Brit kept up a constant soothing grumble. "Now cut that out, sorry I had to smack you back there, I don't know what you thought you were doing, you were nice as pie yesterday, easy now for cryinoutloud, when I need you to be sweet you act like the silliest, stupidest"—she stopped to wrench the handle of the prep stall up and yanked the sliding door open.

And there in the middle of the brand-new grass-green carpet, on a dark stain that hadn't been there yesterday, was the bloody ruin of a man.

Brit took a breath to scream, and taking that as signal, Breathless screamed with her, rearing, and shaking her head to loosen Brit's grip on the lead. The other horses in Tretower stalls whickered and called.

Brit tightened her fist, turning and reaching to soothe. "No, no, sweetheart, that's a good girl, whoa Breathless, here now, here now." Pulling firmly, she reached again to stroke. "Easy, easy, easy," she crooned as the horse responded, then leaned in herself to rest her face on Breathless's warm, steamy shoulder. "It's okay, it's gotta be okay." The filly's head came around to nuzzle Brit's neck in return, and the two stood like that, taking and giving comfort, until after a last "I'm here, I'm here," call from the stallion, the other horses subsided as well.

"Easy, easy, easy," murmured Brit one last time, then turned and leaned a little sideways to see if she had really seen what she thought she had seen. Oh, he really was in there all right, crumpled into a clumsy heap, his legs folded up in an uncomfortable way. He wore light brown pants and dark brown vest and a white shirt with the sleeves turned back as if to show the expensive gold wristwatch on a forearm the delicate, unreal color of cream of wheat.

Snap. *"Second call, second call to the barn for weanlings. This is your second call. AOTS. Let's see what you've got."* Snap.

His throat was all black and shapeless, and his hands were thick with darkness, as if he'd tried to scoop up the blood and put it back. Oh, God, it wasn't a vest, it was blood, blood that had poured down and soaked, thickened and dried all over the front of him.

But what if he were still alive? She stepped away from Breathless and stood on tiptoe to get a different perspective on the body, holding her breath. The upper arm had fallen back, tilting the ribcage against the thickened shirt. She looked until her own diaphragm lurched and she had to begin breathing again—but still the shirt was motionless. No, it was impossible that he could be alive.

She looked around. No one had been attracted by her scream, mixed as it was with the filly's, and the impulse to scream was gone now. And anyway, yelling would send Breathless right back into fits. Also, the people who would come running, when they saw who it was, they might think she did it. Brit, listening to her heart still thundering in her ears, murmured, "So what do I do?" She looked at her watch: 6:50. Kori and Danny should be here any minute. Maybe she should just wait. No, this was an emergency. What should people do in an emergency?

She took a couple more breaths to steady herself, then petted the filly until she was calm enough to follow, put her back into her stall, and hurried away.

Up near the main entrance was the barn office, which did, as she recalled, have a pay phone on the wall beside it. She lifted the receiver, heard a dial tone, and dialed *911*. The response was a peculiar chuggle and then a fast busy. She hung up and tried again. Same result. Okay. Lafite didn't have an emergency call system. She pushed down the lever, let it up, and dialed *O*.

After far too many rings: "Operator."

"Hi, I'm Brittany Morgan, out at the horse show at the fairgrounds, and I've just found a dead body in my prep stall."

There was a startled pause, then the operator said, in a voice suddenly gone human, "Could you say that again, honey?"

"There's a man in one of the box stalls we're using to prep the horses for the show, y'know? And he's—he's bled all over himself, and he's dead. Could you send the police? I haven't got a quarter, that's why I called you."

A middle-aged man wearing an impeccable English riding habit went past her out the broad main door. He was leading a tiny chestnut foal whose fuzzy tail stood up like an ostrich feather on its little rump. Down the aisle from which she'd come, Hilary was walking toward her, leading a sedate Marvin, whose tail, tied in a knot, had gone dark and stringy from his bath. They turned in to a side aisle. The whole barn was alive now, with horses snorting, whinnying, or clattering their metal shoes in the cement aisles, radios blaring six different stations, people talking, laughing, giving orders. It was all so incredibly familiar that Brit was startled when the operator spoke.

"Hon, I asked, how sure are you he's dead?"

"Huh? Oh, gosh, I'm pretty sure. I mean, the blood's dark like it's dry, and he isn't breathing. But I didn't go touch him or anything. I was too scared."

"Well, I'll send an ambulance anyway. You're at the fairgrounds?"

"Yes, in the horse barn."

"Is there like a main entrance?"

"Sure, I'm there now."

"What are you wearing?"

"I'm in jeans and a gray sweatshirt, and I'm wearing a blue baseball cap with a little teddy bear sitting on the bill."

"And your name again?"

"Brittany Morgan. Please, tell them to hurry. This place is full of people." Brit hung up and turned around. Amelia Haydock was standing right there, her dark eyebrows nearly into her maroon hairline and her painted mouth a small *O*. She was immaculately turned out in a green pantsuit, complete with vest and tie, a green-and-gray striped silk blouse, and green patent leather boots. Her friendly-judge outfit, for the amateurs who would be riding horses into her ring today.

"Who's dead?" she demanded.

"Keith Bulward."

"*Not* Danny Bannister, then. You sure he's dead?"

"Oh, he's got to be. I mean, oh God, Ms. Haydock, I just about walked in there and he's . . . he's . . . so awful"—Brit sobbed once and Amelia immediately stepped forward to take Brit in a close hug, mashing her face against a firm chest.

"Not now," she said, thumping Brit very hard on the back, "Police coming to ask questions. After, lots of hysterics. Okay?"

"Yes'm," said Brit, gulping because her sobs threatened to turn into laughter, and struggling out of the smothering hug. The thumping had helped, too, being painful enough to shift her attention.

Amelia kept her strong hands tight around Brit's upper arms. "You okay?" Brit nodded. "Sure?"

"Yes, thank you."

"Good. Go on out. Where is he?"

"Aisle B, center set of stalls."

"I'll guard the body." She turned on her Cuban heel and went tapping briskly down the aisle.

Brit went to stand in the open doorway, wiping the last of the tears away, drying her hands on her jeans. The doorway was a big affair, high enough and wide enough for a team of Shires to walk through.

"*Last call, this is the last call for Arabian weanling foals. We're opening the gate to bring them into the ring. Last call, AOTS weanling foals.*"

A teenaged girl in pants and jacket with a Western cut to them trotted past attached by a blue nylon lead to a dark brown foal even tinier than the chestnut. It skittered on dime-size hooves, now in front, now behind the girl as she angled across the broad street toward the arena. God, they're weaning them younger and younger, thought Brit.

Judging by the puddles, it had rained again last night. It was very chilly, but the thin fog that softened the outlines of buildings and greening trees was already shot through with sunlight. Brit could see her breath curling away into the still air. A robin chirruped boisterously nearby, and by the smell, the sweet-roll stand had added bacon to its menu.

All the doors to the barn were open now. The street in front, and probably the one on the north side as well, were a parade of horses, some saddled and bound for the open-air exercise paddock; others, wrapped in coats, just out to have a look at the day.

The twinkling flash of red lights reflecting off walls and the mist announced the squad car before it turned the corner. It gave a brief, warning growl of siren, and she lifted an arm in signal. Horses turned inquiring heads as their equally curious handlers moved them out of the way.

The car pulled up, lights still flashing. There were two men inside. The passenger got out, tall, thickset, hatless, with a seamed face and tan hair. His zipped black leather jacket had a silver badge pinned to it, and his trousers were gray-blue with a navy blue stripe. The gun in his holster was ridiculously big, even for him. He was carrying a very large transceiver.

"You Brittany?" he asked in a deep voice, giving her sweatshirt a long look. Embarrassed, she brushed at it. The logo on it was a wheelbarrow surrounded by the words "Manure Movers of America."

"Yessir. If you'll come with me, I'll show you what I found."

The cop bent and said something inaudible to the driver, who dropped the squad into park and sat back, prepared to wait.

Brit noticed the heads turn as they walked past the side aisles toward the one where the body lay, calling attention to themselves by the spurts of static and unintelligible chatter from the policeman's transceiver. But no one followed; everyone was too busy to do more than stare them out of sight.

They turned into the third side aisle, and, down near the

other end, in front of the open stall door, Amelia Haydock stood on sentry duty.

The jacket of her green suit was cut long, which helped disguise her height; Brit noticed the policeman's small start of surprise as he came up to her and found that she was not a woman he could loom over.

"What's the story here?" he asked. "And who are you?"

In her own deep voice Amelia replied, "Amelia Haydock. Keeping scene intact." She stepped aside with a gesture as abrupt as her speech. "In there. Dead man."

"Oh, yeah?" said the cop, and went in. His heartfelt "Christ!" brought a tiny smirk to Amelia's lips. The exclamation was not loud and he began to speak even less loudly, apparently into his transceiver, a sentence that was mostly numbers beginning with ten. The transceiver spat and muttered a brief reply Brit interpreted as ten-four.

He came out and asked, "Anyone know who it is?"

"Keith Bulward," said Brit, when Amelia looked at her, but Amelia nodded agreement when the cop, taking out a notebook, glanced at her for confirmation.

"Friend of yours?" he asked Brit, his tone suspicious.

"No." Brit began to feel alarmed, a feeling that grew as she realized the cop was aware of it.

"Any idea how he came to be here?"

". . . No." She was feeling so lightheaded with terror that she could hardly get the word out.

"You okay?"

"J-just scared."

"What's the setup here?"

"We're here . . . for the, the Fourth Annual Lafite . . . All-Arabian Horse Show." She swallowed and took in a breath, let half of it out, then continued more clearly, "I'm the groom for Tretower Farm . . . and these eight stalls are ours for the show."

"Mr. Bulward work for Tretower Farm, too?"

"No, he owns Morning Glory Farms. His stalls are near the main entrance."

"So how'd he end up over here?"

"I don't know!"

"You sure? Is there some connection between Tretower and Morning Glory?"

"No! I mean, not exactly. I mean, I used to work for Morning Glory."

"But you quit them to work over here," guessed the cop. Brit hesitated, and the cop was quick to suggest, "He fire you maybe?"

"No!"

The cop consulted his notebook. "Your name's Brittany Morgan, right?"

Her throat tightened again. "Uh-uh-huh . . . yes."

He added a note, gave her a look that warned her to stand fast, then asked Amelia to spell her name. "You the owner of Tretower Farm?"

"No. Sunny Meadow Arabians."

"You a friend of the deceased?"

"Was," said Amelia cryptically.

"You have any idea how he ended up like this?"

"Knife, probably." Amelia's tone was very dry.

"Huh. Do you know anyone who might have done something like this to him?"

"An enemy, obviously."

"He have many of those?"

A brief nod. "Great many."

"Name one."

"That wouldn't be fair," she said, pointedly not looking at Brit, even after the policeman did. When he looked back, she continued, with a disarming, and less telegraphic, frankness, "I quarreled with him yesterday morning. Not sure if that made us enemies."

Brit listened to Amelia's skillful evasions, so contrasting with her own obvious fear, and thought, I've got to get out of this; I've got to get away before they arrest me for murder.

Kori and Danny came around the corner of the horse barn and saw the square, white-and-orange backside of an ambulance, lights blinkety-blinking in a kitty-corner pattern. Beside it was a squad car, empty.

"Someone's hurt," said Kori. "I wonder who." They hurried into the barn.

A glance down the aisles showed a small crowd gathered toward the south end of aisle three—by their own stalls.

"Hey," announced someone as they approached, "here they come!"

"Oh, hell," muttered Danny.

"What if it's Brit?" worried Kori.

"I see they got hold of you," said a redhead as they came up.

"What's going on, Hilary?" asked Kori.

"Didn't they tell you? Keith Bulward's dead. He was found in one of your stalls."

Kori reached out as if to take Hilary by the arm, but halted, the gesture incomplete. "Oh, no," she whispered.

"One of *our* stalls?" demanded Danny, unbelieving. "What happened to him?"

"That's the question the police are asking Brit right now."

Danny and Kori exchanged looks, then began pushing their way through the crowd. The people, most murmuring sympathetic or comforting words, did their best to move aside, and soon they came up against the crime scene ribbon that blocked the entrance to the aisle. Beyond the strip of yellow plastic, they saw two policemen. The taller one was talking to Brit, who appeared to be crying; the shorter was listening to Amelia Haydock's telegraphic exposition. Both were taking notes. No one else was visible, not even paramedics.

"Yo!" called Danny. "Over here!"

The policemen looked, and Brit made a violent pointing gesture at them, speaking to the taller cop. He came toward them.

"You Mrs. Bricker?" he asked Kori.

"Mrs. Brichter," she corrected him. "Yes. May I know what is going on?"

"Would you mind stepping across the line? Follow me."
And he turned back.

"Wait here," Kori said to Danny, and ducked under the
tape.

"I want to go home and they won't let me!" cried Brit
before Kori had reached her. "Make them let me leave!"

"That's enough," said the taller cop.

"Is she being held for some reason?" asked Kori.

"Ma'm, I haven't even told you what the situation is,"
said the cop, his face reddening with exasperation.

Keeping her voice level, Kori said, "I'm asking you what
the situation is, particularly as it relates to the detention of
my groom, Miss Morgan."

The cop consulted his notebook. "It appears that a Mr.
Keith Bulward has been found dead in what I understand is
called a prep or preparation stall, said stall being one of eight
reserved by Tretower Farm for your use during a horse show.
It was Miss Morgan here who found the body. There will be
an investigation, and we'd like her to stay around until we're
sure we've asked all the questions she can answer."

Brit thrust in, "I've told them everything, over and over,
and they still won't let me go! If you saw what I saw, you'd
be scared, too! Keith's in there, all bloody! It must've been
a crazy person, and I want to go home! They can't make me
stay and get killed too, can they?"

"Is she under arrest?" asked Kori.

"No one's under arrest, not yet," said the cop. "But on
the other hand, we're not going to let anyone with knowledge
about this event just walk away until our investigation is
over."

"When did Mr. Bulward die?"

"That's not the sort of thing we can tell just looking.
When were you last inside that stall?"

Kori thought. "Late yesterday afternoon, I suppose, to
make sure it was all set for this morning."

"Who else could have gone in after you?"

"Anyone. It's not locked, and there have been people here

continuously ever since the barn opened for competitors Thursday morning. People were in here all day yesterday, there was a party in the barn yesterday evening, and people slept here all night." She turned to Brit. "Did you hear anything?"

To her surprise, Brit said, too sharply, "Nothing happened! I was asleep all night! Keith Bulward started it, but I didn't do anything, you know I wouldn't do anything like this! So why should I have to stay here?"

The policeman asked, "What was it Mr. Bulward started?"

"Nothing important, just fooling around. I got mad at him and quit, that's all. So don't you listen to anyone who tries to tell you different. I don't have to stay here and listen to lies." She took the first quick step away, but the cop's long arm whipped out and caught her just above the elbow before she could continue running. Brit swung around, fell onto one knee, and began to sob, struggling feebly. "Let me go, let me go!"

"I think," said the cop, reaching for his handcuffs, "that it's time we took you in hand, little lady."

"Wait just a minute!" said Kori, throwing a pleading glance at the cop, who paused doubtfully. She went to kneel beside Brit. "Listen," she said, shaking the girl's shoulder. "Stop crying and listen." She pulled Brit's teddy bear cap off and stroked the honey-colored hair. "I know you didn't do anything, so you must stop acting like you have. Understand? But you're in a bad position, and you need a lawyer to guide you out of it."

"I don't want to go to jaaail," mourned Brit. "Make him let me goooo!"

Kori tightened her grip on the girl's shoulder. "Listen to me. You're not going to jail. But I can't prevent him from taking you to a police station for questioning. As soon as I get a change, I'm going to call Peter. Meanwhile, *you hold your tongue.* Understand? Say nothing further, not to this officer, not to anyone, until you talk to a lawyer."

Brit seemed to stop crying all at once. Her eyes, still

streaming tears, focused on Kori's face. She nodded, just once, then blinked and seemed to become aware of the embarrassment of her position on the floor.

The policeman, frowning at Kori but grateful the storm was ended, hoisted Brit to her feet and cuffed her hands behind her. "Now," he said with weighty finality, "we'll just see what our investigators say when they find we've got this wrapped up already."

▽

5

ELEANOR RITTER WAS A tall and very slender blond with a mild voice and just a little too much nose. She wore a gray wool suit with a gored skirt, and a pale pink blouse with a bow. The heels of her gray shoes were broad and low, and her purse was large enough to hold a gun without showing a bulge or crowding out the more usual contents. It hung by a strap from her shoulder.

The scene near the site where the body lay was, in her opinion, disorderly. The bluesuits had marked off either end of the aisle of box stalls with crime scene tape, but there were people pressed up against it shouting advice and questions to those inside it—particularly to a young woman in handcuffs leaning up against a stall door, her face pink with resentment and determination.

Eleanor ducked under the tape and signaled the bluesuit standing nearest the handcuffed girl toward her. She recognized him as a man whose abilities did not match his ambition. She met him at a point far enough away to be inaudible to both the crowd and the handcuffed woman. His face rearranged itself into a respectful demeanor only after giving her a glimpse of its owner's honest opinion of female investigators.

"What'cha got, Harve?" she asked, mildly irritated.

"There's a body in that box stall over there. White male. They all agree he was Keith Bulward. Looks like his throat was cut. And that young woman we've got handcuffed did it."

Eleanor said, "She say so?"

"No, but she's acting about as hinky as you can get. Tried to run away when I started to talk to her. She used to work for the deceased, and denied there was an exchange of threats before anyone asked her about it. She slept last night in the stall next to where the body is, but says she never heard a thing."

"Are you sure it's murder?"

Harve grinned. "Hey, maybe it's felonious littering, dropping a body in an uncemetarial location without a permit. Whatever, it sure made a mess of Mr. Bulward."

"Who was the last person to see Mr. Bulward alive?"

"Who knows? I told you, we didn't need to do any of that chickenshit stuff. We walk in, there's the body, and there she is, trying to get small almost before we ask her anything. Open and shut."

She went to the door of the box stall for a look at the body. She muttered a bad word, backed one step, and squatted for a close look at the area around the sill of the stall. On the drift of dust and dirt just under the sill were two small dribbles of reddish brown. She made a face and straightened.

"Attention in the barn," said a metallic voice. *"First call for yearling fillies, Amateur Owners to Show. Start bringin' 'em over, the weanlings will be finished shortly."*

Eleanor's frown at Harve was both angry and consternated. "You mean," she said to the cop, "you let the show go on? Didn't you think it might be a good idea to secure the perimeter? Canvass for witnesses?"

Harve lifted his hands and shoulders. "Well, why? We secured the crime scene, and we collared the suspect. There wasn't any reason not to let everyone else go about their business. In fact, it helped keep the numbers of gawkers down."

"You goddam better hope you're right, Patrolman Wilson!" she said. "You goddam better hope you make detective out of this, because if you're wrong, you're gonna be pushing a squad car for a long, long, *long* time!" She raised her voice. "Get some backup out here, now! I want the whole barn secured! I want everyone who's in here to stay in here, and anyone who's not in here not to come in, got me?" She turned to look at the crowd, and saw Harve doing the same, to see if someone broke loose to run for an exit. No one did—but that might be because Harve and his partner had already given any other possible suspects ample opportunity to leave.

More quietly, she ordered him to request investigators, the medical examiner, and a forensics team to come out. Harve nodded and left in an anxious hurry.

Then she went up and down the aisle, looking for more dribbles or anything that did not belong, anything obviously out of place, finding nothing. She went into the five occupied box stalls, speaking in a soothing voice to each horse while she lifted straw with a toe, looking for blood, and finding none. The one empty stall was that, clean and empty. She spent a few minutes in the stall where Brit had slept, careful to disturb nothing, only looking, finding nothing out of the ordinary, except that the equipment was of high quality and, though not new, well cared for. There were five horses brought by—she glanced at the label on one of the chests— "Tretower" to the show. One of her friends had five horses, and he was of the "use up, wear out, and make do" school. Tretower must be a high-class operation.

She came out of the tack stall and for the first time looked hard at the civilians waiting for her attention. All three were women. One was tall, approaching fifty, weathered in an honest, healthy way, except that her short hair was dyed an ugly purple-red. She was sitting on one of the director's chairs, legs crossed, her face expressive of grim patience. Her green pantsuit had enough of an exotic cut and exquisite fit about it to be tailer-made, and one of the several rings on her fingers appeared to be a genuine emerald. Eleanor had noticed the green-and-wine color motif that marked the Tretower area and wondered if this woman was declaring herself by the color of her clothes to be the owner.

The second woman was standing near enough to the crowd at the other end that she could speak with a man on the other side of the tape. She was much younger, maybe twenty-five, slender, and dressed in a pinstripe suit, the pants flaring enough to nearly cover her low-rise boots. Hatless, she had tucked her dark hair into a big bun at the nape of her neck, except where it had escaped to hang in thin, spiral strands in front of her ears and down her back. The effect was attractive—or maybe it was just that she was beautiful. The beautiful woman looks beautiful no matter what she wears or how her hair is fixed, thought Eleanor, who gave careful consideration to what she wore and how she did her hair. The man also was young, younger than the woman, skinny, with mud-brown hair and cheekbones so high they made his eyes narrow. Both of them looked worried, and as she watched, the man nodded at what the woman was saying and backed into the crowd so purposefully Eleanor was sure he had been sent on an errand.

"Cullen?" Eleanor said, but not loudly, and the other bluesuit left his position beside the handcuffed young woman, which he had assumed as soon as Harve had gone.

As he came over, he said, "Help you?" in a manner that was overtly disrespectful. He was about five feet nine inches, a weight lifter so muscular he looked like a short-legged frog.

"Cullen," she said quietly, "a young man, about twenty-two, wearing faded blue jeans, a red-plaid flannel shirt, and blue windbreaker jacket just left the crowd at that end. Follow him, but don't stop him unless he tries to leave the barn."

"Sure." A sullen tweak tugged Cullen's mouth, and he left. Eleanor pulled out her notebook and pen, found a blank page, and printed the date, the location, and the officers' names as a memo to herself.

Then she turned her attention to the handcuffed woman. She was tall, not quite as tall as the green pantsuit, but bulkier. She had the softness of youth and hearty appetite in her face and under her chin, but the pad of fat around her middle was less apparent than one might expect of someone who weighed at least a hundred and sixty pounds. Big-boned, thought Eleanor, and muscular; possibly even stronger than she looks. The face was not unattractive, but was spoiled by its expression of terrified determination, which became more emphatic as the girl became aware of Eleanor's regard.

Eleanor walked toward her. The girl had been leaning against the door of a box stall. She straightened, biting her under lip, doubtless reminding herself to be brave.

"Good morning," said Eleanor as gently as she could. "How's this for a terrible beginning to what may turn out to be a fine day? Were you out in that rain last night?"

The girl shook her head. "No, I slept in here."

"Lucky—except it must have been cold. Turn around, I want to unfasten your hands." The girl, surprised, obeyed. "I imagine you heard the rain. Must've been like sleeping inside a drum."

"Huh, I'm used to sleeping in barns." The girl pulled one hand free and shook it. "And I have this down sleeping bag, so I didn't know it was cold until I got up"—she stopped and her guard went up again.

"You slept in there?" Eleanor bent her head toward the tack stall.

"Yes." She rubbed one wrist and looked secretive.

"Where did the others sleep?"

"At a motel in town. It's mostly grooms who sleep in the barn at shows."

"So you must be the Tretower groom."

"Just for this show, probably. I mean, they've only got eight horses altogether, so they don't need a full-time groom. Danny and Kori can handle it by themselves."

"Danny and Kori are . . ." Eleanor paused expectantly.

"Danny—Daniel Bannister—he's the trainer, and Kori

Brichter is the owner." The girl's glance flicked, not to the
green pantsuit, but to the beautiful woman still standing
near the tape, the one who had been speaking to the young
man. Who was probably Danny.

"And you are . . ."

"Brittany Morgan." She moved her shoulders experi-
mentally.

"What's your address?"

"Depends on the time of year—seriously. I'm a full-time
student at the university in Champaign-Urbana, but sum-
mers I try to work full-time at different horse operations. My
folks live in Rockford. I'll be a junior at the U this fall."

"At present your address is . . ."

"Care of Mr. and Mrs. Morris Morgan, in Rockford." Brit
gave a street address, adding, "That's just until I get a job,
unless I get one near Rockford and it's not a live-in one, so
I'll live at home."

"Okay, Brittany—do they call you Brittany?"

"Brit, usually."

"Brit, then. I'm Sergeant Eleanor Ritter, an investigator
with the Lafite Police Department. I want to talk to you
about what might have happened here that led to that body
ending up in that box stall. You don't have to answer any of
my questions, and if you decide you will talk to me, you can
consult with an attorney before you do. If you want to talk
with an attorney, and can't afford one, I'll arrange for one for
you before we go any farther. Do you understand?"

Brit appeared torn. "What's the matter?" asked Eleanor.

"You seem to be okay, not like that other guy, but I kind
of think maybe I shouldn't say anything more. Kori said I
shouldn't, that she was gonna call . . . someone."

Eleanor nodded. "That's fine. We'll just stop right now,
until you make up your mind."

She stepped back, trying not to show any reaction to
Brittany's stare of surprise, gratitude, and—disappointment?
Interesting.

"Why don't you sit down," said Eleanor. "Take one of the

chairs from over there, and bring it back up here so those people won't be bothering you."

"Okay. Thanks. Is this going to take long?"

"Hours and hours and hours."

Kori watched the police officer nod at the woman investigator and slink off after Danny. She watched him with equanimity; Danny wasn't going to make a getaway, he was only going to call Peter. She glanced toward the woman, caught her looking back, her expression making clear she'd noted Kori's reaction.

Be careful, thought Kori; this is serious, and that woman may know what she's doing.

Kori had been married to a police detective long enough to tell when an investigation was being poorly handled. There should have been more questions from those two officers. They should have looked for clues or, for all they knew, more bodies. It was all right for them to think Brit might be guilty, but that shouldn't have stopped them from talking to everyone else. The shorter of the two officers seemed particularly wrong, as wrong as his swollen shape. His behavior toward his superior had been patently rude, which no police department allowed. She hoped he wouldn't interfere with Danny making that call. She wanted Peter here. He would know how to talk to these people, and ensure that a real investigation took place. Because that rude behavior might also mean that the investigator was not as competent as she appeared.

And, although Kori didn't want to admit it, she had this desire for a strong, competent, trustworthy man to come in and be on her side. Not someone she could go flying into the arms of, weeping all over the front of his shirt, of course; but someone to admire as he used the right police words to make these people do their job properly.

She looked over and saw the investigator unfastening Brit's handcuffs. Brit was taking it well, listening to the woman and nodding, and answering calmly. Not breaking for the exit like before—stupid, stupid!

Of course, all this must be frightening to Brit. But soon it would become clear to the investigator that it was impossible that someone as thoroughly gentle as Brittany Morgan could have waylaid Keith Bulward and killed him.

Which, of course, brought up the question: Then who?

Cullen walked down the aisle well behind his subject, feigning disinterest, but closing the gap as the kid approached the main exit, which now had a strip of yellow plastic across it and Wilson standing at parade rest just outside. A chorus of sirens told of the approach of more squads. The kid, however, didn't so much as glance out the door; he crossed the broad aisle, headed for the pay phone on the other side. Cullen turned away, to walk down the broad cross-aisle.

There was an amplified *click*, then a voice said, *"Second call, second call for yearling fillies. Bring 'em over, they're judging the last foal right now. Second call for yearling fillies."*

Cullen made a U-turn after he was out of the kid's line of sight, coming back on noiseless feet close enough to overhear the conversation. He had seen the kid was making a long-distance call, looking at a card in his hand and punching in a whole lot of numbers. Now he waited for someone to answer.

"Sarge?" he said. "Boy, am I glad I caught you in! No, no, she's fine; we're all fine. Well, except Brit, maybe. She's under arrest, for murder."

There was a brief pause, probably for an exclamatory demand for clarification. "Hell, I don't know; Kori and I just got here from the motel. We walk in and there's these two cops got our stalls blocked off with yellow plastic ribbon, and Brit's crying. And in handcuffs. Yeah, the whole nine yards, looks like. What? No, Kori got waved across the line and she's still in there. Me? Well, she kind of sneaked over and told me to call you." Pause. "Keith Bulward. He was found dead in our prep stall." Longer pause. "Well, yeah, Kori's sure it wasn't Brit. Hell, it could've been anyone; he wasn't exactly popular. He's a trainer, and he also buys and sells other

people's horses." Another pause, then an attempt to interrupt. "Yeah, but—look, all I know is—what? Uniforms,
both of 'em." Pause. "Yeah, some lady's there now, talking
to Brit. No, I didn't get her name, but I guess she's the
detective. Thin, blond, not bad looking. No, Sarge, listen:
These two cops take one look and slap on the cuffs. You
know? So Kori says, can you come?"

There wasn't a pause this time, there was a lengthy wait.
The kid spent it looking around. He spotted Cullen, raised
an I-see-you eyebrow at him, then turned away to let his eye
be caught by the bulletin board next to the phone. He spent
the next several minutes pretending to be deeply intrigued
by the announcement of another horse show in the region,
an ad for a fly repellent, and the two three-by-five cards with
ballpoint messages beginning For Sale. Finally, his attention
was recaptured by the person on the other end of the line.

"Yeah, I'm still here; what'd he say? Well, shit! When,
then? Okay, I'll tell her. Meanwhile, how about telling Dad?
Maybe he can—thanks. Huh? Oh, that's easy. Take Route 7
to 49, turn north, and it will bring you right by us. Look for
the sign that says Fairground about half a mile this side of
Lafite. What? Oh, the Best Western, on Sycamore and Main.
Room . . ." The kid dug into a front pocket and produced a
motel room key. "Mine's 107 and she's next door, so it's
either 105 or 109. No, Brit's sleeping in the barn. Or she
was; if they take her to jail, then I get to." He did not sound
happy about this. "How's Jeep? Yeah, uh-huh. He did?" He
listened, then laughed. "Yeah. Yeah, I'll tell her. Say hi to Jill
for me, okay? See you tomorrow. Early, I hope. Thanks,
Sarge!"

Which was kind of a funny nickname for a lawyer, thought
Cullen, annoyed that one was being summoned so promptly.
Most lawyers didn't get their start on screwing things up
until after their clients made bail. The kid really did head
for the main entrance now, so Cullen moved to stop him.

"Hey, you," he said in his best Clint Eastwood growl.
"Where do you think you're going?"

The kid turned around. "Just looking out the door."

"What's your name?"

"Daniel Bannister. Why?"

"Where do you live?" Cullen pulled out his notebook.

"Tretower Farm, Route 1, Charter, Illinois." He spelled "Tretower" and waited for Cullen to write that down.

"You own Tretower Farm?"

"No, I'm the trainer."

Cullen looked sideways at the kid, his interest piqued, but made a doubtful up-and-down. "What kind, low-impact aerobics?"

Danny could not help grinning. "No, sir, I train the horses."

"Ah." Interest fading back to the professional, Cullen looked around at the box stalls that lined the broad aisle. There were colorful draperies, video displays, fancy lettering on the signs, even real sod laid on the pavement and further ornamented with tubs of tulips and white wrought-iron benches. The smell of money was almost as strong as the smell of horse. "What are they, show jumpers?"

"They're Arabians."

"You train them to do tricks?"

"No, just the basics."

"Such as?"

Bannister shrugged. "To follow when led, to respond to voice and rein, to carry a rider, to stand properly if they're to be shown at halter, to be strong and flexible if they're in one of the performance classes. To not bite, not kick, to get into and out of a trailer when asked, and to be a nice, polite animal in the barn."

Cullen snorted, but faintly, not sure if Bannister was pulling his leg. Could someone make a living doing something like that? "Who was that you were talking to on the phone?"

Bannister hesitated, then said, "How about you ask my boss, Mrs. Brichter, about that? She's the one who told me to make the call."

"But you're the one who made it. You got a reason for not telling me?"

"No, but how about we get a for-real detective to ask me questions, all right?"

Cullen suppressed the warm fury that response brought, and took his time writing down his opinion of this evasive behavior. Then, "All right, come with me."

The woman detective asked Kori to step farther down the aisle. She gave her name as Sergeant Eleanor Ritter and offered a mild reading of the Miranda warning, which Kori waived.

"So you're willing to answer a few questions, then?"

"Sure."

"Do you know what happened here?"

Kori replied, "We got here after the police did; someone told me Keith Bulward was found dead in our prep stall."

"Correct. If you had anything to do with his death, I want you to tell me now."

The structuring of that question suggested formula, or ritual. "No, I didn't."

"Do you know who did it?"

"No."

"Were you a friend of the deceased?"

"No."

"But you knew him."

"Yes."

"For how long?"

Kori thought. "Maybe two and a half or three years."

"What did he do for a living?"

"He was a horse trainer, and he also would take horses on consignment to sell. He owned Morning Glory Farms, but I don't think he had any horses of his own."

"This may call for some speculation, but I assure you I'll keep your answer confidential. Can you think of anyone who might be involved in what happened to him here?"

All of these questions seemed patterned, and the last especially formulaic, but the answers were important. Kori's eyes shifted away, then back, before she said, "No."

Eleanor sighed and looked at the horse in the box stall they were next to. A bright bay stallion with a long forelock had come over to make soft whuffling noises at them. "What's this one's name?" she asked, a break in the ritual.

"Copper Wind," said Kori, looking at the horse.

"Nice, pretty even."

Kori felt her attention sharpen. She wanted to reach this investigator as a person, to make her understand that an injustice was being done to Brit. "You like horses?"

"Sure. A lot of my friends own horses. Is there a name for his color? I mean, he looks sort of the opposite of a palomino."

"He's a bay."

A palomino is technically a chestnut; his mane and tail are lighter than his body. A bay's mane and tail are darker. Copper Wind's coat was the rich red-brown of an emery board, and the black of his mane and tail also marked his lower legs, his nose, and the tips of his ears. He had the short, dished face, large eyes, and small, shapely ears that define the classic, or "typey," Arabian.

Eleanor put her hand up flat against the wire mesh, and Copper Wind shifted at once to inhale and then blow warm air over it. "Friendly," she remarked.

"Yes. And anyway, he's hungry."

"You want to tell me who it is you suspect, so maybe we can get things going and you can feed Copper Wind and the others a little sooner?"

Kori brushed at a strand of hair that had fallen across her nose. "I shouldn't have broken eye contact, should I?"

Eleanor looked slantwise at her. "Who's been teaching you interrogation techniques?"

"I'm a horse trader." She smiled and added, "Also, my husband is Detective Sergeant Peter Brichter, with the Charter Police Department."

"Is he now!" said Eleanor with respect.

"You know him?"

"We've talked on the phone, and I met him in person at

the FBI National Academy in Quantico last year. Very sharp."

"I'm glad you think so. Perhaps I should tell you I sent— uh-oh."

Eleanor turned to follow Kori's look. Cullen was pushing the young man she'd sent him to tail under the yellow tape. Cullen was trying to look confident, which meant he wasn't sure he'd done exactly as ordered. She waited for the two to get close before speaking.

"Did he try to leave the barn?"

"Yes, ma'm," said Cullen in his firmest voice.

"Did not," said the young man, but quietly.

"You first," Eleanor said to Cullen.

"I followed him, like you told me to. He went to the pay phone up near the front door, where he placed a long-distance credit-card call to a lawyer he calls Sarge, asking him to hustle out here because 'Brit' was under arrest for murder. When he hung up, he walked right to the open door of the barn, at which point I called him back. He says his name is Daniel Bannister, and he *says* he makes a living teaching horses to have good manners."

Eleanor looked at Danny. "I'm the trainer at Tretower Farm," he said, raising his eyebrows as if that should be not only self-evident from Cullen's statement, but not in the least suspicious or surprising.

Eleanor looked at Kori, who nodded. "That's right."

Eleanor asked Danny, "Did you try to leave the barn?"

"No, ma'm; but I did want to go over and have a look. I'd heard sirens on my way to the phone and I wanted to see if something else had happened."

"I assume 'Sarge' is Detective Sergeant Peter Brichter of the Charter Police Department?"

Cullen took a swift, angry breath, and the young man blinked in surprise, then exchanged a Captain-may-I/yes-you-may glance with Kori. "Yes, ma'm. Is your name Ritter?"

Eleanor smiled. "Yes."

Danny said to Kori, "He says to contact Sergeant Ritter

of the Lafite police if you can, because she's sharp; meanwhile, he has to meet with the county attorney, and he can't break that appointment. He'll call you tonight and be here tomorrow." He grinned suddenly. "Also, he told me that Jeep . . ." As fast as he had grinned, he looked embarrassed. "Never mind. I'll tell you later."

"Maybe you better tell us now," growled Cullen.

Danny looked at him and as suddenly as it had gone the grin was back. "Sure," he said, and said to Kori, "Sarge says this morning Jill told him that Jeep woke her up with the pan to his potty chair in his hand. He was so proud that he'd gotten up all by himself and did good that he brought it to show her."

Eleanor bit her lip and Cullen made an angry sound of frustration. Kori put her hand over her mouth to hide her smile, but her eyes had the hurt look of a mother whose child has announced an important growing-up step to the nanny, rather than herself.

The metallic voice spoke. *'Attention in the barn. This is the final call for yearlings, final call. They—what! Who the devil—!''* The voice cut off.

"About time," remarked Eleanor.

"They aren't going to like this," said Kori.

"Who isn't?"

"The show officials. One of them will be over here any minute wanting to know why they can't just scratch Keith's entries from the classes and go on with it."

"Send him to me; I'll explain why," said Eleanor. "Ah, here's my crew and the coroner. You, Danny," she said to him, "go back outside the line, but hang around so you'll be available when I have time to interview you properly. And then maybe we can let you and Brit take care of your horses."

"Yes, ma'm."

She turned to Kori. "Can you wait here just a couple of minutes while I get these people started?"

"Of course."

* * *

Lafite could not afford a proper, full-time medical examiner. Its coroner was an M.D. with a regular practice; he served as coroner on the side. He was a short, rotund man with wire-rimmed spectacles and a thick brown suit. He raised his eyebrow in inquiry as Eleanor walked toward him, and she pointed to the prep stall, then changed course to meet him at the door to it.

Dr. Burke was a qualified pathologist, but to remind everyone that he was mainly a family practitioner, he carried an old-fashioned doctor's satchel to murder scenes. But there was no denying his look of happy anticipation as Eleanor slid open the prep stall door. She said, "He's cold but not stiff. I don't think it happened in here."

The doctor nodded and went in. Eleanor shut the door after him and turned to the other two men who had come in with the coroner. One looked very young, with big, thin hands and a complexion spotted with moles; the other was much older, his short, dark hair well sprinkled with gray, his square-cut face professionally expressionless. Everyone exchanged nods. The young one said, "This one's all yours, Nell. What do you want us to do?"

Eleanor quashed her feeling of surprise before it could more than flicker across her face. Lead-investigator assignments were made in turn; this was the first time one of them involving homicide had been given to her. Then she smiled. "First thing's the log. I want everyone who crosses that line"—she turned and pointed to the ribbon Kori had ducked under earlier—"to log in and log out. And I mean everyone, even the chief. I want the other end"—she pointed—"closed to any entry. Find me two bluesuits to enforce those instructions. And I want four more to stand at each of the four entrances to this barn, to make sure my perimeter's secure. There's going to be some screaming in pretty short order, people wanting both in and out, so warn them to hold the line. That should keep you busy for a few minutes, while I finish talking with Mrs. Brichter there."

The pair nodded and departed. Eleanor returned to Kori

and said in the identical quiet voice she'd been using before
they were interrupted, "You want to tell me who it is you
suspect?"

Kori smiled her surprise, then said, "Oh, all right. But first
I want to say it wasn't Brittany Morgan, that young woman
who was in handcuffs when you arrived. It's true Bulward
tried to assault her a few weeks ago and threatened to con-
clude matters if she ever got within reach. She didn't know
he was going to be here, and we had to talk her out of leaving
on the spot when she saw him. But her instinct was to run,
not fight. I don't think I've ever seen a kinder, gentler young
woman. I simply can't believe she is capable of murder."

Eleanor wrote for a while, then started, "Who might—"
but was interrupted when someone called, "Yo! Sergeant
Ritter! The cavalry has arrived!"

Eleanor turned to see a young black man with close-
clipped hair waving at her from inside the yellow plastic
strip. Behind him, still straightening, was a white man of
the same age, height, and build, his brown hair also cropped
short. He was burdened with a necklace of cameras and two
medium-sized suitcases, heavy ones by the way he was staggering to get himself upright.

"Dave, Roger," she said in greeting. "Over there," and
pointed to the prep stall.

She turned back to Kori. "You were saying . . . ?"

Kori, who had obviously been thinking during this interim, said, "Keith Bulward came out of the blue. His grandfather was one of the best trainers in the country, but his
father wasn't interested in horses. It was like, one day no
one had ever heard of Keith Bulward and the next he was
showing quality horses at halter, and walking off with ribbons. It happened so fast that there was talk that he traded
on his grandfather's name to get clients and that he
'cultivated' judges. But he was very, very good in the show
ring. So lately the rumors have been even more vicious: that
he used cruel and even illegal methods to prepare horses for
showing. If someone sent his horse to Keith for training and

got it back crippled by his methods, he might be very angry. Which is not to say that happened, or even that I know for a fact his methods could do such a thing. On the other hand, I did see him strike a calm and obedient horse with his fist yesterday morning. The owner is Amelia Haydock, the woman in the green suit right over there. She was angrier than I've ever seen her." She paused, trying to think how to sum up. "Keith Bulward was the kind of person who, when you hear he's been murdered, you're shocked, but not really surprised."

▽

6

THE LADY IN THE green pantsuit had been waiting very patiently in the director's chair. She rose as Eleanor came toward her, tugged at the bottom of her jacket, and brushed one lapel; a displacement activity, thought Eleanor, as the jacket needed neither brushing nor adjustment.

"I want to thank you for being so patient," she said, holding out her hand. "I'm Sergeant Eleanor Ritter, an investigator with the Lafite Police Department." Her hand was taken in a warm, strong, callused grip.

"Perfectly all right," said the woman in a deep voice. "I'm Amelia Haydock, show judge."

Eleanor wrote that down, and the other basics, then gave her the warning, coupled with a request for cooperation.

"Yes," said Amelia.

"Do you have some connection with Tretower Farm?"

"No. Came to preserve scene."

"That was very intelligent of you."

Amelia acknowledged the comment with a stiff little nod of her maroon head.

"Do you know what happened here today?"

"Keith Bulward's dead."

74

"Do you have any idea how?"

"Knife, probably." Amelia gave no indication she'd answered that question before.

"What makes you say that?"

"Saw body."

"That must have been a shock, to have seen him like that."

Another stiff nod. "Awful."

"Did you know the deceased?"

This brought a pause, probably to compose an explanation and then lop off any extraneous syllables before answering. Eleanor bit discreetly on the lining of her cheek to keep from smiling as she waited for the result.

"Yes."

Well, that was brief enough. "Was he a friend?"

"Protégé, more like. Until yesterday."

"What happened yesterday?"

"He struck my horse. End of friendship."

"Did you kill him?"

"No." This was said to the floor, and Eleanor sighed. But, when even the ones who knew better could not maintain eye contact, what could you expect of the others? Amelia, hearing the sigh, looked up. "Considered it," she admitted. "But no."

"Nell?"

Eleanor turned to see the coroner gesturing at her from the door of the box stall.

She turned back to Amelia. "We've stopped the show," she said, "so you have no urgent reason to leave, am I right?"

"Fine," said Amelia, replying to the unspoken request that she stay put.

This close to the body, the warm smell of horse and the dusty smell of hay and straw were overborne by the humid, gamey smell of blood and death. Eleanor swallowed her disgust and anger at the sign of the body, but did not deny her feelings; they too often proved a valuable spur to the successful completion of an investigation.

"What happened to my crew?" she asked.

"Dave's gone off to organize a search of the barn. Roger's looking around in the stall next door. Says it looks like someone slept in there last night."

"Someone did. You agree, this didn't happen here?"

"Couldn't have; it would be like an abattoir in here if it had."

"Dave get his pictures?"

"Yeah."

"So what's your official verdict?"

"Interim cause of death will be loss of blood, obviously. There's nothing immediately showing to tell me the method. But let's have a closer look." The doctor, who was not a young man, lowered himself clumsily onto the green carpeting beside the body, which was now face down, and made gestures indicating he wanted it turned onto its back. "Give me a hand, will you?"

Eleanor did. The body was a terrible object, in the antique meaning of the word, that which inspires terror. Under the gore, the cool, pale flesh was faintly mottled, the half-open eyes like set gelatin.

"No rigor," remarked Eleanor.

"Chilling delays onset," replied the coroner. "And anyway, I don't believe this happened earlier than midnight last night, and more likely an hour or two later."

The corpse's throat was open at an angle from just under the right earlobe to near the bottom of the neck. The trachea had been ripped open in passage.

"Once this happened, he couldn't make a sound." The coroner bent forward for a closer look and grunted.

"What?" asked Eleanor.

"Funny sort of wound, as much a tear as a cut." Eleanor leaned in while the coroner picked up the stained hands one at a time and moved the fingers to pull the skin taut on the palms and loosen it again. "Looks like a similar injury to two fingers and the palm of the right hand."

Eleanor looked at that, too. "Defense wound?"

"Possibly."

"So this isn't a suicide." People don't try to fend off a wound they wish to inflict on themselves.

Dr. Burke unbuttoned the thickened shirt to look for more injuries and found none. He removed the wristwatch, then went through the pockets and found a comb, a good eelskin wallet with driver's license and credit cards in the name of Keith Bulward. There was no motel room key, but there was a receipt from a reputable local restaurant, three hundred sixty-four dollars in a platinum money clip set with a sapphire, sixty-seven cents in change, a cardholder with Bulward's business cards in one side and a thin collection of cards from other people in the other, and a short ballpoint pen that looked as if it were made of, or plated with, real gold. There was a key wallet full of keys.

"Robbery not the motive," he grunted.

Burke found faint, bruiselike stains on the parts of the body closest to the floor that didn't actually touch it, evidence that the body had been brought to this site shortly after death. "Or else someone knows about lividity and was careful to put him down in exactly the same pose he found him in." He sat back on one heel and sighed. "Poor bugger, it didn't take long for him to die, but it wasn't pleasant."

Eleanor's mouth pulled tight. She stood up and called, "Roger?"

A voice came from the next stall over. "Here!"

"Come back, and bring your case. We've got some stuff that needs to be tagged and bagged."

"Gotcha."

Eleanor stood, frowning down at the body for a few seconds, rubbing her upper arm. "You know, maybe this isn't murder after all."

With an effort Burke got both feet under him and climbed up on his legs with a groan. "What do you mean?"

"I've got a crummy-looking scar on my arm, right here, that a horse gave me when I was just a kid. I scared him and he reared up and hit me just once. It would have been just a bruise, but he had a loose shoe, and a nail caught in the skin and ripped it for five inches. Suppose Bulward went into a box stall, and the horse in there reared up and lashed out twice, catching his hand and then his throat?"

"Yeah," said Dr. Burke, "and when he'd about bled out, he got up and staggered in here to die. Never minding the physical impossibility, where's the trail of blood?"

"Okay, I was also thinking maybe the owner came along and found a dead man in a stall with his horse. And maybe he'd had a fight with the guy. So he wrapped the body up in something and brought it down here."

"Hm," said the coroner.

"I know it's a long shot, but it needs to be eliminated. And whether someone killed him or found him dead, he was brought here after the fact."

Dr. Burke shrugged. "In what?"

"Something waterproof, or something thick enough to soak up the leakage. A piece of carpet like these people have laid down here would do it. But this carpet shows no signs it was lifted and relaid. I wonder if this business of putting down carpet is unique to this outfit?"

"Beats me," said Burke.

"Okay, we'll check it out, and if it isn't, we'll look for a missing carpet, or a bloodstained one. There's a couple of drops of blood right outside the door, as if when he tilted the body to get it in here—hear that, Roger?" She spoke to the black man standing just outside the door. "Be sure you have Dave get a picture, and then collect as much of it as you can."

"You may consider it done, *kemo sabe*, because it already is." Roger executed a deep bow, then came in with one of his cases. "Where's the stuff you need tagged?"

"On the floor here, beside me. I wonder if whoever moved him chose this particular stall on purpose, and if so, why? And what did he do with the thing he wrapped him in after he finished with it?" Eleanor left off rubbing her upper arm and bit her tongue, thinking. "It took three nurses and two doctors an hour to clean the crud out of my arm. That was the last time I got within a horse's reach. You check his wounds for horse manure, straw, anything like that. I can't tell you how happy I'll be if this isn't murder after all."

"They can't do this to us; they simply can't!" said Sally Reed. "American Horse Shows won't allow it, we have a legal contract, signed and sealed, to run this show on the days we printed in the schedule, in the order we printed in the schedule, without leaving out classes printed in the schedule." Sally was a kind, cheerful, hardworking, middle-aged lady with champagne-colored hair who favored silk print dresses that swirled becomingly around her trim calves, and nice ordinary-size sentences. Only right now, the swirl was gone from her dress as the brevity was gone from her speech. As the joy was gone from her heart.

"Well, what the hell am I supposed to do? You know I can't decide something like that without Hank, don't you? Look, I was told that all I had to do this weekend was turn up, smile, and pose for pictures. 'Figurehead' is the way Maggie described it to me; I distinctly remember she used that exact word. So God dammit, how come everyone's standing around waiting for *me* to be the one to do something?" Bob McIntyre, a handsome, stocky man with silver hair, fumbled for his pipe with pudgy, trembling fingers.

"Because she was wrong, Senator," said Sally Reed. "You're the show manager; that means you're the one who manages this show. Ordinarily, at this point, your work is done, but this time is the one time in a thousand it's different. As assistant show manger, Hank probably could advise you, just as he has all along; he's an experienced show manager. It's not his fault his appendix blew up."

"But can't you help? You know more about these things than I do!"

Sally shook her head. "I'm only the secretary; my job is to take entries and run the show office. Andrew here, he's show steward." Andrew, a young agribusinessman in a fashionable three-piece suit, nodded glumly. "His job is to see the rules get enforced. Our treasurer managed the first Lafite show, but she's stuck outside with her yearling colt, both of them freezing to death because the stupid cop at the door won't listen when she tries to explain that they belong in the barn, they came out of the barn ten minutes before he got there, and couldn't someone at least be allowed to bring Maggie a jacket and the colt a blanket? No, Senator, you're the one with the authority to speak on equal terms with the person running this, this investigation; and more important, you're the *only* one with the power to make that major decision, such as do we cancel the show and give everyone his money back—which will put us severely in the hole since it will be money already spent on the expenses of putting the show together—or do we contact the county and try to extend our rental of the barn and arena to cover an extra day or two, or three, then try to persuade the competitors to stay? Which most of them won't, they having other shows to go to. Can't the police understand how important this is to us? I'm really sorry this is happening at the show where you hold the title of show manager; but since it has, and you do, it's your job to make the decision, and unfortunately we don't have a lot of time to decide." Even Sally was appalled at that spate of run-on sentences. She shut up.

Senator Bob McIntyre, the focus of her concern, was a state senator just turned sixty, who would have greatly improved his noble profile with the loss of forty pounds. Things were just starting to heat up in Springfield, building toward the end-of-June adjournment, but at least he no longer had to juggle that with his workload at the law firm. He had sold his partnership and taken early retirement two years ago when his great-aunt Lucy finally died at a hundred and two.

Which had led indirectly to his being here. She had left a neglected horse farm and three million dollars to him as residual legatee of his deceased parents and two late, childless uncles. It was his sixteen-year-old daughter, pointing out the continuing expense of boarding her thoroughbred, who persuaded him not to sell the farm but restore it to working order. He had, and then she bought another horse, an Arabian gelding, a magically beautiful creature who ornamented the pasture like an end shot on "CBS Sunday Morning." He and his wife sold their townhouse and moved out to the farm, which would have been a mistake had not there now been the money to hire a housekeeper and a gardener and a steady stream of repairmen. Their daughter got two of her horse-crazy friends to help with the barn work in return for rent-free housing of their horses. The senator had enjoyed playing the role of country gentleman when home from state business, getting up early on fine mornings to go out to the fence behind the house just to watch the horses romp or graze. He had mentioned—no, bragged about it to his friends.

Which is probably why these people came to him and asked him to be show manager for the Fourth Annual Lafite Class A All-Arabian Horse Show. He'd explained that it was his daughter who knew what from which about horses, not him. But they had said they wanted an important name to head the committee, and he'd been flattered they thought him important. And, they explained, this would be like being on the board of directors of some hospital or charity. His job would be to set the greater goals—which they trusted would be the same as the last three shows, spelled out here on these two pages for him to study—and be present at photo opportunities. So he'd agreed to do it. To indicate he took the position seriously, he'd borrowed a copy of the current American Horse Show Association's rule book. But, lacking knowledge even of the basics, he found the rules very confusing. Why on earth, for example, should it be deemed necessary for a show official to remove one of a horse's shoes and weigh it? His daughter said never mind, it was the judges who had to be concerned about things like that, not him. And his wife, who would not be coming until that afternoon of the last day, thank you, reminded him that all they wanted was for him to attend committee meetings, agree to anything the committee decided, and sign forms and letters they'd draw up.

So it wasn't fair that all of a sudden some of these same people were insisting that he alone must decide what to do about the show's schedule being held up. And it especially wasn't fair because no matter what he decided, some people were going to be angry. Why, Sally as much as said that some of them might sue!

He sat down behind the big old wooden desk in the show office and spent several minutes wrestling with his pipe, whose refusal to draw offered a nice delay. During that time, he reminded himself that in the state senate there had been some hairy decision making, some of it in states of ignorance almost as bad as this. He closed his eyes and told his frightened brain to get a grip. Immediately, technique number one came to him: Get as many of the facts as you can, both because it might show the way to a solution and because it made possible technique number two: Time spent in collecting facts will delay making an unpopular or even wrong decision. He opened his eyes. "All right," he said in his best statesman's voice. "Do we know how long the barn is going to be closed off?"

"No," replied Sally. "They aren't telling us anything."

"Maybe I can find out how long this is going to take. Who's in charge of the investigation?"

Andrew gestured angry ignorance and Sally shrugged.

"Well, then, it's clear we need more information." Senator McIntyre stood up and said, "I'll find out who's in charge, and ask to talk to him. We can't make any sort of decision until we have more facts."

"And ask him what to do about the horses standing outside," said Sally. "Some of those foals are going to get sick if we can't get them blanketed or under cover soon."

Andrew burst out, "To hell with the foals! Don't even worry about the foals! There's a murderer loose nearby, don't you understand that? What we should be doing is finding out when we can get away from here!" At committee meetings he had been the word of the law, reeling off in an ultra-cool voice chapter and verse from the AHSA and Zone Five rule books. Faced with a situation the rule makers had neglected to cover, he became a squirrel in a tree, making angry, useless noises.

Eleanor Ritter had left the Tretower area, taking her two subordinates with her, but leaving the yellow ribbon up. The coroner had finished with the body and directed the ambulance crew, who had been playing honeymoon bridge in the back of their ambulance while they waited, to take it downtown for an immediate postmortem, along with the new green carpet on which it lay. The forensics pair had taken endless pictures and samples, then put another strip of yellow ribbon across the door to the prep stall and left. A police officer in uniform turned up with a spiral notebook and pen, which he put on a new-looking card table at one end of the Tretower aisle before taking up a guard-post stance beside it.

Danny, regretting the fact that he'd chosen to sleep in another twenty minutes in lieu of breakfast, set the twenty-cup perk to work while he started cleaning up box stalls and feeding the horses. Kori took Brit into the tack stall and sat her down on the cot.

"Now, how about you explain your ridiculous behavior in front of those police officers."

Brit hung her head and touched the folded surface of her sleeping bag on the cot beside her. "I was scared," she mumbled.

"Of what?"

"That they were gonna arrest me."

"So you tried to make sure that would happen by behaving in the most suspicious way you could?"

"I was scared," repeated Brit.

"Why?"

"Because Miss Haydock was doing a pretty good job of pointing her finger at me."

"*What?*"

Brit's head came up. "Honest. She made it sound like she and Keith just had a little quarrel, while 'some person'—and the way she didn't look at me made the policeman look real hard—practically told everyone she was gonna kill him if she got the chance. Oh, it wasn't too obvious what she was doing, she's too smart for that; but the way she was saying things made it look like I was the only person who seriously wanted to do it."

"Why would she do something like that?"

"Probably because she killed him."

"Brit—"

"I know, I know. But she was about as mad as a person can get at him over that Wellaway thing. Here all this time she's been telling people what a great guy he is, and he proves she's wrong by injuring her precious Wellaway right in front of her. It's surprising she waited until last night; I'd've thought she'd've killed him on the spot. Picked up Wellaway and dropped her on him." Brit made a sound of sad amusement.

"Why blame you?"

"Because I was here, right? I mean next door. All night, I was right here."

"Brit, are you sure you didn't hear even the sound of that prep stall door opening?"

Brit halted the denying shake of her head in midstride. She frowned, thinking. "No," she said, still frowning. "But when I went to bed people were still up, taking horses out and putting them away. The people in the row that backs up to us were up; I went to sleep hearing them talking. So if someone did open our prep stall door, I probably would've thought it was them. But I don't remember—but you know, though, that would explain—"

"Explain what?"

"Nothing." Brit picked up the sleeping bag and folded it smaller, working it with her big hands into a compact roll. "Where did I put the cover for this thing?"

*   *   *

As soon as the backups had the enlarged perimeter secure, Eleanor interviewed Wilson and his partner Cullen separately, then sent them out to write down the license plate numbers on every vehicle they could find. That would teach them to grab for glory and ignore proper procedure.

When she first arrived, she knew two things: (1) the scene would have to be preserved and protected until documented thoroughly enough to re-create it in court; and (2) if and when a suspect was developed, it would be necessary to uncover the evidence that would put that person at the scene at the time of death.

But now she was aggravated to discover that: (1) the so-called scene wasn't the real scene after all; and (2) people had been coming and going freely for hours between the time of the murder and its discovery.

She had seven bluesuits helping Dave go from stall to stall looking for blood or other evidence. The civilians in the barn were being brought to one of two box stalls out of the way of eavesdroppers. They were, individually, angry, frightened, curious, and even, once in a while, helpful. There was a slow-moving line at the pay phone, though what they were able to relay to the folks back home as fact couldn't take up more than a minute of conversation. The rest was alarums and speculation, which would generate countless panicked phone calls to the police station in town and probably, considering the average annual income of owners of show-quality Arabian horses, an only slightly lesser number of calls from lawyers with important names.

Eleanor was in another empty box stall facing an outside wall of the barn. She could hear, as background noises, horses being led around, the squeal of the hay car's wheels, and, worst of all, people talking, sharing stories, damaging or altering the individual viewpoints that were like direction finders: Where they crossed could be a suspect. She wished she had the magical power to freeze the barn and everyone in it, making all stay exactly as is until it could be looked at, recorded, and investigated.

She was sitting on a borrowed camp stool, diagraming flow charts. She was a task-oriented person, with a talent for organizing, and she preferred things diagramed, or at least planned out and written down. Since this was at last her turn to be lead investigator, things would be organized the way she liked them.

"Sergeant Ritter?" growled a voice, and someone rapped at the door of the stall.

"Come in, Smitty," she said without turning around. She was sitting with her back to the door, the big pad of paper bent across her lap. She had recognized the voice as that of the veteran bluesuit.

"The press is here," he said, obeying; and before she could even groan in reply, he added, "and Senator Robert McIntyre wants to see you."

"McIntyre?" He's our state senator, right? What does he want?"

"He's also the show manager for this shindig, and he's got some questions he refuses to ask anyone else. Says it'll just take minute."

"Hell," breathed Eleanor. "All right, bring him down—but first, the press. How many and where are they?"

"It's the *Lafite Blazon-Independent*, with a reporter and photographer, WXTV with a minicam crew, and about six more I don't know. Out-of-towners. They're by the main entrance doing interviews and taking pictures of baby horses shivering in the cold."

"What the blazes are baby horses doing outside? Never mind, never mind." She winced. "I remember now; they were being shown when we got here. Well, we can't leave them out there. Tell them—well sure, tell them to go back to the arena. It's heated, isn't it? And it's big enough. What a bunch of dopes, couldn't figure that out for themselves!

"Now, about the press. Find Sergeant Yale, he's good with those types."

Yale had been in blue almost as long as Smitty.

"Is he here?"

"I'm pretty sure I heard his voice a while back. You'll probably find him hiding somewhere with a cup of coffee and a doughnut. Roust him out, give him the poop, and tell him to go play nice. But also tell him I don't want it broadcast that the body was moved after death, or that there was anything funny about the wound—who's our communications person?"

"I am."

"Have we heard anything from Dr. Burke yet?"

"Not yet."

"Then tell Yale to say we aren't even sure this is a case of murder. It's a homicide, which means a human being has been killed. It may be accident, negligence, self-defense, sudden passion, or premeditated. That's what the investigators are trying to find out. Got it? Good, go bring on Senator McIntyre."

Senator McIntyre had straightened his tie, combed his hair, and wiped the nervous perspiration from his jowls and the palms of his hands while he waited for his audience with the lead investigator. He was surprised and then disarmed when it turned out to be this soft-spoken, skinny lady in the dusty suit and no lipstick.

"I think we need to handle one of the lesser items quickly, before it becomes a major one," he began, courteously joining her with him in a leadership role. "We've got some horses outside, just foals, most of them, and it's kind of chilly—"

"That has already been brought to my attention, Senator," said Eleanor. "Pardon me for interrupting, but we're really pressed for time in these early stages of an investigation. I have directed that horses caught outside by the securing of the barn are to go back to the arena."

"Ah." McIntyre pressed the fingers of his right hand into the palm of his left and made a little bow, his sign of unease, roused now by being in the presence of an authoritarian female. Actually, now he thought about it, the solution was a good one, simple and obvious. Why hadn't Sally thought of it? And if she hadn't thought of that, then maybe there was a solution to the big problem that had likewise escaped her. He said, "I think you should know that we have a legal obligation to run this show as scheduled. Your closing of the entire barn has brought things to a halt. There must be some way for us to work around your restrictions, get this show back on the road—"

Again he was interrupted. " 'Pardon me, but did I hear you right? You want me to interfere with a homicide investigation so that you can continue an equine beauty contest?"

"No, no, no, of course not! It just seems to me that since this, er, distressing event occurred in one small part of the barn, it seems unnecessary to close off the whole thing, especially in light of our serious and expensive commitment to continue the show."

"The homicide did not occur where the body was found."

McIntyre frowned at her. "Then where did it occur?"

"That's what we're trying to find out. And that's why it's important that we keep the whole barn secure. We don't want people to walk off, accidentally or otherwise, with what may be evidence."

"Ah. Yes, I see. Do you think you will be able to locate this evidence soon?"

"I'm afraid I can't tell you that."

McIntyre thought this an ambiguous reply and was about to say so, then thought better of it. "Well, could you possibly give me an estimate of how long you will be investigating this, er, incident?"

"I'm afraid I can't tell you that, either; there are investigations that go on for years, and there are cases that are cleared within minutes. This isn't one of the easy ones; we weren't called in time to catch someone standing over the body."

Genuinely astonished, McIntyre said, "Are you saying the barn could stay closed for *years*?"

"Oh, no. As soon as we've finished our search and have interviewed everyone in here, we'll unseal the barn."

"And that may be as soon as . . . today?"

"I'm sure of it."

His tone became jocular. "Well, then, say, half past one? As I said, legal obligations and all that. And we only have the barn and arena through the weekend."

"I'll tell you what. Why don't you check back with me at, say, half past one, and maybe by then I'll have some idea of how long this will take."

"Ah." McIntyre did his odd little bow again. "That will have to be—ah, satisfactory. Thank you, uh, do I call you Miss Ritter?"

"Sergeant Ritter will be fine."

"Very well. Until half past one, Sergeant Ritter."

It was Maggie who found the buckets in the paddock behind the barn. She'd gone looking for buckets after she found a hay cart standing between the barn and the paddock that had, from its soggy appearance, been sitting out all night. She filled the buckets at the outdoor horse shower, loaded them into the cart, and trundled them over to the arena so the horses caught outside could have a drink. She was bringing the buckets back for refills when she saw Sally standing at the barn office window, looking out sadly. She waved.

Sally immediately opened a window. "Is everyone all right over there?" she called.

"We're fine!" bawled Maggie in her cheerful whiskey tenor. She was a very dark woman with strong features, of middle height, in her late thirties, slat thin. She was wearing cowboy boots of turquoise blue ostrich skin, snug-fitting black britches, a heavy silk Western-style shirt the same turquoise as the boots, thin black leather gloves, and a cowgirl hat dyed the color of the shirt.

"That's a great-looking outfit," said Sally.

"This old thing?" Maggie struck a pose, then laughed raucously; the outfit was brand-new and had set her back two thousand dollars. It was like her to risk it carrying water for horses belonging to her competitors, though that might not have been the case had it still been raining. "What's going on in there?"

"They're searching the whole place, and taking people away one by one to ask them questions."

"What kind of questions?"

"I understand one of them is a flat 'Did you do it?' "

"Ha!" said Maggie. "They better not ask me. I might confess just so we can get on with things. I'm filling these buckets at the outdoor horse showers; I hope that isn't against the police rules."

"I don't see how it could be. How'd you come by the hay cart? They aren't allowed out of the barn."

Maggie did an elaborate shrug, pulling her wide mouth down. "It was outside when I came across it, and I saw no reason to shove it back inside. Gotta go; there's a pack of thirsty young 'uns waiting."

"Wait a second, Maggie; there's something important I need to ask you. What *do* we do about the show? Cancel? Rebook? Try for an extension? The senator can't cope, and I've never had this happen before, so suggestions gratefully received."

Maggie let go of the cart's handle, crossed her feet at the ankles, tucked her left hand under her right elbow, and pressed one long, black forefinger into her cheek while looking upward. She should be a mime, thought Sally; she does things like Person Thinking so well.

"Whatever you decide, you have to call American Horse Show in New York for clearance."

"You mean on Monday?"

"I mean today. Someone's there to answer twenty-four hours, seven days. They have to authorize any change in the schedule or you're in abeyance or something. They can authorize a change over the phone. If they disagree with your decision, the show will be canceled or declared unofficial and we're in even deeper poo-poo. But don't worry. I happen to know they allowed a show down south to change its printed hours with no notice because they had a sudden, unseasonal heat wave and the horses were too stressed to be shown during the day. I should think a murder is at least as good an excuse for some kind of change."

$\triangledown$

7

PAUL AND AL, THE two assistant investigators, found two empty stalls a row apart and cobbled them into setups that seemed nonthreatening and vaguely officelike. Then they started to interview people. They mixed hot questions ("Do you know who did this?") with cool ones ("What is your function at this show?"), rated each response as truthful, neutral, or deceptive, and wrote down the names of those persons worthy of further questioning. They took the list to Eleanor. There weren't many names on it.

Sergeant Yale found a room in the arena building for the press. They went reluctantly and peppered him with questions the whole way—anything combining animals and murder meant airtime or column inches. They demanded a press conference with the lead investigator; Yale crossed his fingers and said he'd ask about it. Then he told them what he could, giving enough color that they could get their initial releases done, but not so much detail that their stories would compromise the investigation. He put off more questions by saying he had work to do, and went off to help in the search for the leakproof thing that had been used to carry the body to the prep stall.

* * *

Kori and Brit went to help Danny take care of the horses. Danny complained that one of the hay carts was missing.

"There's only four carts in the whole damn barn to begin with," he griped. "The two metal ones are for manure, so there's only the two wooden ones for fresh straw—except now there's only one, and five people are ahead of us in line for it!"

"Well, where's our own?" asked Kori.

"It's at home." Danny lifted and crossed both arms in a mock show of terror. "I know, I know," he said. "*Frutus*, right?"

"*Frutex*. So, all right, each of us can carry a bale of straw, and if we make two trips, that should hold us until we can get a cart."

"There were two of them here yesterday," said Brit. "I remember seeing both of them."

"Oh, we know where it is," said Danny. "Someone swiped it out of the barn to haul water for the horses in the arena."

"What horses in the arena?" asked Brit.

"The weanlings, some yearlings, and a few other horses caught outside the barn when the cops sealed it off."

Kori said, "Oh. But I thought the rules said no straw carts out of the barn. And how did they get it out? The barn's still sealed, isn't it?"

"Oh, yeah, definitely. You should hear the racket, people wanting in, people wanting out; it's enough to make you feel sorry for the cop standing there. Come on, Brit, quit dreaming; let's go haul some bales."

"Huh? Oh, sure." Brit pulled herself back from whatever distant place her mind had taken her and followed Danny down to sign out.

"What's *frutex*?" she asked.

"Latin for blockhead. You know Sarge—no, you don't know. He likes insults, especially really old ones. He's got some that are even medieval. So she's been one-upping him lately by finding some that are ancient Roman. But you know what's weird? They don't use them on each other, only other people."

Kori sat down in the fragrant straw to watch Copper Wind munch on hay. After a minute he turned his head to look at her.

"We're in trouble," she remarked, and he whuffled gently and came to blow warm air on her face. She reached up to stroke the velvety nose. "If they arrest Brit, I don't know what we're going to do." He snorted and bumped her shoulder with his nose. Obediently,she got to her feet and began to do some serious stroking.

"I know, that sounds as if all I care about is getting a chance to show your daughter, but that's not it. Peter says the first twenty-four hours are the most important if a crime is going to get solved. If they arrest Brit, they'll slack off investigating, and they may not find out who really did it. And Peter won't be here until tomorrow. I think maybe I should poke around myself, see what I can find out, so Peter won't have to start from scratch on a cold trail."

Coppy swished his tail and blew a raspberry. "Thank you very much for the vote of confidence. I wish I could be as sure as Peter is that Eleanor is competent."

"By Eleanor, you mean Sergeant Ritter?"

Kori started, then realized the voice came from the aisle. "Not a bad-looking horse you got there," the voice added.

Kori and Copper Wind both looked to see who was speaking. He was standing against the heavy mesh, a tall man with silver hair and an aristocratic nose. But even the lower planks of the door could not conceal the swell of paunch.

"Good morning, Senator McIntyre," said Kori. "Are you here to tell me the show is about to continue?"

"I'm afraid Sergeant Ritter is not *that* competent. I rather hoped to hear from you what progress they are making."

Kori shook her head. "What makes you think they'd keep me better informed than you?"

"Your husband is a police officer, isn't he?"

Frowning, she went to the door and slid it back. Copper Wind stretched his neck over her shoulder toward the senator, who took two hasty steps back, then turned it into a polite gesture of making room for her to come out.

"Who told you that?" she asked, accepting the offer.

"Oh, I don't remember. Why, don't you want people to know?"

"It doesn't matter," she said, though it did, a little. It could be annoying to field questions from people dismayed, surprised, amused, or disbelieving to learn her husband carried a badge. McIntyre stood there, looking anxious to continue the conversation but unable to decide how. "May I help you with something?" she asked.

Relieved, he launched into an explanation. "As you probably know, we have a few horses, and my daughter wants to get further involved with the Arabian breed. I understand you have a very fine yearling filly; in fact, I understand it is one of the finest of this year's crop. I was wondering if I might take a look at her?"

"Of course." Kori went into the tack stall and got down a woven nylon lead and went to bring Breathless out into the aisle.

The senator seemed dismayed that she should go to that much trouble. "Lovely animal, lovely." He raised a hand in a please-stop gesture.

Breathless stepped toward him, extending her nose in friendly greeting, but again he stepped backward and put the hand in his pocket, as if afraid Kori might invite him to stroke.

A lot of people admire, even love, horses, but become nervous when one threatens to come within touching distance. "It's your daughter who handles your horses, isn't it?" said Kori, recognizing the reaction.

McIntyre, relieved to be found out, confessed, "It was my name, not my vast experience with the animals, that brought me this assignment as show manager." He nodded at Breathless and said, "On the other hand, even someone as inexperienced as I can tell this is a very fine animal."

"Thank you," said Kori, her voice as much a caress as the gentle hand she put on the filly's neck.

"Are you by chance willing to sell her?"

Kori smiled as Breathless nuzzled her, seeking more stroking. In many ways Breathless was very like her sire. "I'm afraid not."

"Seriously, what kind of price would you be thinking of?"

"Seriously, I am not thinking of a price at all."

"I'll give you five thousand for her right now."

Kori blinked at this curious combination of persistence and low price. It had cost more than that to raise her, and her bloodline alone made her worth twice that. "Sorry."

"Okay, you're not a fool. Twelve."

"I don't think you understand—"

"Twenty."

"No."

"Okay, thirty-five, but that's my limit." He was reaching into an inside pocket.

"Look, Senator . . ."

"Call me Bob."

"I repeat, Bob, she's not for sale."

McIntyre looked at her face. He didn't know horses, but he did understand the unmaking of a deal. "I'm sorry," he said, bringing his hand out empty. "It's just that my daughter is looking for a really good mare, and this appears to be one in the making. I tell you what; if you change your mind, will you give me first refusal?"

Kori barely hesitated before smiling and holding out her hand. "In a few years I'll breed her. If she drops a cow-hocked, ewe-necked foal, then she's for sale. Agreed?"

"Agreed." He shook the hand and went away satisfied.

Kori shook her head, turned Breathless, and put her into her box stall.

Then she went to resume communing with Coppy. "Yes, yes, I know," she said, finding his favorite itchy spot under his forelock. "That was very rude of me. But you know something? I don't think he really knows if she's great looking or not; he as much as said he was depending on the opinion of other people." She reached into a pocket and pulled out a small carrot, which she broke in half. Feeding one piece to Coppy, she continued, "I hope he doesn't brag about the deal we made until after the show. He is going to be very angry with me when he finds out I made almost as much a fool of him as Keith Bulward did."

The stallion shook his head, getting strands of his long forelock over one eye. She lifted them off, smiling. "Sooner or later he'll consult his daughter, and she'll point out that a person after a foundation mare wants one that produces foals that are neither cow-hocked nor ewe-necked." She fed Coppy the other piece of carrot.

She leaned against the stallion's warm shoulder and wondered what would have happened if she'd said yes to McIntyre's offer of thirty-five thousand. Who would he have called on to help him lead her away?

"I always thought farm people went to bed when the sun went down," grumbled Paul, the younger investigator. "According to the people I've been talking to, they didn't even notice sundown happening, and they didn't go to bed even when the lights went out." He consulted his notes. "That was at half past ten. They had a party going on that didn't finish breaking up until after eleven. Some of the people went to one of two motels, while half of the others sat up talking for another hour. The other half took horses out to the arena to practice with them, or gave them baths or shaved them— did you know they shaved these horses' faces?"

"Bald?" asked Eleanor doubtfully.

"No, just kind of close. And then they smear on Vaseline just before they show them." Paul shook his head at the peculiar customs of an exotic culture, and consulted his notes. "Anyway, it didn't get anything close to quiet until probably two A.M. And even then, someone was hauling hay around in one of those two-wheeled carts, someone was washing a horse, two people were having a loud quarrel, and another horse woke up in a screaming fit until someone came and settled it down. Do horses have nightmares?"

"Not that I know of," said Eleanor. "But do you have more about that quarrel? It may be significant."

"Yeah," said the older investigator. "I also heard about it from the people I talked to. According to them, it was short, just a couple of sentences back and forth, but real angry. Maybe it was the end of something that started outside."

"Who had the quarrel?" asked Eleanor.

"I got 'two people,' 'two or three men,' and 'two guys,' " said Paul, reading from his notes.

" 'Two men' and 'it sounded like two men,' " said the other. "Both of mine agree that they were mad, and it ended with one of them shouting 'No' or 'Ow.' "

"Anything else?" asked Eleanor. "Sound of a scuffle?"

The investigators shook their heads "But I did get one person saying that the quarrel included the words 'cheat' and 'sick' and 'gimme that' as parts of the quarrel," said Paul.

"Hmmm. Well, let's look some more at that screaming horse," said Eleanor.

Paul turned back two pages of his notebook. "Two people said it was the kind of scream that they would have thought it was a horse being whipped, except there wasn't the sound of a whip. No one was sure exactly where it was coming from, except it was near where the body was found. They said other horses sounded upset, too, but that sometimes it happens that one horse will have a conniption and the horses around it get upset and start whinnying, too. Still—how sure are we that this guy was killed somewhere else?"

"We know he wasn't killed where he was found," said Eleanor, "and I can't find blood or any other sign he was killed right near there, either." She frowned and with a gesture of frustration indicated they should continue.

"I get a report that it was a woman he heard quieting the crazy horse down," said the other investigator. "And I got three different people telling me about this 'yearling filly' who was high as a kite this morning." The older investigator checked his notes. "One of 'em says it was the groom the horse seemed scared of. That would be that big kid who was in cuffs when you arrived. Brittany Morgan."

As midday approached, the results from the barn search began to accumulate. The smear of blood on the wall of an empty box stall reserved by Morning Glory Farms turned out to be not human. "Probably from that horse Bulward assaulted," remarked Eleanor, making a note to ask Amelia Haydock about it during her second interview.

No bloodstained carpet or tarp or plastic suitable for carrying a human body had been found.

And there was still that list of people whose responses to the investigators' questions were false, contradictory, or otherwise off-center. Only eleven names were on the list, but Eleanor had to interview each of them. And Kori Brichter, Danny Bannister, Brittany Morgan, and Amelia Haydock were all waiting for a second interview. Eleanor grimaced, looked the names over, and assigned each a number in line to be personally interviewed.

One name on the list was the show manager's, Senator Robert McIntyre. "I know," sighed Paul; "I mean, for Christ's sake! People with his kind of clout don't need to get physical. But for some reason he's nervous as a virgin in a Hell's Angel bar."

"That's a good analogue of his situation," said Eleanor. "He's a totally inexperienced official in charge of a horse show where someone got murdered. The intelligent reaction *is* to get nervous." Nevertheless, she left McIntyre on the list to be interviewed, because the test was valid, and McIntyre had failed it. But she put him last, because she agreed with Paul.

The first name pulled from the preliminary interviews was that of a trainer, whose sickly, whispered "Good morning" brought with it a stink of yesterday's alcohol. He gave his name as Stoddard Eckiherne.

Stoddard was a tall man in his fifties who retained traces of a once-elegant bearing. His hands were trembling with hangover, and the broken blood vessels in his nose showed this was not an uncommon condition. More careful combing might have disguised his need for a haircut, and though his linen was fresh, his beautiful, elderly tweed suit looked as if it had been slept in. He sat as directed on the metal folding chair beside the card table and offered an exceedingly frightened grin.

"I don't know why your other investigator insisted I speak with you," he said in his drink-roughened voice. "I cannot tell you anything of value about last night." His speech was correct in the way that comes from growing up among people who talk like that.

Eleanor replied, "I'm sure you are aware that solving crimes demands the collection of a lot of extraneous detail because some of it may prove not so extraneous. Why don't you let me decide what's of value, and just tell me everything you did yesterday. When did you arrive at the fairgrounds?"

"Yesterday afternoon, late, about five or half past five. I had only one horse with me, a two-year-old colt. I'm not scheduled to show him until tomorrow, Sunday, but I wanted to see who was here and what my competition might be. My reservations were all in order, so I put Maurice in his stall and went to dinner. Maurice is the colt."

Eleanor nodded, writing. "Go on."

"Things get a little fuzzy after that."

"Why is that?"

"The restaurant I dined at had a liquor license, and I did a little celebrating."

"What were you celebrating?"

Stoddard's pale blue eyes shifted away, then back, bringing a smirk of triumph with them. "My being hired on as a trainer for one of the finest farms in the business."

For several moments Eleanor let that statement lie steaming on the floor between them like the fresh manure it doubtless was. Then she remarked, "I think you should know I check everything I'm told, Mr. Eckiherne."

Stoddard's eyebrows sailed up. He swallowed. "Well, it wasn't exactly confirmed," he admitted. Eleanor waited some more, and Stoddard gestured with an aging but still beautiful hand. "All right, dammit, the thing was good as blown to hell. How was I to know that bastard was going to turn up here with a two-year-old colt of his own?"

"Which bastard was that?"

"Keith Bulward."

Eleanor sighed and made a note. "Did you attend the party in the barn last night?"

Stoddard frowned. "Yes."

"Did you see Mr. Bulward at that party?"

"He was there, I think."

"You saw him?"

The frown deepened. "Yes."

"Did you talk with him?"

"I—no."

"Did you have a quarrel with him?"

A pause, while some inward struggle went on. "No, I'm sure I didn't. If I had, I'm sure someone would have mentioned it to me by now."

"Or to me," said Eleanor casually.

The muscles of Stoddard's face tensed, and he was suddenly far more intelligent than he had appeared only seconds before. "Will you tell me what happened if I admit I don't remember a thing?" he asked.

"No, because I don't know enough about what happened to do that in a way that would be fair."

He considered this and nodded briefly. "That's one reason, probably," he said. He leaned back and massaged his face with both hands. "I'm an alcoholic," he said, as if admitting it to himself, or reminding himself. "I have blackouts. When I found out Keith Bulward was here with a flashy two-year-old colt, I knew it was all over, that I wouldn't get the job with Barty, that I'd never come back as a trainer. So

I went to a bar instead of a restaurant for my supper, and by the time I left to come back here to check on the colt I was three sheets to the wind. I remember arriving at the party, and bits and pieces of conversation, but I can't remember leaving or where I went afterwards, though I think it was to my motel. And I don't know how this happened." He held out his left hand, balled into a fist, to display the bruised and scabbed knuckles.

Eleanor leaned forward to look, then sat back. "Is that the suit you had on yesterday?" she asked.

He straightened and pulled in his chin to look down at himself. "Yes," he said, brushing at a wrinkle in a lapel with the injured hand.

"Will you stand up so I can look it over?"

The ghastly grin reappeared, and he swallowed before saying, "If you like," and getting slowly to his feet.

She made a close inspection of the suit. It was a greenish gray tweed, tailor-made for him years ago, before his figure had slopped downward. It was wrinkled, and in need of an airing, if not dry cleaning. There was dust and dried mud around the bottom of the cuffed trousers, but no dark stain or suspicious speckles anywhere.

She thought hard about it, but there wasn't quite enough evidence for an arrest. "I'm not going to hold you, Mr. Ecki-herne," she said, to his patent relief. "But I would like your permission for a member of my crew to photograph your injured hand and to remove some scrapings from under your fingernails."

This frightened him all over again, but he agreed, and also agreed that he would not leave Lafite County without telling her where he was going. She sat a long time after he left, thinking and making notes to herself. Someone must have seen him leave; someone may have seen him come back. She made a note to find out what kind of car he was driving.

The next two names on the list were Morning Glory grooms. One, a very scared girl named Missy, blurted after several minutes of fencing that she was only fourteen, although she had told Mr. Bulward she was sixteen.

"See, I want to be a trainer," the child explained, "and we live in town so I'd have to board a horse if I got one, and we can't afford that; so the only way I can get the experience I need is to work for someone else. You won't tell on me, will you?"

Eleanor agreed not to, and since that was all Missy had to offer, dismissed her.

The other groom, a pretty blond woman of eighteen, gave her name as Fran Obermeyer. She wore dusty jeans, scraped jodhpur boots, and a sweatshirt with an Illinois University seal on it. Her hair was just short of shoulder length and had been crimped to look like closed venetian blinds. She was initially evasive, weaving a maze of contradictions it took Eleanor some while to unravel.

What finally became clear was that she was possibly the last person to see Keith Bulward alive. It seemed that she and Keith Bulward had been sleeping together for several weeks, and that in fact she had been with him in his trailer last night.

"His *trailer*?" Grimacing, Eleanor made a note. When no motel key had been found on the body, that should have set off an inquiry as to where Bulward was staying. "Where is it?" she asked, sharply, because she was annoyed. "What does it look like? Do you know the license plate number?"

Fran sat up straighter. "No. But it's like this Airstream, a big one and they're not common. I think his is the only one out in the lot. You know what they look like, don't you? Silver and kind of round at the front and back?"

"Hold on a second." Eleanor sent the bluesuit standing outside the door of her office-stall to find the two plainclothes investigators, and to tell them to find and search a big silver Airstream parked with the other RVs and trailers. The key would be in the wallet found in Bulward's pocket. Then she came back to Fran Obermeyer. "Why a trailer instead of a hotel?"

"It's more private. And closer. And his is really nice inside, like a house, all neat and clean, not like some men let theirs get. Not that I've been in all that many of them," she added, misinterpreting the look in Eleanor's eye. "He's been really good to me, Keith. He said the next time I spotted a good performance horse coming through The Glory to be sold he would try to cut a deal for me with the owner."

Eleanor blinked to wipe the look away and nodded. "Nice of him. What time did you leave his trailer last night?"

Fran's shoulders drifted upward just a little. "I'm not sure of the exact time. It was after two, but not half past two yet. He got this phone call and said he had someone coming to see him right away."

"Phone?"

"It's like a cellular."

That would indicate a local call. "Man or woman?"

The girl thought. "I was using his shower, so I didn't hear him talking. And he didn't say."

"Could he have made up the phone call, as a way to get you to leave?"

Fran shook her head. "I heard it ring; it's on the kitchen counter like right next to the shower."

"And it was what, sometime after two? Kind of late for a phone call, wasn't it?"

"Well, yeah, I guess so. He said I had to go back to the barn, and he wouldn't even give me time to fix my hair." She touched the pale, crimped mass in a tending gesture. Obviously she'd taken the time to fix it this morning.

"Was the person he was going to meet coming to the trailer?"

"I suppose so; like, why else would he want me out of there? But Keith was going to meet him somewhere else, I think, and bring him to the trailer. Because he walked me back to the barn, and he doesn't usually do that. I figured it was because his truck was in the car lot behind the barn."

"He walked you back to the barn and left you at the entrance?"

"No, at the tack room in our section of the barn. It's a

box stall, really; but we keep bridles and stuff in there, so we call it the tack room."

"Was the child groom, Missy, sleeping in there, too?"

"Yeah."

"Did you talk to her when you came in?"

"Uh-uh. She was already asleep, and I was really beat, so I just got undressed and fell into my cot and was dead to the world in five minutes."

"And Mr. Bulward . . ." Eleanor paused expectantly.

"I heard him go into one of the other stalls, and come out again almost right away, and walk off."

"He went to check on a horse?"

"I don't think so. Like for one thing, he doesn't do that. And for another, I think it was the prep stall he went into."

"Why would he go in there?"

A shrug. "I dunno. I heard him come out and walk away, and then I went to sleep."

"Do you know Amelia Haydock?"

The evasive look came back. "I don't think so."

"Do you know a horse named Wellaway?"

Fran became interested in her left thumb. "No."

"Come on, Fran; everyone knows Keith borrowed Wellaway to ride in a competition, and that when the horse didn't perform well, he struck it."

An elaborate shrug. "Then why ask me about it?"

"Because I want to know what Ms. Haydock said to Keith when she came to get her horse back."

A long silence.

"I assume you were there, and saw it." Eleanor assumed this from the silence.

Another silence, then, "Yeah, I saw it."

"But you don't want to tell me about it."

Fran gave an embarrassed grin. "Well, no, but you want to know, don't you?" Eleanor didn't reply and Fran sighed, and said, with slow emphasis, "She was really, really pissed. She was white as a sheet, her lipstick and blusher looked like Halloween makeup. She comes up to me and she goes,

'Where's Wellaway?' Now I had just seen Keith take her into her stall, which was kind of unusual, since we untack the horses in the aisle. So I pointed and followed after her when she went over there. And first thing I saw when I looked over her shoulder is blood slobbering out of Wellaway's nose. I wondered how she knew the horse had injured herself, but Keith was yanking the saddle off her like he was mad, which he wouldn't be doing to an injured horse. And he didn't hear us walk up, so when she goes, 'Come out of there, Bulward,' kind of quiet, Keith jumps back and Wellaway jumps back and he holds up the saddle like it's gonna protect him against the horse, like he's scared the horse will bite him. Ms. Haydock opens the door and he comes out kind of sideways and he's holding the saddle like he's afraid of her now, and he backs away. And she goes in and talks real gentle to Wellaway, takes off her bridle and puts on her halter, and then she leads her out and gives Keith a look as they walk off. And I thought 'Whoa!' Because I hope nobody *ever* looks at me like she looked at him."

The driver slowed, downshifting, and flipped his turn signal on. The bottle-green Mercedes 350 SL moved obediently into the right turn lane. The small sign said Lafite County Fairgrounds. He made the turn onto the narrow blacktop road and wound his way through the empty fairground streets.

The rain had stopped a while ago and the blacktop was drying, but puddles here and there had wet the tires of cars going through them, and the driver, figuring the traffic had been bound for the horse show, turned a corner to follow the trail.

He was a tall, runner-thin, dark individual in a silver-gray suit set off with a densely flowered tie. He wore gold-rimmed glasses set halfway down his noble nose, and had an unlit cigar tucked into a corner of his mouth. His curly hair had a lot of individual gray hairs in it.

He found a space in the parking lot beside the arena and

got out. In one hand was a big, worn attaché case. He was Phillip Bannister, Danny's father. A talented criminal defense lawyer, he was frequently a thorn in the side of the Charter Police Department, which didn't mean Peter hesitated to call him when his wife's employee needed help.

Phil walked up to the yellow ribbon that barred entrance to the barn, produced identification, and said with gentle authority to the weight lifter guarding the entrance, "I am here to represent Miss Brittany Morgan. Please notify the person in charge of this investigation that I wish to speak with Miss Morgan, and if there is any interrogation ongoing, it must stop immediately."

▽

8

THE NEXT SEVEN NEEDING to be interviewed had proved to be nervous types; they were so frightened at the prospect of being suspects that they stumbled over every question. Eleanor, her quiet voice and gentle manner a decided contrast to the chill suspicion of the men, calmed them and allowed each to establish his or her innocence in a few minutes.

Now, that done, she sent for the last person on her list, Senator McIntyre, and while waiting reviewed her notes.

"But I just want to see her for a second," insisted a woman's voice from outside the door.

Eleanor's head came around, listening. The voice sounded familiar. "Who is it?" she called.

"It's me, Brittany Morgan!"

Eleanor closed her notebook, stood, and went to slide back the door. Standing outside in the aisle were a bluesuit, State Senator McIntyre looking much less confident than he had earlier, and Brit.

"I believe you asked to interview me at this time," said McIntyre. "But if you wish to interview her first, I have a great deal to do and would be very happy to be excused for now. I can come back at a later time."

"You don't have to go," said Brit; "this'll only take a minute, I promise."

Eleanor turned to the bluesuit. "Find the senator a chair and bring him a cup of coffee."

She looked at McIntyre, who threw up his hands in resignation. "Black," he said to the cop.

"You," Eleanor said to Brit with a follow-me gesture, and went back into the stall.

Brit nodded impatiently through the rereading of her rights, and then said, "Yeah, yeah, forget about all that. This is about carrying the body."

"What is?"

"I heard you say look for a piece of carpet or a tarp, but it wasn't either of those."

Eleanor inhaled lightly and tried to keep all expression from her face, anxious not to disturb whatever it was that brought this girl to the point of confession. Funny, she thought, how many confessions begin with some extraneous detail. "What was used to move the body?"

"The hay cart."

"Which hay cart?"

"There's supposed to be two of them, but there's only one. Well, there's four, actually. And some people bring their own, too; but there are four that belong to whoever runs this horse barn. Two have metal bins and they're for manure, and two have wooden bins and they're for straw. Danny was complaining that someone is using one of the barn's straw carts to take water to the horses in the arena, and Kori wondered how it got out of the barn with cops guarding the door. Then while I was carrying a bale of straw I heard someone say a hay cart got left out in the rain last night. So see? That has to be what got used."

Eleanor sighed again, less lightly; this was not a confession after all. "I don't understand."

"That cart wouldn't have been left outside, don't you see? And not just because of the rule. If someone took the cart to bring stuff from their truck to the barn, which he shouldn't've done, it would end up back in the barn, right? Why wheel it all the way back outside again, especially when someone might see you?"

Eleanor gestured impatiently. "Maybe they were taking something away from the barn, and didn't want to get caught bringing the cart back in."

"No, yesterday everyone was still coming, nobody was going yet. I've been trying to think how it could've ended up outside, and all I can think of is the rain. Because the murderer was hoping the rain would . . . wash it off." Brit swallowed at the thought, but her eyes brimmed with earnestness. "See?"

"Hmmm, yes I do."

Brit stood, "I just had to tell you as soon as I figured it out, because I'm sure the buckets being carried in that thing are sloshing over, and washing it even more."

"Wait a minute, will you?" said Eleanor. "Stay right here."

She left to tell the bluesuit to find one of her forensics crew and have him find, impound, and check a two-wheeled cart with a wooden bin apparently being used to carry water to the arena.

She came back to find Brit pacing the stall. "Look," said Brit, "I have kind of a question to ask you."

"Yes, but I have kind of a question to ask you first. Sit down, Brit."

The girl sat, her face gone wary.

"I want to talk to you about Breathless. What happened last night that upset her?"

Before Brit could answer, Cullen knocked on the stall door, pulled it open, and stuck his head inside. Without the weight lifter's body to deflect attention, he was a young man with fine, almost delicate features. "I'm real sorry," he apologized, "but there's a lawyer outside the main entrance, says he's Brittany Morgan's attorney. He wants to see her, and says we should stop any questioning of her right now."

Eleanor turned to Brit. It isn't the lawyer who stops the questioning, but the suspect. "Did you call a lawyer?"

"No, uh-uh. But maybe Mrs. Brichter did. And if she thought it was that important, maybe I should talk to him before I talk any more to you."

"Mrs. Brichter?" said a voice with a mild air of irritation in it. Kori turned to look and saw Sergeant Ritter ducking under the tape. Brit was behind her, signing into the log book.

"Yes?" said Kori, leaning the push broom against a stall door.

"Did you call an attorney to represent Miss Morgan?"

Danny stuck his head out of an open stall door. He had a curry brush in one hand and an interested look on his face. If a defense attorney had been called by Kori, he knew who it would be.

But Kori frowned and said, "No, should I?"

"Someone already has. Miss Morgan seems to think it was you."

"No, it wasn't."

Eleanor looked at Danny, who shook his head. "Not me."

Kori said, "Maybe Peter did—Brit, who is the attorney? What's his name?"

"I haven't seen him yet," replied Brit, putting down the log-in pen and ducking under the tape. "I was talking to Sergeant Ritter here, and a policeman came and said a lawyer was asking for me. I thought you sent for him, so we came here to see him."

"Here I am," said a new voice, and Brit and Eleanor turned toward the man who was standing at the yellow tape. Beside him was the weight-lifting cop, who looked more than prepared to escort him away if so directed.

"Hey it *is* Dad!" said Danny, hopping out of the stall. "What are you doing here?"

"Hi, Son. Peter called to say there was some kind of problem with one of his wife's employees and he couldn't get away until tomorrow, so would I come for a look. So here I am." He looked at Brit with kind interest. "Are you Brittany Morgan?"

"Yessir," said Brit, staring at him. He looked very expensive.

"My name is Phillip Bannister, and I am here to see that your rights are protected, if that's okay with you."

Brit turned to Kori. "Do I need a lawyer?"

"I think you need at least to talk to one."

Phil asked, "Is there a place we can talk in private?"

"Use the tack stall," said Kori, gesturing, and Brit led him away, a little cowed by this fresh reminder of the seriousness of her position.

Kori asked Eleanor, "Is she still your suspect?"

"She's on a list of suspects."

"Why?" asked Kori. "I can't believe you seriously suspect her. She is totally incapable of murder!"

"She's lying to me. I get suspicious of people who lie to me. Now, if you will excuse me, I have another person waiting to be interviewed."

"Wait a second. Just what is it you think she is lying about?"

"I'm not prepared to share that kind of detail right now. On the other hand, I'd like to know why you're so sure she's innocent. May I send for you in a while?"

"Sure."

Senator McIntyre referred to the murder as "this deplorable event," and seemed to wish more than anything that if Keith Bulward had to be murdered he should have had the courtesy to be killed somewhere, anywhere, else.

"Did you see Mr. Bulward at the party in the barn?"

"Party? Oh, yes, someone said there was a party. No, I wasn't there."

"But you were here on Friday."

"Of course, during the day. I was in the barn office, mostly; but also the show office, and I had a look at the dressage setup in the arena, and I walked through the barn once or twice to see if everything was all right. At about six I went to my motel room. I called home from there. My wife likes me to check in when I'm on the road. Then I went out to supper about eight, and back to the motel for the night."

"Your wife's not here with you?"

"No, she and our daughter are coming Sunday—tomorrow—for the finals. I recently bought a show-quality mare for Birdie—that's my daughter—and she wants to meet some of the judges."

"So you are involved in showing horses."

"Me? No. Birdie would like to be. Now that we have the ranch, you see. She's always had horses, but now, with the pastures and barn, she's just been crazy to make a serious try at raising them. And she likes the Arabian horse. I investigated, of course, to see what we might be getting into, and it was an eye-opening experience. This showing business is far more complex than most people understand. Of course, I have a long way to go before I can say I really know anything about it; I probably know just enough to be dangerous." The senator smirked to show he was being self-denigrating.

"So why did they ask you to be the chief official at this show?"

The senator shrugged helplessly. "They were looking for a Name. Someone well known. They said it attracts people. Fortunately, I have a very experienced staff to assist me, and everything has gone very smoothly, until now. In fact, if it had not been for this absolutely deplorable event, I'm sure we would have been one of the best-run Class A shows in the State of Illinois." The senator swelled like a courting frog, and Eleanor thought it had taken some effort on his part not to put "the Great" in front of "State of Illinois."

"You stayed in your motel room all evening?"

"Yes, I wanted to be alert and well rested for today."

"Alone?"

The senator looked a trifle scandalized. "I told you I called my wife at home."

"And no one else shared your room."

"No, of course not." He was surprised that she might think a Name would be expected to share his room.

"Did you receive any phone calls in your room? Or make any, later on?"

"No. But would it be all right if I called home now and warned them not to come? I don't want them walking into the middle of all this."

"That's up to you, Senator. But first, how well did you know Keith Bulward?"

"I had met him, and he seemed very personable. He is—er, was—I am given to understand, an excellent judge of horse-flesh, and a fine trainer. Though I had lately heard rumors about his methods. Just this morning someone told me that he had struck someone's horse with his hand, hard enough to injure it." The senator made a fist and contemplated it. "I would not have thought that possible. They are beautiful creatures, but when one gets up close, one can see they are not, er, frail."

"Did you kill him?"

The senator's eyebrows went up and he glanced around, as if to check for eavesdroppers to this highly inappropriate question. "Why on earth should *I* kill him?"

"I haven't asked you why, yet. Only whether or not you did."

His look was direct. "No. No I didn't."

"Do you have any idea who might be in any way responsible?"

"No. Except I can't think it was anyone connected with this show."

"Why not?"

"Horse people are—well, they're decent folks. Not the sort who murder one another. It must have been something else, a mugging that went wrong, perhaps."

Eleanor did not care to speculate with the senator on the likelihood of a mugger choosing a horse barn in an otherwise deserted fairgrounds in which to find a victim, so she sighed and dismissed him with the standard request that he not leave without telling her where he was going.

*   *   *

Phillip Bannister studied his newest client. She was a big girl, five feet, seven inches at least, and solidly built. She wasn't beautiful by *Cosmo* standards, but her features were regular, her skin clear, and her big blue gaze was sweetly shy.

"I was scared," she was explaining in a voice rather light for her size. "When I opened the prep stall door and there was that body, I about—er, fell over. Scared Breathless, too. Took me a minute to get her settled down."

"Who?"

"Breathless."

Bannister blinked. "Breathless is . . ."

"Yearling filly. By Copper Wind out of Blue Wind. It was her I was gonna prep, see. For the show."

"Ah. But there was no one else, no one human, around when you found the body."

Brit gestured impatiently. "There were people all over the place. Mucking out, feeding, prepping—it gets busy real early at a show."

Bannister removed the big, unlit cigar from his mouth. He began every working day with one, and chewed his way through it and another before he went home at night. "It was because they were busy that you chose to tell the police rather than one of them you had found a body."

Brit looked askance at him, not sure if he were testing her or just ignorant. "No," she said. "Look, it only took a second to see Mr. Bulward—"

"You knew who it was right away?"

"No, at first all I could see was . . ." She gestured. "You know . . . I mean, first I saw it was a guy who hadn't died of a heart attack. And I wanted to scream for help, but then I thought, if I do, half the barn will come running, and everyone knows you shouldn't invite a crowd of people to go sightseeing around a murdered person before the police get a chance to do their stuff."

"I suppose Sergeant Brichter told you about that."

Brit blushed. "Okay, what happened was I did scream, but so did the filly, and by the time I got her calmed down, I was calmed down myself. So I called the police instead."

"So at that time you weren't scared."

"Sure, I was! Just looking at him, wondering who—"

"I mean, you weren't scared the police would think you did it."

Brit looked away. "It was kind of getting around, about me and Mr. Bulward. So I didn't want people to come running and find me and—him, like that. Because they might think . . . But I couldn't just pretend I hadn't found him, because when Kori—Mrs. Brichter—got there, I was supposed to be prepping Breathless, and you do that in the prep stall. I don't think I really thought it through like I'm telling you, I just couldn't think what else to do but call *911*. Only they don't have *911* here, so I dialed the operator. Because I didn't have a quarter."

Bannister sat back in his director's chair and replaced the cigar. He stroked a hollow cheek with a long, knobby finger. Interesting child, open, innocent. Or was she? His dark eyes, warm and friendly behind the gold rims, were nevertheless probing deeply. "Suppose, after all, you are charged with the murder of Keith Bulward," he began, and at once held up a hand to cut off her protest. "Let me finish. Suppose you are brought to trial for this murder. Can they prove you did it?"

Brit hesitated. "Sometimes they find innocent people guilty, right?"

Bannister nodded.

"But that's usually because the police screw up somehow and don't arrest who really did it, isn't it?"

Bannister shrugged, unwilling to get into these waters out loud until he knew what her point was going to be.

"But Sergeant Brichter will be here tomorrow. And Danny—is he really your son?"

"Yes," nodded Bannister shortly. "But that's not relevant. Go on."

"Well, Danny says he's really good. Sergeant Brichter. So I don't have to worry, do I? Because he'll find out who really did it, and the rest of us can go home."

Bannister smiled at her naïveté. But he also relaxed, just a little. "Who do you think really did it?"

"You won't tell if I say?" asked Brit.

"Only the confessional is less violable than the confidence between lawyer and client." Brit raised a pair of puzzled eyebrows, and he clarified, "Wild horses couldn't drag it out of me."

"I think Stoddard Eckiherne did it."

"Is he someone here at the show?"

"Yes, he's a trainer, like Mr. Bulward was. But Mr. Eckiherne used to be a lot more famous than Mr. Bulward, until he turned into an alcoholic. Someone told me he's an old-fashioned gentleman, but I think he's kind of snooty. And Mr. Bulward was . . . flashy. They didn't like each other."

"That hardly seems to be a motive for murder."

"Yeah, well, some people who drink, it's like they're always looking for something else to blame instead of the alcohol. Talk was, even when Mr. Eckiherne had the better horse, Mr. Bulward would steal the judge's attention with his flash. Mr. Eckiherne believed it, from what I hear. He got fired from his last job over a year ago, and everyone said he's history. But then he turns up here, and he's got a really nice colt from Baron Barty's farm—that's a top breeding farm, and Mr. Barty is looking for a new trainer—and all he has to do is take first and he's got a really nice new start."

"But?" prompted Bannister.

"But, Keith Bulward turns up here, where no one expects him, and he's got a nice colt, too—and the judge likes flash. Y'see?"

"Yes, I see."

"We all saw Mr. Eckiherne at the barn party. He was really, really drunk. And I saw him this morning looking nervous, scared. And you should see his hand. His knuckles are all scraped, like he's been in a fight."

"Do the police know this?"

Brit nodded solemnly. "I hear he told them he can't remember a thing about what he did last night. Danny says

Mr. Eckiherne's an old man, but I say, he may be old, and he may've been drunk, but he hated Keith Bulward, and when your life's at stake, you'd be surprised what you can do."

When Eleanor slid back the door of her interrogation stall to let Senator McIntyre out, she was surprised to find Kori Brichter standing a little way off with an air that seemed to indicate she hadn't just arrived.

"Mrs. Brichter," said McIntyre with a stiff little nod.

"Senator."

"You know each other?"

"Not well—" they began, then looked at each other with confused smiles.

"He's not from my district," explained Kori.

"By reputation only, until today," said McIntyre. "She has a very fine line of Arabian horses." He nodded at Eleanor, again at Kori, and departed with long strides.

"Come on in," said Eleanor to Kori. Inside she looked Kori's pinstripe suit up and down and said, "Is that what they call a riding habit?"

"Sort of. I mean, it's a fake. The trousers are, anyway." Kori extended a foot and looked down at her leg. "See, if it were a real riding habit, there would be big cuffs turned up at the bottom. Because," she added, seeing Eleanor's surprise that deep cuffs on bell-bottom trousers might be useful, or becoming, "when you sit on a horse, your trousers shorten, just like when you sit on a chair. And to make these long enough to cover your boots when you're riding, they have to be too long when you're standing."

"So why are you wearing a fake riding habit? Don't you ride?"

"Oh, yes. But this is my costume for showing at halter." Seeing the same nonunderstanding look again, she explained. "The horse wears the halter, not me. All I do is lead her in and try to get her to pose for the judge."

"Hey, don't overestimate my ignorance, okay? I know about horse beauty parades; it was the expression 'at halter' that threw me. For a second I was picturing people riding bareback and using halters instead of bridles. I've got a friend who rides like that sometimes."

Kori nodded. "I've done it too."

"Sit down, Mrs. Brichter." Kori sat. "Tell me why you're so convinced Brittany Morgan is innocent. Have you known her a long time?"

"Well, no. But I've talked to people who have. She's worked as a groom since she was ten years old. And everyone agrees, she is a very gentle person."

"How long have you actually known her?"

"Not quite four weeks. For the last ten days, she's worked at my farm full-time, because I wanted to get a look at her before we came. My old groom left, and I'm looking for another, and it's important to me that I hire someone who has the same attitude I do about handling my horses."

"And you're the kind who uses gentle methods."

"Yes, emphatically. But because I needed someone for this show, I was also looking for someone who knows what she's doing, someone I don't have to train."

"And Brit fit both those requirements."

"Yes."

"So you think because she's nice to your horses there's no way she would kill Keith Bulward."

Kori hesitated. "I didn't say that. If he caught her in a corner somewhere and came at her, really scared her, she would have defended herself. Anyone would."

"Is that what you think happened here?"

"I'm not sure what happened here. What I *think* is that if Brit did it, then as soon as it happened, she would have told someone. She's the one who called the police, remember, as soon as she found the body."

Eleanor's chin came up just a trifle. "I see. So why is she lying to the police now?"

"I don't know if she is. What do you think she's lying about?"

"Last night one of your horses created an uproar that woke

some people up, and didn't shut up until someone went in to calm it. Yet Brit told me nothing happened last night. Do you think that's possible?"

Kori thought, then shook her head. "No. She's a responsible person, and very attached to horses, particularly one of mine named Breathless. If the horses were upset enough to be making a lot of noise, I'm sure the one who went to calm them was her. No, what I think this is about is the way she was treated by the first officers on the scene. They saw a body, they saw her acting scared, and so far as they were concerned, that was that."

"You know, she may have been about to open up about last night when my interview of her was interrupted by the arrival of the attorney."

Kori had the grace to blush. "Do you want me to talk to her, persuade her—"

"No!" interrupted Eleanor. "I don't want anyone to do anything that might spoil this case. If it was brought out that I encouraged you to persuade someone to waive their rights . . ." She sighed.

"Yes, of course, how stupid of me. But can I offer to help you if you have any sort of questions about horses or horse shows? I'm sure this wasn't a chance murder, and that means whoever did it had a motive connected to showing Arabian horses."

"Maybe you can. For instance, you mentioned the business about Amelia Haydock. Anyone else with a similar motive?"

"Not that I know of, not that similar. But at the party last night Keith was bragging about selling a sterile mare to a man who didn't know enough to have the animal checked by a vet before paying for her. And this morning Senator McIntyre came by and made a determined effort to buy my yearling filly, and was pleased when I said I would consider his offer if Breathless had a cow-hocked, ewe-necked foal."

"I take it you wouldn't want a cow-hocked, ewe-necked foal."

"No, those are severe defects."

"If he knows so little about horses, why did he try to buy yours?"

"Breathless is an exceptionally good-looking horse, anyone with an eye will tell you that. I'm sure Senator McIntyre has heard people saying so. I think he's aware that people know that Keith's sucker in the horse sale is him, and is trying to make up for it by acquiring Breathless. I shouldn't have made a fool of him again; but he was so persistent, and so ignorant, I couldn't resist."

"Have you told anyone about his offer for your horse?"

"No, but I probably will, if I get a lot of offers for her. I won't mention the business about the ugly foal; all I want is for people not to pressure me about selling her. They can go pressure him instead."

"Anyone else?"

Kori thought. "Well, Stoddard Eckiherne was very drunk last night, and I was told it was because he thinks Keith Bulward kept turning up at places he was showing to spoil things for him."

"Do you think that's true?"

"That Keith was doing it on purpose? No. That things were getting spoiled for him? Yes."

"That's very interesting."

Kori looked at her and waited, but Eleanor didn't say anything else, so she said, "May I ask a question?"

"Shoot."

"It's almost lunchtime and some of us ate very early this morning. I'm starting to covet my horses' oats. Is there some way we can get food delivered?"

"How about, since it was you who needed to remind me we've got a whole barn full of hungry people, you be the one to find Sergeant Yale and tell him I said to organize a run to a local takeout. No, send him to me. There's a place in town that sells a really good corned beef on rye with dijon mustard and sauerkraut . . ." Eleanor was suddenly aware that her own stomach had been complaining for some while.

"That sounds delicious."

"Now wait a second, they couldn't handle all these people. I'm thinking more along the lines of pizza or hamburgers for you all."

"But surely they could handle two sandwiches. Or three, if Sergeant Yale wants one, too. I'll buy if he'll fly."

Eleanor knew when she was outmaneuvered; it was surrender or eat lukewarm pizza with everyone else. "Okay." She nodded. "But don't go bragging about the deli even if— no, *especially* if—you like it."

"Agreed."

Stoddard sat stiffly erect on a bale of hay in his prep stall. He could feel his hands trembling against the insides of his thighs. His left hand complained mildly that the friction was painful, and he put the hand, bandaged side up, on his knee, where it still trembled. Part of the tremor was hangover, of course. But a lot of it was fear.

Christ, why did Bulward have to do this to him?

A sound like a snort escaped him. As if Keith Bulward got himself killed just to spite Stoddard Eckiherne.

But what if Stoddard Eckiherne had murdered Keith Bulward? Then the fear was more than understandable; it was mandatory.

The colt next door whickered; it was time he was fed. Stoddard's prospective employer had been trying out the new theory that frequent, smaller feedings were better for horses. It sounded right; big, twice-daily feedings had to stress a digestive system evolved for all-day grazing. And statistics seemed to show that horses treated to frequent feedings were far less plagued by colic. The problem with the new theory was that it was work intensive. Used to be, you went through the stable in the morning doing a feeding, then had until evening for training, repairs, upkeep, raising children, grocery shopping, gardening, haying, reading up on the newest theories, selling a horse, buying a horse, negotiating with your farrier over his bill, or trying to catch up on your sleep after your mares had kept you up six nights running with foaling. With the new method, there was still all that, plus the constant interruption of running to the barn to dole out the next installment.

Like now. He groaned and got to his feet. Barrel of oats, where was the goddam barrel of oats? He picked up a plastic bucket with traces of feed in its bottom and looked around for the big covered feed barrel, which he eventually found under a horse blanket he had neglected to hang up.

He was standing in the stall with the colt, watching it scraping around the bottom of the feed bucket with its prehensile upper lip for the last few grains, when it struck him.

A thin fragment of straw bounded gently off his nose, tumbled slowly down his chest, and landed on the colt's white mane. Stoddard, frowning, picked it off and looked up. A pair of sparrows were perched side by side up in the rafters of the barn. One had a beak full of straw and the other, half squatting, was chirping excitedly, fluttering her wings and crouching definitively.

"Don't do it, Son," Stoddard advised him. "We're only here for the weekend. Come Monday, we're gone and all our grain with us, and your family may starve before they book another show into here."

But the one with the beak full of straw dropped his burden and scrambled aboard.

"Pah!" Stoddard waved the drifting bits of straw aside. The colt, spooked by his voice and the movement of his hand, jumped back, the muscles under his golden coat suddenly prominent.

"Here now, here now," soothed Stoddard, and the colt came forward to accept a caress. "It's only us humans who can imagine the future," he explained. "That's why we get ulcers and sparrows don't." The colt shifted his attention from the caress to the empty bucket, snorting his disappointment to find it still empty. "And that's why you horses eat till you founder and we don't." He looked at the still-trembling hand he'd used to brush away the falling chaff.

"Funny, you'd think it would keep us from getting hangovers, wouldn't you?"

But how else to make a temporary getaway from visions of the future? Like the one of his arrest for the murder of Keith Bulward?

He didn't know how he should be feeling about that prospect, because his attempt to blockade another dismal view of the future had led to a blackout of a vitally important part of his recent past.

He pushed the colt aside gently and went out of the box stall. As he was closing the door, a new thought occurred: Maybe one of the reasons they thought he was guilty was that *he* thought he was guilty.

How would he be acting if he thought—no, if he *knew*—he wasn't guilty?

Well, for one thing, he wouldn't be so goddam sorry Bulward was dead. He might even be relieved.

Or glad even, because, with Bulward dead, that meant he, Stoddard Eckiherne, had the first-place ribbon in the two-year-old class as good as in his hand. And with that win, he was in as Baron Barty's new trainer.

Maybe he wasn't guilty. He hadn't gotten physical with anyone for years, drunk or sober. And it was entirely possible he'd gotten his scraped hand in a fall. He'd done a lot of falling lately. And it was only the hurt hand that made him think he was guilty, right? So probably he wasn't guilty. He forced a halfhearted sigh of relief.

But falling down would have to come to an end now, because Mr. Barty would not keep a drunk on his payroll, no matter how talented.

And it was true that every time previously he'd tried to sober up, he'd discovered what a horrible mess he was in and immediately dived back into the bottle. But now, oh yes now, he would find himself landed in a pot of jam, a nice, safe, warm, responsible, honorable, praiseworthy pot of jam.

With such a prize within his grasp, and conditional on his drying out, how could he not stay sober? Respectability, honor, prestige, an important position with an important farm, his now for the taking.

He went to rinse out the feed bucket and, on his way back, found himself humming, something else he hadn't done in years. He put the pail away and decided it was time to take a little walk around the barn, look at the competition. Because it might even be possible that he'd take not only the two-year-old class, but the championship itself.

The first shower checked, of course, showed no sign of blood. Swearing under their breath, Dave and Roger began to look very carefully at every square inch of the second.

The still-damp walls were covered with tan tiles to a height of seven feet. The grout between them was old and fairly porous, but none of the darker spots tested positive for blood. Dave borrowed a three-legged stool from a nearby exhibitor and began an examination of the narrow ledge that marked the meeting place between the tiles and the boards above them. "Well, I'll be dipped," he muttered after getting about halfway around. "Looky here."

"Whatcha got?" asked Roger.

"Something dark and dry."

But Roger climbed up for a look and sneered, "You're a hell of a forensics specialist; can't you tell blood from bird doo?"

"Guess I haven't been shit on as often as you, Rog. Let's take a look at the floor."

The floor was cement, new looking, with no obvious cracks or repairs. It sloped toward a big-bore drain in the center, which was covered with a round metal plate punched with holes. The plate was not screwed down, and Roger lifted it easily. The trap was full of cold, still-sudsy water. He removed his jacket, rolled up his sleeve, and put his hand down the drain. "Yech. Hair. Oops, wait a second." He groped deeper and came up with something, a medium-size knife with a wooden handle. The last inch of its curved blade was bent sharply back, as if it had been used to loosen a paint can lid. He held it up, his hand draped with strands of wet mane and tail hair. "Whadaya think?"

Dave squatted for a closer look. "Could it've gotten in there by accident?"

"Hardly. That cover fits into a rim. And what would you bring a knife into a horse shower for?"

"What am I, a cowboy? I didn't even know they gave horses showers." He looked at the blade, frowning. "Maybe someone used it to pry off a horseshoe."

Roger made a doubting face and took a closer look at the knife. It wasn't rusty and didn't look old or abused, except for the bent blade. "Sharp," he said, gingerly testing it on his thumb.

They bagged and tagged the knife, then Roger began a duckwalk around the perimeter, where cement met tile. In the back corner, there was a tiny gap, little more than a crack. Roger stuck a plastic pin into it and brought it out coated with a tarry substance. "Yo, Watson," he muttered; "the game's afoot."

He took a slip of filter paper and touched it to the pin. A dark red stain climbed up the paper. He waved the paper to dry it, while Dave poured a small amount of a benzidine solution into a glass test tube.

When the paper had dried, a piece of it was dropped into the test tube, and they waited. A color started to develop in the tube, and Roger held it up to the light. Blue-green, a positive reaction.

"A hit," murmured Dave; "a very palpable hit."

∇

9

KORI, NOTING THE NUMBER of people beginning to wander
around, went to the end of the aisle, the one through which
no one was permitted to leave. She nodded to the uniformed
police officer on guard and turned on the VCR.

"You're going to get awfully sick of this, I'm afraid," she
told him.

"What is it?"

"An ad for our farm."

Music started—a brisk version of "The Entrance of the
Queen of Sheba" on a trumpet—and there was Copper Wind
galloping across a meadow, his mane and tail flowing like
black silk in the wind. A somewhat muffled voice began
describing the stallion, naming his ancestors, and listing the
championships he had won, both at halter and in English
Pleasure performance. The music stopped abruptly and a
new scene began, the birth of a foal, then the foal dry and
romping beside its mother, and then all grown up and showing off her blue ribbon outside an arena. The muffled voice
described the new horse as Summer Breeze, typical of the
fillies Copper Wind sired. The voice then went into raptures
about Tretower Farm (shown as an attractive Queen Anne–

style house with well-kept barn and outbuildings, set among big, old trees), where Copper Wind lived, and where his small harem (shown galloping across their own meadow) regularly produced the kind of splendid horse (a shot of three adorable weanlings) you, the discerning Arabian horse owner, should buy to complete, complement, or begin your herd. Nothing as crass as price was mentioned, a warning to the slender of purse, and the program ended with a soft-focus shot of Kori walking in knee-high grass along a narrow stream, with Copper Wind following like the gentle pet he was, while the voice encouraged the viewer to contact Kori Price Brichter at the address shown on the screen.

The picture faded to black, then to snow, then the Queen of Sheba began her entrance again. The cop sighed.

A dark woman in an expensive Western costume gave a caw of recognition and stopped with her companion to look at the video. "Wonderful, isn't that just wonderful?" She saw Kori and held out her arms in an invitation to a hug. "*So awful!*" she bawled when Kori came within reach, grabbing her by the shoulders and touching cheeks. "I don't know *how* you're standing it, so brave! *Isn't* she brave, Adam?"

The man standing beside her made a subtle shrugging face. "Mrs. Brichter," he said in greeting. "Any sign this will be over soon?"

"I guess not, Mr. Croy."

"Oh, you two aren't on a first-name basis? I don't believe it! Kori, this is Adam. Adam, Kori. Now shake hands and be friends."

Kori and Adam both knew Maggie well enough to smile, shake hands, and repeat first names at one another.

"What are you doing in here, Maggie?" asked Kori. "Someone told me you were carrying water to the horses in the arena."

"I was, but two men came and took away the hay cart I was using, and brought me in for a little third degree; and, so long as I was in, and had started out in here, they let me stay. If I'd known they were going to do that, I'd have asked to bring Magic Dancer with me. He's the weanling I was showing. He won, did anyone menton that? That's the second Polka Dancer foal to win a blue at a Class A show, and Polka Dancer's only four. Not bad, hey? And Polka Dancer's gonna win a ribbon in performance—or he will, if they ever let us get the show back on track. God, I can't *believe* this is happening to us! Polka is so ready for this show it's a crying shame. And I've got a real chance at a blue now they've changed the rules."

"Why, what rules?" asked Kori.

"AQHA issued new guidelines for judging Western Pleasure. Didn't you know? No, you ride English, don't you? Let's see, the ears can't be lower than the withers, no traveling in slow motion, no more tired, skinny, dried-up look. Isn't that *great*? Christ, it was sickening to walk through a Quarter Horse show barn and find some unfortunate creature with his head tied way up high for *hours* so's his muscles would give out and he'd drag his nose in the dirt when performing! And with the Quarter Horse people cleaning up their act, everyone showing Western will do it, too."

"Say, we Arabian judges never did give ribbons to the thin, the tired, the poor—"

"Maybe not, Adam, but that horse you made reserve in Chicago last fall couldn't't've passed the ears-above-the-withers rule if he was half *jackrabbit*! Now if you judges would only start paying attention to some of the other crap that goes on . . ." She turned and hit Adam in the shoulder with a small, hard fist.

"What crap, Maggie?" he asked, but not as if he really wanted to know; this was obviously going to be the chorus of an oft-heard song.

"Peeled ginger up the ass! You walk into the show ring nowadays, and it smells like stir-fry in there! And makeup? Some people's prep stalls look like a booth at an Avon convention! Sure, it's illegal, but everyone does it because everyone gets away with it!"

"Now, Maggie, not everyone does it. And we can't watch

every horse being prepped, so what am I supposed to do?"

"Goddam excuse 'em!" barked Maggie. "You walk around the back end of a horse and smell ginger, you say in that voice all you judges practice up on, the one makes your soul wither up inside you, '*Thank* you' and let the steward show 'em the gate. A horse comes in with eyes like Tammy Faye Bakker, '*Thank* you,' an' out he goes. A horse comes in so hot the trainer can't hardly control him, '*Thank* you.' "

Maggie drew breath to continue, but Adam said hastily to Kori, "I understand you've got a pretty nice yearling filly with you."

"Yes, we think she's beautiful. I'd invite you in for a look but you have to go around the other side and sign in."

"And I suppose you're stuck in there," said Maggie. "Poor *thing*, that can't be any fun."

"No, actually, we're not." She gestured at the other end. "So long as we sign out and back in, we can come and go as we please, too."

"Well, you give yourself a break—and do yourself a favor," said Maggie. "Go take a look at that colt Stoddard brought. *Very* nice and over fifteen hands. I think you should consider Baron Barty's stallion. You could use a little size on your horses; that mare you rode in dressage yesterday looked like a *pony*. Can't get a good trot out of a horse that small."

There was nothing whatsoever wrong with Blue Wind's trot, but Adam was judging the English Pleasure class in Chicago next month, where Kori planned to compete. Maggie's daughter was also riding in that class, and hinting that Blue didn't have much of a trot in front of the judge of the class couldn't hurt. Maggie might be against physical tampering, but she wasn't above verbal sabotage.

Kori smiled ruefully at Adam, who smiled back, and Maggie, catching their exchange, cawed with unrepentant laughter and began dragging him away.

Still, Kori decided Maggie's advice about going out for a look at the competition wasn't bad. She checked on Brit, who was polishing a pair of boots in the tack stall, and told her she had ordered a pizza in her and Danny's name.

The sign-out log was an ordinary spiral notebook guarded by a uniform cop because, Kori knew, the notebook would become part of the case file. Noting that Phil had not been back since he signed out an hour ago, Kori wondered whom he was talking to. She wrote her name, signature, and time out, tucked the pen into the spiral, and left the Tretower aisle.

The barn was subdued, partly as a reaction to the murder and its investigation, partly because there were no classes to be getting the horses ready for. People wandered from group to group, and talked in low voices, their words lost in the clash of radio stations. It was usual to play music to the horses in their own barns, then play the same kind of music at a show, on the grounds that the more things around the horses were familiar, the less stress they would feel. Since the grooms had to listen to it as well, and since the grooms were universally young people, the music tended to be very contemporary, which, one might think, undid its purpose of soothing the horses.

Kori walked toward a group that included Adam Croy *sans* Maggie, and redheaded Hilary. Their sudden silence told her the subject of conversation. "It's okay," she smiled, "talk all you like. I'm ready to hear anything that might be useful."

"Are you working with the police on this case?" asked Hilary.

"Not at all."

A man in a working cowboy's outfit with authentic wear marks on it said, "But your husband is a policeman, a detective, isn't he?"

"Back home, yes. But that cuts no ice with these people, as it probably shouldn't. And in this case, it may well be that *I'm* a suspect." But Kori smiled when she said it, and the muffled snickers of the others showed they didn't take it seriously, either. Still, they didn't want to plunge back into speculation with her present and there was an awkward silence.

Finally Hilary said, "You know, Marvin had pneumonia this past winter. He's nineteen now, and it took him a long while to come back. We thought he'd maybe be a little bit unhappy at hitting the show circuit right away, but when he saw the trailer out in the driveway, he just about dragged me up to it, he was so anxious to go."

"He's an old campaigner," said Adam, who had given him more than a few ribbons over the years.

"Unlike our show manger," said the cowboy. "Where they got the audacity to ask someone as ignorant as him to serve, I don't know."

"You mean where he got the audacity to accept, don't you?" said Kori.

"It's practice for him, accepting nominations," said Adam. "He's hoping to be nominated for governor one of these days."

"Meanwhile," said Hilary, "shouldn't he be at the state capitol raising our taxes or something?"

"No, they don't work on weekends till closer to the end of session," said Adam.

"You talking about McIntyre? I hear he wants to be governor so bad he can taste it," offered a newcomer, a man whose green Western shirt had long white fringe and whose felt hat was an immaculate white.

"Huh, who'd vote for him?" asked the real cowboy.

"My uncle works in the state attorney's office, and he says Bob McIntyre is a pretty good state senator," Hilary offered.

"Yeah, but that was before this business of buying a sterile foundation mare came up," said the cowboy. "It's okay for him to retire from his law firm so he can make a fool of himself with inherited money, but when he's coming up with a budget for my tax money, that's a whole 'nother thing."

"Bulward was probably exaggerating," said the fringed shirt. "He had a tendency to do that."

"Yeah, but he was cutting so deep so far as Senator McIntyre was concerned," said Adam, "that the truth must've been pretty pitiful."

Hilary said, "Hey, now, remember how Keith was careful never to mention the sucker's name? How come you're all so sure it was Senator McIntyre?"

"Hell, we all know who he was talking about," said the cowboy. "And don't think McIntyre didn't know we all knew."

"You don't suppose . . . ," said Adam, lifting an eyebrow.

"Aw, he hasn't got the guts!" sneered the cowboy.

"And," said the fringed shirt, "even in today's climate, committing murder might endanger his political career."

"But that means it's one of the rest of you," said Adam.

The cowboy laughed. "What's this 'rest of *us*' shit, Adam? I don't think his family will ask *you* to give the eulogy. You were the one going around saying Bulward should be investigated for fraud over his horse dealing."

The fringed shirt said, "Yeah, but a lot of us were mad. Horse traders like Bulward give all of us a bad name. And the way he treated his horses—hell, they could arrest anyone in this barn and make a damn good case he did it."

"Not me," said Hilary. "I've got a one hundred percent alibi. I wish they'd name the people they know didn't do it, and let us go home. I'm not used to being scared and bored at the same time. And I'm getting hungry. Where's that pizza we ordered?"

"We ordered fifty pizzas," said the cowboy; "it's gonna take a while."

"I don't want to go home without competing in Western Pleasure," said the fringed shirt. "I feel a blue coming on. Why don't they just arrest that girl they were talking to at first? Everyone knows she did it."

"Hey," objected Hilary. "Don't say that." She tilted her head in Kori's direction.

But the shirt didn't pick up the hint. "Why not? It's true."

"It isn't true," said Kori. "Anyone who knows Brit knows it can't be true."

"You just say that because she's your groom," scoffed Hilary, speaking to Kori but looking at the shirt, who winced hard and looked away.

"That isn't so. Brit may be a big girl, but she's gentle as a fawn—gentler. My horses already love her because she's so kind to them."

"She said she'd hurt Bulward if he came near her," said Adam. "Several people said they heard her say that, just last night."

Kori said, "And having said that, I'm sure Keith was too smart to take her up on it, because if she turned up injured we'd all know who should be arrested. And she was far too scared of him to go start something."

"I agree," said Hilary. "She's just not that kind of person."

"I think it was Stoddard Eckiherne," said the cowboy. "He was a scared mess this morning, and he *says* he can't remember a thing that happened last night."

The fringed shirt said, "You know, I was there when Alek told him Bulward was at the show. It was like he let all the air out of Stoddard's balloon. Stoddard went into his tack stall and after a while he started throwing things, swearing up a storm. He really thought he was in clover with that Baron colt. No wonder he drank enough to forget last night."

"I don't care how drunk you are, if you kill someone, you've got to remember at least parts of it," said Hilary.

"Maybe he's lying about not remembering," said the cowboy.

"Maybe he's not," said Adam, and on that note the little group began to break up.

"Adam," said Kori, "could I talk to you?"

"What about?"

"Amelia."

Adam winced. "What about her?"

"Not here. Why don't you come back and take a look at Breathless?"

"I don't know . . ."

"It's okay, you're not judging at this show, so you can look at anything you like."

Adam smiled. "Okay."

* * *

"What kind of a manager is he, anyway, sweatin' like a nigger at election!"

"Jonathan!"

"I don't care, he is! And you know it!"

Phil Bannister paused outside the open stall door to listen.

The woman said, "I mean, your way of putting it. Sweating like a—Jonathan, you know better than that!"

"Oh, for Chrissake, Carole! My father used that expression, and from what I know of elections back in his day, they had good reason to sweat, them not having much say, and the white folks' choices being between bad and worse, so far as the black folks were concerned."

"I don't care, it doesn't sound very . . . nice when you say 'nigger.' "

Phil stuck his head in. "Jon? I thought I heard your voice."

"Bannister!" said a slightly built man with thinning hair, rising from the camp stool. He held out a hand to Phil, who came in to accept it.

"Carole," he said to his wife, who was about his size and weight, with a big chignon, "this is Phillip Bannister, a fellow attorney. He's from Charter."

"Bannister, from Charter?" she said, reaching out her own small hand. "Are you any relation to Danny Bannister?"

"He's my son," said Phil, somewhat taken aback. He was unused to people thinking of him as someone's father.

"Fine trainer, going to be one of the best," said Jon. "You must be here to see him in action. Wish he were mine."

"Well, thank you," said Phil, who had a standing offer with his son to pay his way through any college course he chose, so long as it didn't involve horses. He said to Jon, "I heard you taking someone to task. May I ask, who is it?"

"Oh, it's Bob McIntyre. I wish he was running this fall; I'd truly enjoying campaigning against him."

"But he's not from your district, is he?"

"What's that got to do with it?"

"Now, Jonathan," said Carole. "He's been in the State

Senate for years, and you've never said a thing against him until now."

"Yeah, well this is the first time I've seen him in action. And I don't like it."

"Why, what's he doing?" asked Phil.

"It's been all morning and half the afternoon, and still they're holding up the show. I don't know what they're waiting for, and it's clear the senator isn't busting his buns getting them to open the barn."

"Now, Jonathan," said Carole, "this is his first try at managing a show. And who expects a murder? Even an experienced manager wouldn't know what to do."

"Hell, that isn't the whole story about him." He turned to Phil. "Did you hear what happened at the party last night? Keith Bulward was making fun of some jerk who bought a mare from him without checking its veterinary records first."

"So?"

"Well, it seems the sucker is none other than McIntyre. And I happen to know that the senator is up for a position on the State Finance Committee this fall. You want a fiscal idiot making decisions about how our tax money is spent? I think I'll write a couple of letters when we get home."

"Wheee-ew," Adam whistled a few minutes later. "Unless she falls and breaks her neck real soon, you're going to have the hottest mare in the business."

Breathless, who never minded being the object of admiration, lifted her head even higher and gave him a sideways glance.

"Good girl," said Kori, and Breathless turned around to give Adam the benefit of her other profile. Kori went in to stand in front of her, stroke her neck, then hold the palm of the hand high in front of her and pull it back; Breathless followed the gesture with her nose.

"Jee-zuz," murmured Adam, his eyes sweeping the filly's topline. "I don't suppose you'd care to sell her?"

Kori made a mock-regretful face. "I'm so sorry, Senator McIntyre and I have kind of an agreement."

"McIntyre? Are you serious? And since when did he get such good taste?"

Kori chuckled. "Don't worry, I set such conditions that the sale probably won't go through. Not that he realizes it. That's what makes the Keith Bulward business so shabby."

"But you don't think he killed him?"

"How well do you know McIntyre? He's from your district, isn't he?"

"Yes." Adam nodded. "But I'm not too involved in the political scene. We've met at social events a few times. I like his wife. His daughter talks politics and horses exclusively, and tends to snub anyone who isn't prepared to do the same; but she's only sixteen and may outgrow that. As for him, I just don't know. He's all politician, which means the real man is carefully concealed. He can be very charming, and he's a hard worker. Someone told me he has the instincts of a street fighter, but that person had just failed to get a favor out of him. What do you think?"

"Politicians don't usually do their own murders, do they?" Kori said it with a smile, then sobered. "On the other hand . . ."

"Ah, yes," nodded Adam. "Amelia Haydock, the real reason you asked me back here. Okay, that lady would easily kill someone she caught hurting one of her horses, especially if the horse were Wellaway. Which makes me surprised they didn't find Keith right there outside the arena looking like Beetle Bailey after Sarge gets through with him."

"I agree," said Kori. "And, she was here in our part of the barn when we got here."

Both of Adam's eyebrows went up at that. "Here?" he said. "In the barn?"

"I know," said Kori. Judges are not allowed in the barn after a show begins.

"Did you tell the police that?"

"They know it; she was here when they arrived. And they

arrived before Danny and I did. And, he'd made a fool of her after he'd been her favorite for so long."

"Not that long. None of them last that long. Amelia's always making a fool of herself over good-looking young men, but it rarely lasts more than nine months or a year."

"Yes, but this was maybe a little different," said Kori. "Keith's reputation kept getting brought up to her, and she'd come right back, saying it was all lies. And then he proved she was wrong by hitting Wellaway where other people could see him do it. I saw her at the party last night, and she was so angry it was scary."

"What did she say?"

"I asked her if she'd made up her mind what she was going to do to Keith, and she said no, but with a look on her face that made me think otherwise."

"You know," said Adam, "if I was Amelia, I wouldn't want him dead."

"What?" said Kori. "Why not?"

"There's things she could have done to him that could have made his life really miserable."

"How miserable?"

"Well, sooner or later Bulward would have had a horse up in front of her. If you were a judge and someone you hated trotted a horse up to you . . ."

Kori made a dismissive noise, but Adam lifted a hand and said, "I assure you, by the time she was finished with him, she'd've run him out of town. He'd've sold Morning Glory and changed his name and moved to Boise by the time she was done with him."

"How could she do that?"

Adam said, "If I were a judge and absolutely certain a trainer was crooked, I'd pray for him to bring horses to me so I could never give him a ribbon. If one of his horses was really spectacular, I'd pull out seven horses, including his, and give the other six the ribbons. If the class was so small there were more places than horses, I'd place him fourth of four, fifth of five. And I'd do it as often as I got the chance."

"God keep you from ever getting mad at Danny!"

"Amen. Because if I thought he deserved it, I would do it to him. Or anyone. Some people should be run out of the business."

"I saw a judge last year in Chicago . . ." She paused. "Listen and tell me what you think: A trainer showing halter brought his horse to be judged, and just as he got it set up, the judge asked him to set it up again, as if he hadn't done it right. When he set it up again, she asked him to do it over. By then he was rattled, and he set his horse up wrong, everyone could see that, and the judge just waved him away. There was laughter in the audience, but even at the time I thought it was her; she was doing it to him on purpose."

Adam blanked his face and raised his hands, a cautious refusal to comment. But Kori dared him with her expression and he shrugged. "Okay, I was at that show, too," he said. "The owner of the horse was waiting outside the arena to fire him."

"Did he deserve it?"

"God, yes."

Kori nodded and stored that away for later reference; she had been thinking of buying a horse from the trainer. "On the other hand," she said, "we both saw the judge do that. Other people probably did, too. If someone saw Amelia's monkey business, why wouldn't he ask her why she didn't give the best horse in the class a ribbon?"

"He might." Adam smiled and, deepening his voice, said, " 'I really liked that horse, but that trainer obviously has no idea his farrier is ruining its feet. The way that horse was traveling, I couldn't possibly place it.' "

"I see."

"The horse show world is very incestuous; everyone knows everyone else. Once Amelia started in on Keith, especially after she was so nice to him for a while, other judges would've figured she found out something, and they'd've quit placing his horses, too. And people would have stopped giving him horses to train."

Kori said, "And other trainers would have stopped trying to emulate him, which wouldn't be a bad thing, either. I'm getting very tired of trainers flashier than their horses. Now we have a whole new reason to be sorry someone murdered Keith Bulward."

Stoddard met Kori in the main aisle near the front entrance. He had just come from taking a look at the four-year-old mare Clover Lake would be showing against Maurice if they both got into the finals. If this show ever got under way again.

"Congratulations on that comeback in dressage," Stoddard said. "And someone told me you have a lock on the blue in the yearling filly halter class. If visitors are permitted in your area I would like to come by—?"

"Of course. But she's not for sale."

"Ah." He turned to look at the elaborate Morning Glory Farms layout, with its real sod and potted tulips and white iron fences. "Looks like a cemetery, doesn't it?"

"Don't say that, Stoddard!" she replied. "Anyway, they can't tear it down until the police are finished in here."

"You know about things like that, I suppose, your husband being a policeman."

"It's only natural that one might take an interest in what one's spouse is doing, don't you think?"

Stoddard flushed. His divorce had been loud and messy. Resolutely, he continued, "Still, you've talked with the police about it?"

"A little."

"Have they told you whom they suspect?"

"No, of course not."

"Who do you think did it?"

"I don't know, except it wasn't Brit."

"How about Amelia Haydock?"

"Why her?"

"Because she always had a better-than-you attitude, as if being a judge of horses made her a judge of people, too. And

Bulward showed the world how wrong she can be about people, so . . ."

Kori frowned doubtfully. Then, "*Delata*!" she said. "You're hoping I'll help you spread that idea, aren't you?"

"Oooh, she speaks Latin, doesn't she? Naturally, I'm doing all I can to assist the police in thinking it wasn't me. But maybe I'm wrong; maybe Brit Morgan did kill him."

"You had better not repeat that!" she said with bared teeth.

"Hey, take it easy," said Stoddard, lifting both hands. "I was just talking to someone a few minutes ago—"

"Mr. Eckiherne?" said a new voice.

He turned, and there was a policeman looking at him. "Yes, I'm Stoddard Eckiherne."

"Sergeant Ritter has sent me to ask you to come and see her for a few minutes."

Stoddard looked rocked, but recovered quickly. "Of course. If you will excuse me, Mrs. Brichter," he said and walked off with the cop.

Whew, he thought as he went down the aisle beside the officer, that cat needs her claws drawn. Would she repeat her opinion of his gossip? Would it matter, so long as the gossip got handed along? A fragment of yesterday evening came into his head, a scene between Kori and Keith. Keith was barking at her, like a dog. *Cave canem*, that was part of it, Bulward's punch line to a story he was telling. Of course she was showing off her Latin then, too; saying it was *caveat emptor*, unless Bulward was speaking of himself. Then Keith had begun to bark at her. Stoddard had laughed at Keith's clever comeback, but it seemed to him now, in the cool light of sobriety, that it was she who had been the sharper in that exchange, too. Had he gone too far with her now? He had better stay out of her way until this was over.

Eckiherne stared a long seven seconds at the knife in the plastic bag before shrugging with careful nonchalance. "It's a hoof knife, obviously."

"It was found in the drain of the horse shower."

"Really? How did it get there?"

"Is it yours?" asked Eleanor.

"No. No, I'm sure it's not." But he didn't look very sure.

"Then you won't mind if I send someone along to help you look for yours. Unless you didn't bring yours along?"

Stoddard hesitated, wanting badly to use this way out. But he looked at Eleanor, already prepared to ask if someone might look through his things anyhow, and he said, "There should be one in the kit I always travel with."

Fran looked at the plastic bag. "Hoof knife."

"Yours?"

"You mean like mine personally, or Morning Glory's?"

"Do you own a hoof knife?"

"No. I've seen them used, but I've never had the guts to use one myself. They're sharp suckers, take your finger off if you're not careful."

"Does Morning Glory Farms own one?"

"At least one. Keith was always asking someone to put a twitch on this or that horse so he could pare those hooves down nice and thin."

"Twitch?"

"It goes on a horse's upper lip. Distracts him, and can hurt if he won't stand still. Keith cut a little too close sometimes. If you get the front hooves real sensitive, the horse gets his hind legs under him so they can carry more of his weight, and the effect is nice, and a buyer thinks like he'll do good in English performance."

Eleanor looked slantwise at this, but Fran looked back with a don't-blame-me expression. Eleanor asked, "Did he bring a hoof knife to the show?"

"Always. It's in the prep stall."

"I'm going to send someone along with you to bring it back, okay?"

"Sure."

*   *   *

Eleanor picked up a labeled plastic bag and showed it to McIntyre. "Can you tell me anything about this?"

The senator leaned forward to look at the object inside the bag, then shied back from it. "It's a knife."

"Do you know what kind of knife?"

He leaned forward again. "A knife with its blade bent back at the tip."

"I mean, do you know what it's used for?"

He shrugged and without looking at it again said, "It's too big to be a paring knife and too small to be a carving knife and rather sturdy to be a steak knife . . ." He thought. "A hunting knife?" he guessed. "Probably a good one, to allow the blade to be turned back on itself like that without breaking."

"It's a hoof knife, Senator."

He nodded vaguely. "Oh."

"It was found in the drain of the horse shower."

He nodded again. "Somebody dropped it, perhaps?"

"I don't think it was dropped."

"Oh?" His eyes met hers. He swallowed thickly. "You're sure?"

"Yes. What would you say if I told you someone saw you put it down the drain?"

"That's impossible." He shook his head vigorously. "You must be mistaken. Or they must be mistaken. I wouldn't know how to go about killing someone. Especially with a knife." He wiped his hands on his trousers, his mouth pulled back in a fastidious grimace.

Eleanor wrote something down, then tapped her pencil on the notepad while she thought. "Do you have any idea who might say they saw you do that?"

He began slowly to writhe all over, like a schoolboy in the principal's office who doesn't want to tell whom he saw break a window.

"Did you see Amelia Haydock at the party last night?" she asked, guessing whom he would accuse.

"No," he said, surprised. "I told you I didn't attend the party."

"So it wasn't from her you heard about her horse being struck by Mr. Bulward."

"No."

"Who was it?"

He shrugged. "I don't remember. I mean, more than one person was talking about it, and I don't remember who was first."

"Then what is it you don't want to tell me?"

He sighed and pursed his lips, and took his pipe from his pocket to look at it before putting it back. "A young woman came to me yesterday, when I was alone in the office. She was . . . upset."

"What about?"

"Keith Bulward. She said she used to work for him, and that he fired her because she refused his sexual advances. She said he had threatened her. I could see she was upset, but there *is* that sort of hysteric who will exaggerate, or even lie, to get a man in trouble. So I asked if she wanted me to phone the police and have him arrested, and she said it would only be her word against his, so no. I told her it was impossible to send him home because of some alleged offense, and she said okay, then be aware there would be trouble if he tried to pick up where he left off."

Eleanor asked, "Who was the young woman?"

Again the reluctant writhe, then, "Brittany Morgan. She's a groom with the Tretower Farm. I wouldn't mention it, but the body was found in one of their stalls, and . . ." He shrugged.

"Why didn't you mention this to me before?"

"Because last time you asked me, I hadn't heard the story about how he came up on her in the horse shower last night and she said if he got close enough she'd hurt him bad. And now you say that knife was found down the drain in the horse shower."

When Eleanor opened the stall door to release McIntyre, she saw Bulward's groom Fran waiting with a young bluesuit.

Fran was near tears. "This is crazy, this is just crazy!" she was saying.

Eleanor waited until the senator had left before asking, "What happened?"

"We can't find that knife for hooves," reported the cop.

"I asked Missy and she says she didn't move it," whined Fran, kneading her hands as if she were shaping them in clay. "And I know it was in the prep stall, I remember seeing it right on top of the kit when we set up Thursday afternoon. I can't think where it could've got to!"

Eleanor brought her in, sat her down, and calmed her, but before she could ask her anything, they were interrupted by a sharp knock on the stall door.

It was Stoddard, a triumphant, relieved grin on his face. He was holding a knife in his hand. "Right where he said it would be," said the bluesuit with him.

"First place we looked."

"Wait a second, that looks like our knife!" said Fran, peering around Eleanor.

"Nope, not a chance," said Stoddard. "See, I burned my initials into the handle."

Eleanor took the knife, which appeared older than the one in the plastic bag. Its blade was narrower, worn down by numberless sharpenings. Near the end of the handle were the crudely cut initials SE. The carving had been done long enough ago that the edges of the lettering were smoothed down. But, most interestingly, the blade of this one was bent exactly like the murder weapon. She turned to Fran. "Is the blade of your knife bent like this?"

"Sure. All hoof knives have a blade like that."

She said it as if she were surprised Eleanor didn't know that, and Eleanor handed the knife back to Stoddard. "Thank you, Mr. Eckiherne." He took it and left, and Eleanor turned back to the groom. "Sit down, Fran. Let's talk some more." She waited until the sound of footsteps faded away. "Now, about Missy. Could Keith have been sexually abusing her?"

"*What*? No, of course not! He wouldn't do anything like that! Anyway"—her voice changed and her eyes dropped—"he knew we were kind of keeping an eye on her."

"Because you thought perhaps Mr. Bulward would try something with her?"

"No, because she's practically still a baby."

"What do you mean?"

"You didn't ask her? No, sure you did!" scoffed Fran. "You asked *me* how old *I* was!"

"How old is she?"

"She says she's sixteen, but the way she talks about boys, the stuff she says she's studying in school—she can't be more than fourteen!"

"Then why did Keith hire her?"

"Because he offered her a dollar less an hour than minimum, and she not only took it, she worked just as hard as the rest of us. Harder, sometimes."

"And she didn't resent that?"

"Are you kidding? She was thrilled to death to be working in a real horse barn. She thought she was on her way to heaven when Keith asked her to come to this show."

"Hmmm." Eleanor made a note. "You say you were watching out for her. Would you have noticed if she got up and left after you went to bed last night?"

Fran nodded emphatically, relaxing because she was not under suspicion. "Her cot was against the wall, and mine was right up next to hers. She would've had to've climbed over me to get out, and I don't care how tired I was, that would've woke me up. As long as I was there, she was there."

Eleanor sent for Kori, and showed her the bag.

"Hoof knife."

"Yours?"

"It looks like ours—but it looks like everyone else's, too. That's a popular brand." Kori looked closer. "May I look at it?"

"So long as you don't take it out of the bag."

Kori picked it up and turned it so she could see the underside of the handle. "No, thank God, it's not ours. I have this tiny branding iron, and I burn our logo onto anything I don't paint it on or embroider it on. It should be right here, three little towers." She touched a spot where the handle sloped toward the blade. "There's nothing on this one."

"If I come with you, will you show me yours?"

"Yes, of course." She put the bag down and wiped her fingers on her trousers, an unconscious gesture that curiously echoed McIntyre's. "So this is the weapon, is it? No wonder Brit was so upset over finding Keith's body. If someone used a hoof knife on him . . ." She wiped again.

On the way to the Tretower section of the barn, Eleanor asked, "Had you spoken with Keith here at the fairgrounds?"

"Sort of, at a party last night. He was bragging about how he suckered a man into buying a sterile mare, and I remarked to the effect that he was un untrustworthy dog. He barked at me."

Eleanor smiled, but asked, "Did that make you angry?"

"Not really. I think my bite was worse than his bark, not that he noticed."

Eleanor, seeking information, allowed herself to become friendly. "I take it Mr. Bulward wasn't your favorite example of a horseman?"

"His horses always showed at their best in the ring, but his methods were rumored to be questionable. The trend today is definitely away from the quick and dirty methods."

"What do you mean by 'quick and dirty'?"

"Mean. Cruel. You can use kindness to teach a horse, but it can take time. And patience. The old-fashioned ways are a whole lot faster, but there's getting to be a lot of resistance to them. Even with the kindest methods, though, show horses suffer a lot of stress, enough to cut years off their lives." Kori drew her shoulders up. "Sometimes I think I should quit showing. The rewards aren't always worth the heartbreak."

"Amelia Haydock apparently didn't know about Bulward's methods."

"She'd heard the rumors; it would be impossible for someone as involved in this business as she is to not have. But she chose to disbelieve them."

"What about the other rumors, about his sexual aggressiveness?"

Kori frowned. "Sexual—oh, you mean like with Brit. Were there rumors? It fits, I suppose; but no one ever repeated to me a rumor about him being that way."

"No? Well, here we are. Where do you keep your knife?"

"In an old wooden carpenter's box. I found it in an antique shop. It's great for carrying the clutter of last-minute things you need to get a horse ready. In here." Kori led the way into the prep stall, stooped over a smooth and shining but stained and scarred carrier, and spent an anxious minute taking items out before finding the knife wrapped in a rag. She handed it to Eleanor with a sigh of relief.

Eleanor checked it, found the tiny chesslike towers, and handed it back. "Thanks." She looked around the prep stall, noting the missing carpet. "Are you going to replace the carpet?"

"Not during this show," said Kori. "But yes."

"Where'd you get the idea of putting down carpet?"

"Oh, everyone does it. You have to avoid the dust and dirt any way you can."

"I see. Okay, can I talk to"—she checked her notebook; Brit was off limits for now—"Danny?"

"Sure; he's grooming Copper Wind, the stallion you admired earlier."

10

DANNY WENT WILLINGLY WITH Eleanor and sat down in the interrogation stall relaxed and prepared to talk.

"Did you see Keith Bulward yesterday?"

"Yes, at the party. I went to see him earlier, but he wasn't home."

"At his trailer?"

"No, up by his setup near the front door."

"What did you want to see him about?"

Danny offered a shrug, then a sly smile. "I've never been what you could call a friend of Bulward's. When I heard he slugged a horse in front of witnesses, I wanted to go pick on him a little about it. Good trainers—and he's always let it be known he's a good trainer—will tell you that no matter how angry you are, you don't take it out on the horse. His doing that to Amelia Haydock's Wellaway was like borrowing a gun so you can shoot yourself in the foot. I couldn't help going to see how bad he was limping."

"How well do you know Amelia Haydock?"

Danny opened his mouth, then closed it again. "I see her at all the shows," he said.

"Talk with her?"

149

Danny grimaced. "Sort of. I mean, she's kind of out of my league, a judge and all. And she has this way of using one word when anyone else will hand you a paragraph, y'know?"

Eleanor bit her tongue and nodded.

Danny continued, "Everyone says she's real close to her horses, takes a personal interest in them. And that Wellaway was like her favorite child." Danny shook his head. "I can't believe Bulward was so stupid. He, better than most of us, must've known what she was like."

"So Amelia's not one of those trendy multimillionaires who got into Arabian horses because it was the thing to do."

Danny raised his eyebrows at her. "You've certainly been asking lots of questions, haven't you? Well, no, she isn't." But then he waved the denial away. "I mean, not trendy. She had Arabians before everyone wanted one, and she stayed after the movie stars sold out. But she's got to have money; she's got a big place and has been known to pay big bucks for a horse. She trains them herself, and she's a judge as well, which adds up to not having time for a regular job." This was obviously the first time Danny had really considered Amelia from this angle; he spoke slowly, as conclusions came to him. "She's never been married, either, so the money's her own; there's no husband or ex-husband supporting her. So yeah, there's money, probably old money from the way neither she nor anyone else talks about it." He looked across at Eleanor. "But she's not one of those sables-in-the-stable types, either. She knows the location of every hair on the coat of every one of her horses, and can recite their lineage back to the pair that came off the Ark. Her one blind spot is pretty young men. She thought Keith Bulward was the greatest thing since the stirrup. It must have been quite a shock to watch him bloody Wellaway's nose."

"Did you see him do it, too?"

"No, but my boss did, and it's been a big topic of conversation here at the show. Or was, until they found Keith's body."

Eleanor made a note. "Does Amelia Haydock own a hoof knife?"

"I'm sure she does. We all do, practically. Take a walk through the barn; you'll find them everywhere. But I'll bet you a month's pay hers is at home. She doesn't need it because she's here to judge, not to show. So that one in the bag can't be hers." He gestured at the object on the card table.

There was a pause while Eleanor made another note, this one lengthy. While still writing, she asked, "Can you give a horse a bloody nose with your hand?"

"Depends on the horse. Easier to use a fist."

"Still, you must have to hit it pretty hard."

"It helps if you're really mad."

She looked up at him. "Have you ever done it?"

"No. It's not a good tactic; it doesn't make you any smarter, and only confuses the horse. And a horse like Wellaway, who would die for you if you asked her—well, what Keith did made me mad."

"How mad?"

Danny hesitated. "Oh, not very—no, what the hell, I was pretty pissed. There were people who've said Keith was hard on his horses, and people who said he wasn't. I thought maybe he was, but I didn't know for sure. I mean, there are horses who could make St. Francis reach for the whip. But Wellaway? Jeez! I knew when the word got out, there'd be a line around the block of people waiting to punch Keith's lights out."

"And where would you be in that line?"

"Nowhere. But in the audience? Definitely." Danny gave a single sharp nod, grinning.

"In strictest confidence, who do you think killed Keith Bulward?"

The grin vanished as if by sleight of hand, but Danny thought before answering. "I don't know."

"Who do you *think* might have done it?"

Danny took a breath, then let it out slowly. "Does it matter what I think? I mean, it could be anyone. At the party last night, I saw Amelia, and she was furious. And Stoddard Eckiherne was plastered out of his mind because he thought

Bulward was here on purpose to ruin his comeback. And Keith was making fun of Senator McIntyre—no, wait; McIntyre wasn't there to hear him. But like I said, anyone. Heck, even *I* got mad all over again when Brit started telling us she'd actually seen Keith whipping the horses he was training."

"Were did you go last night after the party?"

"To the motel."

"Were you there alone?"

Danny began to look alarmed. "Yes, but not until after about one. Kori and I sat up talking in her room."

"About what?"

"The show, mostly. She was nervous about showing Breathless. This is only her third try at amateur showing, and the filly is something special so she wants to do her justice."

But the look in his eyes was evasive, so Eleanor persisted. "What else did you talk about?"

Danny looked away in silence, but she waited. He sighed. "Okay, Brit. We were both worried about her, because of Keith. I thought maybe we should have sent her to the motel and left me in the barn."

"What might have been different about last night if you had done that?"

"Nothing!" said Danny, and repeated, only a little less fiercely, "Nothing!"

After another few minutes, Eleanor dismissed him. She went back to her investigation stall and sent the bluesuit on guard there to look for Amelia Haydock. A few minutes later she looked up from her notebook at the sound of footsteps. But opening the door, she found fellow investigators Paul and Al approaching. "Got time for a talk?" asked Al.

"Sure, come on in."

"American Horse Show Association."

By gum, there was a real human being answering! McIntyre, doubting Sally's assurance that the place was always manned, had briefed himself to leave a message on a recorder, so it took him a moment to change gears. "Ummmmm—I mean, hello! We're calling from the Fourth Annual Lafite County All-Arabian Horse Show, and we've got kind of a problem here."

"Yes?" prompted the voice. She sounded very young. "Who is this calling, please?"

"I'm State Senator Robert McIntyre. Someone's been killed, murdered."

A pause. "You mean, someone at the *show*?"

"Yes. And it's stopped the show, y'see. Because they won't let anyone take their horses over to the arena."

"Why are . . . who said . . . I mean . . ." There was a sound as of a deep, calming breath being taken. Then the young woman asked, in a poor replica of her professional tone, "Is this a Class A show?"

"Ah, yes it is. Class A. I take it that's significant."

"Are you an official at this show?"

"I'm the manager. In name only, of course. I mean, all I know about horses could fit inside a flea's belly butt—"

"One moment please, sir."

There was a click, an electronic series of notes, then the sound of a phone ringing. It was interrupted on the second ring, and another woman said, "Hannah Germaine, may I help you?"

"Ah, yes, I hope so. I am State Senator Bob McIntyre, manager of the Fourth Annual Lafite County All-Arabian Horse Show here in Illinois, and our barn has been closed because of a murder. The police came, of course, and they won't let anyone in or out of the barn. I understand I have to consult with you about what to do."

There was a lengthy silence on the other end, then Hannah Germaine asked in a shocked voice, "Where did you say you were?"

"County fairgrounds, Lafite, Illinois."

"And you say someone has been *murdered*?"

"Yes, ma'm. I think it was a robbery gone wrong, some kid

looking for drug money, but the police are talking to every-one."

"Was it a show official who was killed?"

"No, a trainer, here to show some horses."

"I've never heard of such a thing happening at a show before! What do you want—of course, you're calling because you need authorization to revise the show schedule."

"Yes, that's correct."

"Ah, okay. How long has the barn been closed?"

"Since about eight o'clock this morning. We'd finished one class, the, er, weanlings."

Hannah Germaine's voice grew calmer as she focused on a problem she could solve. "And what time is it there now?"

"Almost half past one. I hear they'll open the barn pretty soon."

"How many classes did you have scheduled for today?"

McIntyre consulted his schedule. Fortunately the classes were numbered. "Thirty-five. So we've got thirty-four to go."

"When does the show end, tomorrow or Monday?"

"Tomorrow."

"So you have to make up as much as you can today. What you'll have to do is start up again right away, as soon as the barn is, er, opened, and continue until you finish all of today's classes or until midnight, whichever comes first."

"Why midnight?"

"Because you have to have an eight-hour break between 'days' of your show. If you go until midnight, you can begin again at eight tomorrow morning and go on until you're finished. If you don't experience any more . . . delays, you should make up most if not all of that by running into the evening today. There's no time specifically scheduled except the start, right? So just keep calling your classes by number, and you're filling the legal requirements."

"So we're authorized now to do this?"

"Yes. I'll write a letter confirming our conversation, but you're authorized as of right now to continue the show as I've outlined. I can't believe it; what's going on out there?"

"Nobody knows for sure. Mr. Bulward wasn't a very popular person, so the police are treating some of our other entrants as suspects. It's all very distressing."

"I can imagine. Or maybe I can't. Well, good luck."

"Thank you, Ms. Germaine." McIntyre hung up. That had been far easier than he had anticipated. Maggie had spoken of AHSA like it was God and His angels, but McIntyre had found dealing with the association to be very easy sailing. And why not? He was an important person, too. Maybe he should quit letting others lead him around by the nose; his task was not to be an expert on horses, but an expert on being in charge. Which he was, and which was what this whole process needed. And if he did it well, he could take credit for it without wincing. Right, then. He turned to Maggie and with confidence relayed Hannah Germaine's instructions.

"Not that typing the blood in the hay cart is going to help all that much," said Eleanor, using her tongue to lift a flake of sauerkraut from the corner of her mouth. Her conference with her investigators had been interrupted almost before it began by the arrival of lunch. "Bulward had blood type O, and so does 60 percent of any random gathering of people. Of course, if it's not type O, that might prove something."

"Yeah," said Paul, stuffing a rolled-up slice of cold pizza into his wide-open mouth. Not only did he look like a teenager, he had the vast appetite and overdrive metabolism of one. "It would prove that somebody else bled into that hay cart, which means we may have a body unaccounted for."

"I take it," said Al, sipping a Diet Coke, "you've got a preliminary report from Dr. Burke?"

"I borrowed a hoof knife from the show farrier—that's blacksmith to us ignoramuses—and sent it to him, and he agrees that a hoof knife could easily be the weapon that cut open Keith Bulward's throat. And he has found no crud in the wounds that might indicate it was a horse with a loose shoe that did it. You can find these hoof knives all over the barn."

Al picked up the plastic bag with the hoof knife in it. "Yeah, but in this case, was the blade bent before or after the murder?"

"The knives come like that."

Paul frowned and shook his head. "Weirder and weirder."

Al said, "So how does it look? The killer needed a weapon and saw this lying around and picked it up?"

"It wasn't lying around," said Eleanor. "So far as I can determine, these people are fairly neat, and especially anxious to keep sharp objects away from their horses—who seem equally anxious to hurt themselves, probably so they can go home, away from this nonsense." She turned to look at one of the several annotated charts on the wall. "Right now my suspects are Brittany Morgan, Amelia Haydock, Stoddard Eckiherne, and, maybe, Robert McIntyre. Brittany, Stoddard, and Amelia were likely to know exactly where to put their hands on a hoof knife, but only Amelia and Robert came to the show without one already in hand. And the senator didn't know what kind of knife it was when I showed it to him."

Al looked around at the many lists, flow charts, and diagrams on the walls. "So there's method in this madness," he said.

" 'Truth lies in the details,' " Eleanor, quoting an FBI instructor.

"While suspects lie in the interviews," snorted Paul. "For example, someone told me there's this famous stud horse, he lives in Minnesota, he gets fresh orange juice every morning in his own plastic cup. Can you believe that?"

Eleanor nodded. "There's a white stallion here, and his owner says he's for sale, a real bargain at only a hundred thousand dollars. I bet that Minnesota horse not only has his orange juice, he could have champagne every evening, and drink it out of a crystal goblet, if it would keep him happy. This Arabian horse business is a very strange thing, believe me."

Al drained his can of Coke, crushed it, and said, "Any profession is strange when you start taking a close look at it. Even ours. Especially ours."

"Anything else new?" asked Al.

"Actually, there is something," said Eleanor. "I was hoping one of you would have it too, but since you didn't: The only knife that's missing is Bulward's. His groom Fran was genuinely confounded when she couldn't find it; and she's so quick to insist the murderer couldn't be her underage roommate that I'm sure Fran herself isn't the murderer. I mean, I'd sure as hell be throwing suspicion anywhere I could if it was me who killed him."

Al said, "So you think Bulward had the knife with him. And the murderer took it away from him."

"Possibly in self-defense," said Eleanor. "But you see how that puts Senator McIntyre back on the list of suspects. He didn't need to bring a hoof knife; he didn't even have to know what it was. And he is certainly capable of taking a knife away from someone like Bulward. So are most of them, for that matter." She sighed, turned away, and stopped to make some notes on a chart on the wall. "I wish I could eliminate just one of these people!"

"Well, it was two men having a quarrel, right?" asked Al. "Not a man and a woman."

"So what's next, Nell?" asked Paul. "A lot of people want to know when we're gonna open the barn."

Eleanor nodded. "I think we've gotten just about all we can from the site itself. Is there anyone we haven't talked to?"

"Nope."

Al added, "Everyone we've asked not to go home just yet has agreed to stay. And Dave and Roger finished up some time ago."

"I don't think any of them will leave," said Eleanor. "Showing is a big part of this business, it affects the price of these horses, so they can't let something as trivial as murder stop the show."

"Lighten up, Nell," said Paul uncomfortably.

"Why should I? This really should matter to them! It's one of their own that's been killed! But every fourth person we talk to asks when we're going to open the barn and let them pick up where they left off!"

"I understand one of the participants is the wife of a friend of yours."

"Then you'll be glad to hear she's one of those who didn't ask!" Eleanor pushed her chair back in an angry gesture, almost tipping it over. "Sorry," she mumbled.

"Hey," said Paul, "did you hear about the senator trying to buy a horse?"

Eleanor said, "What about it?"

"A couple people told me about it. Said he kept raising the price, and . . ." Paul frowned and began to dig out his notebook. "Something about a foal . . ." He began to turn over pages.

"The horse couldn't have a foal!" exclaimed Eleanor. "It was sterile, right?"

Paul looked confused. "No, he can have the horse if it drops a cow-hocked foal." He read that again, and his confusion fell back on itself. "What does that mean?"

"Beats me, but maybe you could ask."

She stood, and Al opened the door—and standing outside, hand raised to knock, was Amelia Haydock. She looked curiously at the lists and charts on the wall before saying, "You said you would interview me a second time."

Eleanor, moving to block her view of the interior replied, "Where's Morecraft?"

"Who?"

"The policeman who is supposed to be standing outside this door."

Amelia looked around and shrugged, then saw a uniformed policeman making those little adjustments to his clothing that told them all where he had been. When he saw them looking, he increased the tempo of his approach.

"Follow me," said Eleanor to Amelia and led the way to the interrogation stall. She gestured at Al to come with her.

Paul pointed in the direction of the exits, indicating he would go take the tapes down, and Eleanor nodded agreement.

Amelia watched the exchange with uncomprehending interest but said nothing. Eleanor could not repress a smile, even while she wondered despairingly if there was any way at all to open up so terse a suspect. "Come in, Miss Haydock. Sit down."

In *The Gentle Art of Interviewing and Interrogation*, Shutt and Royal suggest that first interrogator and subject indulge in small talk, to put them both at ease. "This chill is unseasonable."

"Yes."

"Hard on the horses, especially the young ones."

Amelia nodded and shifted impatiently, which brought Al into her view. He was taking out his notebook and pen. She frowned at him and deliberately shifted back.

Eleanor asked, keeping her voice friendly, "Have you been involved with Arabian horses long?"

"Thirty-seven years."

"Someone said you were a judge."

"Yes."

"But you own Arabians, too. Do you train them yourself?"

"Yes." To show she was trying, Amelia added, "Most judges do."

"Did you teach Mr. Bulward how to train horses?"

"No!" This was barked and Amelia frowned at herself. "No. But his grandfather taught the man who taught me."

"I've been hearing some bad things about Keith's methods. Did his grandfather use cruelty in training his horses?"

Amelia drew her shoulders up, and her lips twitched. She took a deep breath. "Used to be," she began, "the idea was to master the horse. Break him. Old John Bulward was hard, but not cruel. Keith . . ." She frowned. "I now think Keith was afraid of horses."

"Miss Haydock, what first attracted you to Keith Bulward?"

She closed her eyes as if they hurt. "Good manners."

Eleanor wanted to hear that deep voice boom out in anger,

or become shrill. "I understand this isn't the first time you've been taken in by a pretty face. That you have on other occasions gotten taken advantage of by handsome young men who only pretend to be your friend."

Amelia's eyes opened, sick with misery. "Yes," she whispered.

"I'm sorry," said Eleanor, and meant it. "How did you feel when you saw Keith Bulward strike your horse?"

Amelia looked away. "Angry, of course."

"Had you heard the rumors about him?"

"Jealousy," she explained.

"But you had heard the rumors," insisted Eleanor.

"Always are rumors when someone wins a lot."

"And you dismissed what you heard as jealousy, or nonsense."

Oddly, Amelia smiled. "Thought it was nonsense about the Tennessee walker, too."

"What about the Tennessee walker?"

"Public inquiry. Not that they didn't deserve it. But it came from outside, a complaint to the ASPCA. Headlines and the evening news. Take years for them to come back."

"What do you mean, they deserved it?"

"Have you ever seen a walker?"

"Once, at a horse show years ago. That run they make them do looks silly."

The muscle that pulled Amelia's mouth a little sideways seemed to tug her head in the same direction. She also twisted her hand a little in echo of the small gesture, all of which was meant to amend Eleanor's judgment. "They are born knowing how to do a running walk. To sit the rack, as it's called, feels like what people who have never ridden think it's like to ride a horse. But for show purposes, you want it bigger and better. After everyone's already doing it as well as can be, all that's left is exaggeration. Put bigger pads on his front hooves, chains on his ankles, even spiked chains. The gait gets ugly, ridiculous, uncomfortable, and the horse ends up crippled. If you're in a hurry, and dishonest, you sore his ankles, injure them so the chain really irritates. If you're in

a big hurry, you put on special shoes that hurt the frog—"
Amelia caught herself and dammed the flow of words by
clamping her mouth shut.

Eleanor chose to misinterpret her reason for stopping. "I
assume the frog must be a part of his hoof. And I suppose a
horse with feet sored like that will yank them up off the
ground with every step."

Amelia nodded. "Looks like he's got a pretty way of going."

"And the same thing has been happening with Arabians?"

Again the combination of small movements. "Can't. Sor-
ing makes a horse bob his head, which for Arabs is a fault."
She saw the look on Eleanor's face—what stopped this abuse
from spreading was not a concern for the animals—and went
on, "People forget why they got into this business in the first
place, which was because they love the horse. You get a
beautiful horse, you want to show it. But other horses,
horses just as good or even not as good as yours, walk off
with the ribbons and you decide the only way you can win
is to play the game." Amelia made a gesture of frustration,
and this time did shut up.

"What do you think should be done to the cruel trainers?"

"Anyone involved in cruelty—trainer, owner, groom—
should be prosecuted, tossed out of the Association, and
forbidden to own or train a horse again for the rest of his
life."

"Not executed?"

The smile appeared again, this time with barbed wire in
it. "Not for a first offense."

Walking around the barn to work off his tension, Stoddard
had learned a few things. One, there were no other colts at
the show as fine as his, except Bulward's. And Bulward had
no one qualified to be his backup, so his horses had been
scratched.

Two, there were perhaps three stallions and one mare fit
to compete with him for best halter horse. Of course, that
was only his opinion; the judges might think otherwise. But

it appeared Baron Barty's colt was in the running for the halter championship, a very satisfactory situation indeed.

Meanwhile, three: It seemed that Kori Brichter's groom had had some kind of ongoing problem with Bulward, which escalated into a quarrel just last night. So the body turning up in her area of the barn was a very bad sign for the groom.

And four: The reason Bulward had socked Amelia Haydock's Wellaway in the face was he had a piss-poor showing in the Training Level dressage competition. Amelia should have known better than to loan a horse to Bulward, but she was still steaming about it as late as the party last night. It was Stoddard's opinion that Amelia was a butch lesbian who would have enjoyed avenging her horse by slicing a man to ribbons, and he had said as much to several people, though in more careful terms.

It had been scary to find he was considered a serious suspect. The occasional sharp look and avoidance of conversation sent icicles down his spine. But, having started, he continued spreading his normal behavior far and wide, passing along whatever he learned that might tip the balance still more deeply in someone else's, anyone else's, direction.

He heard footsteps and looked to see a detective, the one he had talked to initially, walking with very obvious intent toward him. He froze, feeling the blood fade from his face. He had done so well, finding his knife where it belonged—what had they found now? He tried to smile and nod, and knew the effort to be a failure.

To his utter astonishment, the detective only nodded back and kept going, obviously having some other errand. Stoddard, staggering with relief, tottered to a stack of hay bales along the aisle and sat down. He pulled a handkerchief from his breast pocket and wiped a brow suddenly wet. When he uncovered his eyes, he saw Kori, stopping at a crossing place in the aisles to rest her burden of a bale of straw, looking at him consideringly. Had he been able, he would have risen and stalked away.

*   *   *

When Kori went into the tack stall to put the straw fork away, Brit was there, rubbing hard at an already shining stirrup. She did not look up. "I didn't know you were still in here," said Kori.

"You must be crazy," Brit said. "The Arab market like it is, you should have taken that offer for Breathless. Thirty-five thousand is good money."

Kori almost laughed. Brit had been holed up in this stall since before lunchtime, yet not only had the story of McIntyre's offer reached her, the sum mentioned was accurate. "Not for Breathless. Anyway, if I'd agreed to his offer, he couldn't have taken me up on it; he's too scared of horses to be able to lead her away. No, he's up to something else."

"What could he be up to? His daughter wants a good mare; he said so."

So the story had come directly from McIntyre. Interesting.

"And if she knows Arabs, she'd be thrilled to get Breathless for what he offered. But I can't think he'd buy his daughter a horse without getting her in on the deal before he pays for it. He admitted that she's the one who knows horses. Besides, he's a piker."

"What do you mean?"

"In two years I'll be turning down ten times that." Kori leaned the fork in a corner. When she turned around, Brit was gaping at her. She smiled. "I've already talked to Tallmadge, and he's reserved a place in his stud calendar for her. Abu ben Salim is not only a halter champion, he's blowing the competition away in dressage. If Breathless fulfills her promise, and breeds true, their foal will be a living legend. And *him* I'll sell."

Brit laughed. "If you won't sell Breathless because she's so wonderful, you won't sell her foal, either."

"Maybe you're right," agreed Kori with a chuckle. "You'd better put that stirrup iron away before you wear a hole in it."

"Sure." Somewhat pink-faced, Brit got up off her cot and went to obey.

"Why are you hiding out in here?"

"People keep coming by." She sat down again. "Have you got anything I can do for you in here?"

"You shouldn't let them intimidate you, Brit."

"What can I do? Some are sorry for me, some are scared of me, some are mad at me. But all they want to talk about is Keith, and I can't stand it." Brit's chin trembled, and Kori came to stoop and take the girl's hands in hers. They were cool, almost cold.

"Brit, did you hear anything at all last night?"

Brit looked at the ceiling, blinking, shaking her head.

"Don't lie to me!" said Kori sharply, and the cold hands leaped.

"I'm not lying." Her clear blue eyes, awash in tears, looked directly into Kori's. "I didn't hear anything."

Kori got up with a worried frown and began to wonder if the solution that was forming in her mind was perhaps wrong after all.

Eleanor sat for a few minutes after Amelia left, thinking this case over. Keith Bulward's next of kin had been notified; his mother and two sisters were on their way, would arrive late this evening. She felt a sudden clutch of anger at the murderer. By most accounts, Keith Bulward was not a nice man, but his suffering was over, while his family's had just begun.

On the other hand, Bulward's last minutes had been unpleasant indeed. Unbidden, Eleanor's first look at him returned in memory: the pale skin, the blood-soaked clothing, the odd pose. Now known for fact, it seemed obvious from his position that he had been dropped in that box stall postmortem. Thanks to Brit the hay cart had been impounded, and had tested positive for traces of human blood.

What a terrible ordeal that must have been, lifting that corpse into the cart. Eleanor tried to put herself into the nighttime barn, a murderer with a fearsome task. How clumsy the body must have been, how gruesomely sodden. How loud the squeal of wheels must have seemed as it was wheeled to its destination. And then the horrid task to do in reverse, lift and pull the body into the stall.

And then the filly, catching the scent of blood, screaming in terror, waking Brit, and unknowingly trapping the murderer in the prep stall with the body until Brit finished calming her and went back to bed.

Because that seemed to be the sequence of events. But was that the way it happened? Eleanor made a gesture of frustration. If she could ask Brit one question, she would know if the scenario she was building was the right one.

The intercom system crackled. *"Attention in the barn. Attention in the barn. We have been given permission to resume the show."* People in the barn began to cheer as the announcement continued, *"We will begin with . . . Class Number . . . in about fifteen minutes . . ."* But the rest of his announcement was drowned out by the cheering, and when Eleanor came out of her stall to look at the excited horse lovers, a man saw her expression and bellowed "SHADDUP!" so loudly it sent a wave of silence rolling through the barn. But Eleanor gestured wearily that they should go on about their business, so he turned to a groom and ordered her to run over to the arena and ask the announcer to repeat his message.

11

THERE WERE FEW IDLERS in the aisles; everyone was either prepping horses or in the arena watching the resumption of the show. McIntyre was alone in the shabby barn office, reading an old issue of *Equus* magazine. Al looked through the grilled window and, when McIntyre did not notice him, cleared his throat.

McIntyre threw the magazine onto the desk as if it had burst into flames and began sorting through the papers on his desk. As quickly, he aborted this effort to look busy. "Yes?" he said, looking at last toward the window. "Can I help you? Oh, Jesus!" He got to his feet.

Al closed the leather folder that held his ID card. "Sergeant Ritter and I would like to speak with you for a few minutes, if that's all right."

McIntyre looked sick with dismay. "Of course, of course. Come around to the door, I'll let you in."

By the time they got around to the side, the door was already standing open, with McIntyre waiting to gesture them in.

"It looks like the show is getting back on track okay," said Eleanor.

"Yes, it is," agreed McIntyre. "And I want to thank you

166

for allowing that to happen. We have people whose time is very valuable. Quality people. Can't think how this terrible thing could have happened among people like we have here. Sit down, sit down."

Eleanor took the wooden office chair McIntyre had vacated, and the senator drew up a gray metal chair with a torn plastic seat. When Al gestured briefly that he'd rather stand, the senator took the seat.

"Anything I can do to help you," he said, "just ask." The offer was sincere, but colored with a hope there was nothing.

"Where were you last night?" asked Eleanor.

The senator's eyebrows went up. "In my motel room. I told you that."

"All night?"

"Yes, of course."

"Alone?" asked Al, his tone brusque.

"Certainly. My wife and daughter were to join me here today, but I've phoned and told them not to come."

"What time did you get to your motel last night?" Eleanor asked.

McIntyre sighed at having to cover ground already covered and said, "About nine or a little after. I knew I had a long day ahead of me today, so I wanted to get a good night's rest."

"Did you see or speak to anyone at the motel?"

"I asked the clerk for a wake-up call at six A.M. when I got there—I have a travel alarm, but I can sleep through it."

"That was when you checked in."

"No, when I returned for the night, at a little after nine."

"Anyone else?"

McIntyre made a show of thinking about this. "No. Sorry."

"Did you phone anyone from the motel?"

"I phoned home to say I had arrived—but that was earlier, when I checked in. About two in the afternoon."

Al, feigning impatience—he and Eleanor were doing a Mutt and Jeff—said, "We've covered all this, I think. Let's get to the real point. I understand you bought a 'foundation mare,' or tried to."

McIntyre began to fumble in the side pocket of his suit coat while he stared at him, dark blue eyes boggling. "Ahhh," he said, drawing out the sound, trying to think of an answer. None came, so he resorted to the truth. "Yes." He produced a pipe, and began to fumble in the other pocket.

"Tell us about it."

"The truth is, Keith Bulward sold me an Arabian mare. I believe I told you earlier I knew just enough about the breed to be dangerous? That danger proved to be to my wallet." McIntyre smiled at Eleanor, who did not smile back, so he tucked his away with a sudden movement of his lips. "I was at a horse show in Chicago, last year, with my wife and daughter. Birdie—that's my daughter—pointed out a mare in one of the classes and predicted it would win. And it did. She also said she would like to own a mare like that, because if it produced offspring as pretty as itself, it could be the foundation mare for our new stable. So I checked into it. The mare had a foal, a male foal—"

"Colt," prompted Eleanor, impatient with his ignorance.

He produced a tobacco pouch and a little box of wooden matches. "That's right, a colt, about nine months old, which had already won a class at that same show. Mr. Bulward had been assigned as broker as well as trainer, and he told me they were for sale as a pair, mother and son, an arrangement I understand is common." He opened the pouch, stuck the pipe in, and began some hidden maneuver involving it and his fingers. "Well, the price he quoted seemed reasonable enough, but it turned out to be an outrageous price, because the mare had caught some kind of infection, er, postpartum, that left her sterile; and, of course, a male colt, however good-looking, could not make up for that when you are looking for a foundation mare."

"And you were upset when you found out."

"Naturally. I went back to Mr. Bulward, but he said a deal is a deal, and I should have done the usual thing and asked to see her veterinary records before I bought her. Which I didn't know was the usual thing, so he took advantage of my ignorance. But that's why they call it horse trading, you know." He twinkled ruefully at Eleanor, pulled the pipe out of the pouch, and used his thumb to begin pressing the tobacco he had scooped into it. "I think I made up the ground lost today, however. Mrs. Brichter and I have entered into a verbal agreement that I have first refusal of Leaves You Breathless after she has her first foal."

Al lifted his chin at Eleanor, whose smile was so brief it was emotionless.

"So you have accepted your loss and aren't angry about it," said Al.

McIntyre stuck the pipe in his mouth and spoke around it while he opened the box of matches. "Of course I'm angry! It was a fair enough price for the horse I thought I was buying, but an outrageous price for the horse I got." He struck a match, applied the flame to the bowl of his pipe, and began puffing. "The man was a crook"—puff, puff—"a con artist." McIntyre waved the match to extinguish it and tossed it into an ashtray on the desk. "But what could I do? Technically, what he did wasn't illegal. He took advantage of my ignorance, that's all." He blew a plume of smoke at the ceiling.

"What else were you mad at him about?" asked Eleanor gently.

McIntyre puffed again at his pipe, reached again into a pocket, and pulled out a little metal tool, which he used to tamp down the burning tobacco. He looked cross-eyed at the glowing stuff in the bowl, puffed several times, and looked at Eleanor through a milky fog of smoke. Then he removed the pipe so he could speak firmly. "He was making the name McIntyre a laughingstock in the horse show world. Making it difficult for my daughter, as my daughter, to break in and show her horses. That's what I objected to, more than anything, the harm it was doing my daughter, an innocent party." He looked at the stem of his pipe, then snapped at it like a dog biting an enemy.

"Did you know Keith Bulward was coming to this show?" asked Al.

"No." Puff, puff.

"What would you have done if you knew ahead of time he'd be here?"

McIntyre frowned and drew longer at his pipe. "Don't know," he said thoughtfully. "I don't know if anything could have been done. I mean, when that young woman, Brittany Morgan, came to me with her complaint about Bulward, a far more serious complaint than mine, there was nothing I could do."

"What did you say when you saw him here?" asked Eleanor.

"Nothing, I didn't see him. Wouldn't have said anything if I had." Puff, puff.

After a little silence, Eleanor remarked, "You probably aren't the first person he's taken with his shady deals. A lot of people seem unhappy with him. In fact I can't find anyone who's truly sorry he's dead."

McIntyre gestured with his pipe. "I'm sorry, for one," he said. "Because I and a lot of innocent people are being put through hell as a result." He added with heartfelt sincerity, "I'd give a million dollars to have him walk up to that window right now and start telling me what a miserable excuse for a horse trader I am."

"This is your last call, last call for yearling fillies. Class Number Two, yearling fillies, AOTS. Bring them over, ladies and gentlemen. Last call, AOTS, yearling fillies."

"Hup," said Kori. "Hup, baby." She lifted the lead and Breathless obediently lifted her head, putting weight onto her haunches. Danny was walking around her spraying coat sheen; Brit was combing out her tail, letting strands of it fall into silvery darkness. Brief, silvery darkness; Breathless's tail was still more a promise than an actuality. They were in the aisle, not the prep stall.

Kori was herself brushed and combed and polished, though her unruly hair was already lifting itself out of the

knot at the nape of her neck and forming tendrils in front of
her ears. She wiped impatiently at a fine curl that swept
becomingly across her forehead.

"Fy'n galon!"

She turned at the words, Welsh for "my heart," and the deep
baritone voice that formed them. "Peter!" Detective Sergeant
Peter Brichter was a narrow man with a harsh, Germanic cast
to his features. His thinning hair was pale mouse in color,
and his eyes were the chilly shade of old pewter. He wore a
stern black suit, serious gray shirt, and dark maroon tie.

Kori's tense face went joyous. "Oh, Peter!" She dropped
the lead and came running to him, threw her arms around
his neck, and held him close. For all her elegant costume,
she smelled strongly of horse, hay, and fly repellent, and only
faintly of Chanel No. 5. This did not prevent him from
returning the embrace, because when she made a display
like this in public, she was sorely in need of comforting.

"So, what's the story here?" he asked.

"The story is," said Danny firmly, "we have to leave right
now for the arena. We have a horse to show."

"Peter," said Kori, "I need to talk to you. These people
have it all wrong, I know who did it! But it will take some
explaining—"

"No time, no time!" pleaded Danny.

"Right," said Peter. "Unless a few minutes will make a big
difference?"

She hesitated. "Probably not," she admitted.

"Good. Go on, get over there. You can tell me when you
come back. Is Sergeant Ritter here?"

Danny, who had picked up the lead when Kori dropped it,
started up the aisle with Breathless; Kori had perforce to
follow. "She's got an empty stall at the other end!" she called
over her shoulder. "Wait, Danny!" And she was gone.

Brit, making a frightened face at him, followed. She would
have no role in the show ring, Peter knew, so she was escap-
ing from his questions. He went out into the aisle to watch
her hurry off, his face thoughtful.

* * *

It had warmed up considerably, and the sun lay like a warm hand on Kori's dark hair as she took the lead from Danny and they parted ways. She refused to hurry, but walked Breathless to the waiting area beside the arena. The filly was alert but calm, looking from left to right like a princess taking an official stroll through the streets of a new city, filling her widening nostrils with the odors of this new place. The long gold chain under her throat swayed with the motion of her walking and her moving head, but she had worn it in training often enough that it did not distract her.

Maybe I should have scratched, Kori thought. Except this is important and a few minutes won't matter. So don't make the same mistake you made with Blue; drop everything, concentrate on showing Breathless the best you can. She closed her hand more tightly around the whip Brit had handed her. It was made of tightly woven leather, and had a short tail on a stem about five feet long. She would have been shocked at any suggestion that she might use it on the horse.

She began to study the people and horses already gathered at the entrance to the floor of the arena. There is no rule about attire for people showing horses at halter, except that it not insult the occasion. The other people wore slacks and sweater-vests, business suits, bright sport coats, even, in one instance, a Navajo skirt and blouse. Since "yearling" covers the age from twelve to twenty-three months, the horses in this class were greatly disparate in size. Breathless was fifteen months old, just beginning to fill out and still very leggy. The bay just joining the waiting group looked, by comparison, fully grown, and must be almost two.

Yearling classes tend to be the largest at a show, because no hopes have been dashed yet. There were almost twenty yearling fillies already waiting as Kori joined them. Behind her, two more were trotting up the street. One, who looked to be close to Breathless in age, was all black and truly black, a rarity. Her topline was lovely, her mane and tail already well grown and flowing. She was curvetting at the end of her lead, not in fright but in movements that suggested laughter. Kori bit her lip and turned back to her own filly, whose still-fuzzy mane had to be tamed with mousse. But Breathless was also beautiful, and she had in addition the tranquil air of an animal who has never been mistreated or teased.

"We'll show them, won't we, girl?" she murmured, and the filly dipped her head and blew gently.

The ring steward standing guard by the wooden gate to the arena was a short, officious man in a gray suit. He signaled his assistant to open the gate and pointed at the woman in the Navajo skirt to bring her horse in. He pointed at a man, but held his hand up for him to wait. He would space the horses about fifteen seconds apart. Strategy calls for a showman to bring his horse in early or late, so Kori, hoping to be last, shifted sideways and backward, but three cleverer than she managed to maneuver themselves behind her, so sooner than she wanted, the ring steward caught her eye.

But Breathless, made anxious by the regular departure of the other horses and the growing tension she could sense in her mistress, was glad to run away beside Kori when their turn came. The sudden opening out from a dim passage into openness, the harsh, artificial light, and the applause of the crowd made her dance and snort as she ran, tail up and out like a brief banner behind her.

There was a lot of noisy whooping as they made their entrance, but Kori spared not a second to appreciate it; she was too busy concentrating on calming Breathless as they came up behind the row of fillies stopped along the right side of the arena.

She brought her to a slow walk, watching the animal's hind legs. Just as the near back hoof came down, she said, "Whoa," and Breathless, impeccably trained by Danny, immediately halted, one hind leg forward of the other, exactly as required. As luck would have it, her forefeet were already well positioned. Kori lifted the lead rein to raise the filly's head and put her weight onto her hindquarters. Then, facing the filly, she showed her the butt end of the whip, drawing her attention, made a tiny sucking sound, and moved the whip backward. Breathless's nose followed the motion, and the result was a well-made setup for the judge to look at.

"Whooo!" went someone in the audience. "Whoooo, whoooo!" But the gorgeous black filly was frisking into the arena, so this was probably for her.

Phillip Bannister flinched as Danny whooped and yodeled.

"What's that for?"

"C'mon, Dad; don't tell me you don't see how great that filly is."

"What filly?"

"The one Kori's setting up down there."

Bannister looked, his view a little obstructed by the temporary wooden bandstand in the middle of the dirt floor, and found Kori wearing too-long trousers with an old-fashioned flare. She was holding a whip over her shoulder and a very leggy gray horse with dark mane and tail was stretching its nose toward it as if the handle were a carrot. There was a long string of horses along the wall of the arena, brown, gray, black, light brown, and some of them were trying to sniff the butt end of their owner's whips, too. They all looked great to him. As he watched, a shiny black horse with a long mane came up behind Kori's horse, but it was too excited to be interested in the whip its owner tried to show it.

"I like the black one," he said.

"You're kidding," said Brit, who was sitting on his other side. They were in the front row of the arena, in one of several small areas marked off with blue rope. "I mean, look at her."

"I am looking at her. I like black horses with long manes."

Brit snorted. "Her knees are too high."

Since the horse wasn't lifting her legs at all, Bannister didn't know what that meant. He shrugged and said, "I don't care. I'd give her the second-place ribbon."

"Who gets the blue?" asked Danny.

"Kori, of course." He grinned at his son. "She's family."

The black horse was drawing a concentration of whoops

and applause from another section of the arena. This concentration of admiration happened for almost every horse, Phil had noted. What purpose a claque served he couldn't imagine, since their concentration proved them claques, not general opinion.

Brit looked past Bannister and Danny to the steps at the end of the row. "Look, it's Sergeant Ritter."

Eleanor worked her way along the row behind them, stopping behind Phil to say, "Mind if I sit here?"

"You want to talk to my client, I suppose?"

Brit said, "I want to talk to her, too."

"I've already advised you—"

"I know, I know." interrupted Brit. "But it's okay, really it is."

"I must object to a public interview," said Phil.

"But I want to see this," argued Brit. "Breathless is my special honey, and I want to see how she does. By the way, Peter's here."

"You mean Sergeant Brichter?"

"Yes, he came in just as we were leaving. He was asking for you," she added, to Eleanor.

"Fine, but let me talk to you, first."

"It is all right if I remain present?" asked Phil drily.

"Sure, if you want to," said Brit, and Eleanor laughed.

The seats behind the trio were empty, and Eleanor moved to a place just on the other side of Brit. Phil shifted in his seat so he could watch them more closely. Danny, while obviously listening, was more interested in the progress of the judging on the floor of the arena.

"Brit, I want you to think back to last night," said Eleanor. "What time was it when you went to bed?"

The girl shrugged. "I'm not sure. Probably a little after one."

"Were Danny and Kori still there?"

"No, they left before eleven."

"Was everything cleaned up and put away before you went to bed?"

Brit nodded. "Pretty much."

"Anything left out in the aisle? Buckets, pitchforks?"

"Oh, no, the aisle was clear." She frowned, then her face changed, and she took a frightened breath.

"Sergeant Ritter—," began Phil.

"Shut up for just thirty seconds, okay?" said Eleanor. "She's remembering something important. What is it, honey?"

Brit said, "I got up when I heard Breathless having a fit. I know I shouldn't have lied about that, but those policemen were treating me like a criminal and I got scared, and then I was afraid to change my story and say I knew anything at all about last night. But I did. The horses woke me up. I don't know what time it was. I couldn't think what was wrong. I could hear Breathless, she sounded totally panicked. The other horses were acting up, calling, and jumping around, and I went to see what was the matter . . ."

"Yes?"

"The cart, the hay cart, it was there. I almost ran into it. I remember thinking, Why did Danny leave the hay cart in the aisle like that? And then I went in and shushed Breathless. It didn't take long, but she was all over the stall there for a minute or two. I couldn't figure out what spooked her. I got her quiet, then I went back to bed. I guess I wasn't really awake, thinking something stupid like that, that Danny had left it there. The cart. Because I know it wasn't there when I went to bed. And in the morning"—Brit's eyes were large and frightened, and she wrung her hands together—"it was gone again. That means he was there, wasn't he? I was in there with Breathless, and he must've been right in the next stall with—with that awful thing."

Eleanor relaxed all over. "Yes," she said. "I think that's exactly what happened."

"You mean—," demanded Danny, then stopped. But they were all looking at him, so he drew his shoulders up and said, "Brit really *didn't* do it, did she?"

"No," said Eleanor and Phil together, and there was an

instant of surprise that these natural adversaries could be in such firm agreement.

"Then who did?" asked Danny. "Or don't you know?"

"I think I need to get a few more questions answered," said Eleanor, but the way she looked at Brit said she had gotten the right answer to an important one.

At major shows, owners were permitted, for a stiff fee, to reserve the boxes in front of the bleacher seats, which they proudly marked with banners or signs. In smaller arenas, like this one at Lafite, where there were no box seats, the front two or three rows of bleachers would sometimes be roped off for the same purpose. The owners would fill these with people who would cheer the owner's horses, and, if they did not win, make cutting remarks about the wisdom or impartiality of the judges.

Peter stopped in the aisle, looking along the roped-off front-row seats. He spotted a standard with a shield-shaped cardboard sign in dark green with maroon uncial lettering: Tretower. And under the lettering the three chesslike towers that were the emblem of his wife's farm.

Beyond the sign were Danny, Danny's father, Brit, and Sergeant Ritter. Peter's left eyebrow came up; he would not have suspected Phillip Bannister would allow Sergeant Ritter anywhere near his client, but they were obviously engaged in conversation. Peter began to work his way along the bleacher seats toward them.

He spared a series of glances at the horses standing in the dirt-floored arena. Peter's years of marriage had taught him perhaps more than he wanted to know about the Arabian horse; he therefore looked with an experienced eye at his wife's competition. There were more than twenty, all sizes and colors, but one gray stood out as if a spotlight were shining on it. Lovely, shining, perfect. He inhaled sharply; then saw it was Breathless, with Kori, and exhaled. All right, he thought, all right. They were near the end of the row waiting to be judged. From the length of a new-forming row along the far wall, he figured judging was about half finished.

When he reached the Tretower section he held out a hand toward Eleanor and said, "Glad to see you again, Sergeant Ritter. Am I correct in assuming you are the lead investigator here?"

"Sergeant Brichter," she replied. "Yes, I am."

"Sit down, will ya, Peter?" complained Phil. "You're blocking our view."

Peter raised an eyebrow at him, but moved over and sat down on the other side of Brit. "Are you all right?" he asked her.

"I am now," she said, and his thin mouth quirked sideways in surprise at the compliment, which she immediately corrected by continuing, "Sergeant Ritter just told me she knows I didn't do it."

His look angled back toward Eleanor, who said, "I'll explain when this is over."

"This must be a hell of a horse show when people who know diddly about horses come and they're hooked," said Peter, surprised.

"It is when it's the kind where one of the participants kills another one," said Eleanor, her attention on the arena.

Peter frowned and looked again at the horses shown and waiting to be shown. Was the murderer down there?

Danny, noting his attention to the judging, asked, "Who's gonna get the blue?"

Peter smiled. If Danny got word at a horse show the world was about to end, he'd say, "Please, just one more class?" Peter gestured. "That chestnut with the big blaze."

"You think so?"

"And the black reserve."

"If reserve means second, then I told you so," said Phil.

"Oh, right, Mr. Expert," said Danny, but he was grinning at his father's unexpected interest.

"And I like that dark gray at the end of the line for third," said Peter.

Danny started to laugh. "Sarge . . ."

"And how about the bay beside the man with the yellow vest for fourth? And the dark chestnut fifth, and the bay with the star-and-snip sixth."

"But what about the gorgeous gray the dark-haired woman is showing?"

Peter leaned sideways, squinting. "I'm sorry, every time I look in that direction I'm blinded by the light."

The bay ahead of Kori was going to be next. Its owner, a big man in a blood-red sport coat, set her up while he waited to be summoned to judgment. His face was wet with perspiration, but the filly went into her pose with no fuss. The ring steward, watching the judge out in the arena, spoke to the man, who released the filly and led her at a walk to the judge, a medium tall man in a gray tweed sport coat and tan trousers. Once there, his hand visibly trembling, the owner tried to set the horse up again. Someone in the audience whooped and the owner jumped, making his filly start and work her feet as if about to run away. "Whoa!" shouted the man, yanking on the lead. "Whoa, whoa!" The filly froze, but after three failing attempts to set her up again, the judge, who had done a walk-around, waved them away, and watched closely as they trotted off.

"Nice hocks, nice," noted Danny under his breath. "Okay, boss lady, here we go."

Kori had Breathless set up by the time the judge turned to her. And the filly walked quietly beside her to the judge when the ring steward ordered them out. Danny waited until she was set up again before drawing breath to whoop, and so was preempted by whooping from across the arena. He joined in, and spread his hands to applaud, but a trickle of applause had already begun near the gate and Danny could only encourage it by making his own applause slow and loud. "Wha-hoo!" hooted Phil. "Eeeeya-hooo!"

The judge said something brief to Kori and then signaled her away. Breathless trotted off with a springy display of flawless legs, and Brit whooped. By now the applause was general, and Danny had a grin so broad you could see his back molars. His clapping grew faster. "Yes!" he said. "Yes!"

Peter, joining the applause, wondered if he did or did not wish that applause might influence a judge. He was pleased to find Danny and Kori's judgment verified by so many others. But a judge was rarely interested in what the crowd liked, which was probably as it should be.

The black filly's claque tried to stir up a general round of applause for their contestant, but failed.

As the last horse was being judged, a very young woman in an ill-fitting and totally unsuitable cocktail dress came into the arena with a fistful of ribbons in one hand and a sullen expression on her face.

The judge made one last sweep of the fillies with his head cocked a little sideways, then walked toward the bandstand in the middle of the arena while writing on a slip of paper. A boy in a white shirt and blue slacks took the paper and handed it to the announcer.

"Ladies and gentleman, the winner of the yearling filly class is . . . Leaves You Breathless, owned by Kori Price Brichter!" The applause had started even before he finished speaking, and his further announcement that the filly had been trained at Tretower Farm by Daniel Bannister was barely audible.

Kori led the filly on a victory run around the arena, her face alight with pleasure. Breathless, sensing she had done well, was willing to race as fast as Kori would let her. They came around and stopped by the gate where the young woman handed her a big blue rosette with four broad streamers, then a photographer took their picture while the assistant to the ring steward tossed dirt into the air to get Breathless to prick her ears at him.

The black filly came in fourth.

When it was over, everyone in the Tretower section except Sergeant Ritter went back to the barn to congratulate the winner, and found Kori explaining politely to two young men that she was not interested in selling the filly at any price.

"How many?" asked Danny.

"They're the third and fourth. The first was waiting for me outside the arena."

"How much?"

"Fifty thousand's the best offer so far. I'm starting to be glad I told Senator McIntyre he could have first refusal. Let them go pester him."

"But you told Senator McIntyre you'd only sell him Breathless if she dropped a sorry foal," said Brit. "That means you're saying no to any deal."

"Right," said Kori. "Hey, they're all from the big-name farms. They don't want to show Breathless as their own, they want to take her out of competition for a year, so their own fillies will have a chance." Kori stroked the smooth neck of Breathless, who bent her head to nuzzle Kori's ear. "In another year, they'll be offering me half a million for her. And I'll be turning that down, too." She handed the lead to the nonplussed Brit, dismissing her, and turned to Peter. "I thought you weren't going to be here until tomorrow."

"And so you just went ahead and solved it by yourself," he grinned. "In between winning blue ribbons."

"Well, I'm only morally sure," she replied. "I don't know how to gather the proper evidence to prove it."

"I don't suppose you're willing to share what you've found out with me?" asked Phil, his smile pulling his unlit cigar back into a corner of his mouth.

Kori looked at Peter, who shrugged. "It's up to you," he said. "I'm way out of my jurisdiction here. On the other hand, I am going to pay a courtesy call on the lead investigator, and anything you don't want me to tell her, you probably shouldn't tell me. Do I smell coffee?"

▽

12

"Come on over here, both of you," said Kori, leading them in the direction of the three director's chairs. Peter followed but kept going, far enough to stand in front of the TV monitor and watch a little of the Tretower video.

"The audio on that is terrible," he remarked, coming back to sit down.

"I know," sighed Kori, handing him a Styrofoam cup. "Phil?"

"Black," he said, and sat down, too.

"Okay," said Peter when Kori had filled her own cup. "Tell me about Brit. Could she have done it?"

The answer was sharp. "No!" Too sharp?

"Why not?"

"You only ask that because you hardly know her. Peter, she's so kind and gentle. She really good with my horses because she never uses more force than absolutely necessary, sometimes less than she should, even."

"Then why did she get put into handcuffs by the first cops on the scene?"

"Because she acted like an idiot." Seeing his next question, she continued, "Because she was scared." And the next, "Because Keith made some heavy sexual advances to her,

182

and threatened to 'finish the job' if he ever got the chance, so she threatened to hurt him—no, kill him, if he tried."

"So Keith turns up dead in a Tretower box stall, she acts guilty, and the cops totally irresponsibly detain her."

She gave him a Look. "The two policemen who answered the initial call were stupid, ignorant, and not willing to listen. They didn't talk to anyone, look for clues, ask for witnesses, nothing. And they were really rude to Sergeant Ritter when she arrived, insolent even—isn't that against the rules? Insubordination or something?"

Peter frowned. "Is one of them a weight lifter?"

"Yes?" Kori said, meaning So?

Peter gave a little nod. "I met him when I arrived."

Phil said, "I had a little set-to with him myself. Thought for a while he was going to run me off the grounds. Thinks he's Clint Eastwood and everyone else is Pee-Wee Herman."

Peter tucked that bit of information away and said, "Okay, *fy'n galon*, who do you think did it and why?"

There was a knock on Eleanor's stall but before she could get up to answer it, the door slid back and Peter stepped into the room.

She made a face. "Did you sell that Porsche 928S?"

"No, why?"

"Took you a while to get here."

"If I'd known you needed my help so badly, I would've abandoned the county attorney and hurried right over."

"Get stuffed, Brichter."

"May I speak with you, just briefly?"

Eleanor hesitated. His tone was suddenly formal, which might mean he was going to ask for a personal favor. But then, Brichter's reputation was for not giving anyone a break, so it was unlikely he'd try asking someone else to give him one. She nodded and said, "Sit down."

"Looks like you've got a murder mystery here," he said, meaning this wasn't a murder involving professional criminals, but the far more difficult kind involving amateurs.

"My favorite kind of crime," she agreed. "I understand you're responsible for Phil Bannister coming here."

"If I'd known you were running the investigation I wouldn't've bothered. I called him when I got a report that the two uniforms who responded behaved less than professionally. Was one of them that blowfish that tried to make me move my car?"

"Blowfish?"

"Juice monkey. Steroid abuser."

"Oh, you mean Cullen. Yes. That is, he was here first, and he's a weight lifter, but I don't know if he uses steroids."

"You might want to try to find out. There's a documented tendency for them to lose control in a big way. You don't want to find a member of the department up for felony assault or worse."

Eleanor frowned. There was a fad current among some of the bluesuits for weight lifting, and a lot of macho posturing accompanied it. "Thanks for the tip."

Peter offered his sideways smile and sat down. He looked around the box stall at the flow charts, diagrams, and lists tacked to every surface. "You look determined not to miss anything."

So he was uncomfortable about coming right to the point, another uncharacteristic behavior. But she replied, "If I make myself write it down, I have to sort it out in my head first. I have a good grasp of detail if it's arranged in some kind of order." She leaned sideways and pulled a sheet off the wall. "Like this one is about the victim. Name, address, occupation, date of birth, reason for being here at this show, everyone here he knew, anyone he had a quarrel with, et cetera, et cetera. See, I've asterisked the names of people he'd quarreled with if they are also here. Then I do a time-line chronology of these people's lives, so I can see where they cross. I index all the details in all the police reports, so I can locate each fact in the case when I need it—and when it comes time to go to court."

Peter shifted his chair around so he could look at the chart in Eleanor's hands. "Jesus, you're even more thorough than I am."

"It really hurts when you lose a case because you missed something."

"That must not happen to you very often."

"Not very," said Eleanor grimly. "Not since I had this hot suspect in a rape case. I mean, I *knew* it was him. But forensics did a saliva test on a cigarette butt found at the crime scene, and it didn't match, not the perp, not the victim. The defense played that butt up like divine revelation, and it was reasonable damn doubt, and I lost my case. And you know what it turned out? Some rookie threw his cigarette away when he saw his sergeant coming, and that's what forensics found, the rookie's cigarette butt. But by the time I found that out, the perp had been exonerated and double jeopardy kept us from trying him again. People say I'm a control addict, but I swore then I'd never lose a case because of something stupid I did, or my crew did."

"That must've hurt," commiserated Peter. "I can see what it did to you, but what happened to the rookie?"

"He made a fortune in real estate right here in town." She turned to fasten the chart back on the wall. "But he's still a jerk. Are you here to chew me out for not collaborating with your wife on this?"

Peter looked startled. "No. What makes you say that?"

"Then what do you want?"

"Tell me what you've found out so far."

Eleanor studied him, but he was a hard read, his thin mouth set and his cool eyes steady. "Do you want in? Why?"

"No, because no investigator appreciates someone moving in on his case." He gestured carelessly. "I have some information, and I want to compare it with what you have."

"What information? You've only been here twenty minutes, and ten of that was watching your wife's horse win a blue ribbon."

"Trust me."

She blew until her cheeks ballooned, but he waited her

out. "Okay, but you have to sit through it all." He nodded and sat back, and she said, "Here's the story as I read it. People started arriving Thursday afternoon for this shindig. One of the earliest arrivals was Keith Bulward. He brought two grooms and six horses, and he spent most of Thursday getting that real pretty setup together right inside the main entrance. One of his horses was a loaner, a mare named Wellaway, trained in dressage—damn silly name—owned by Amelia Haydock. Bulward rode Wellaway in a dressage competition Friday morning, and out of a possible two hundred, he scored fifty-one. He apparently knew he wasn't doing well, because after he rode out of the arena, he got off and hit the horse with his fist hard enough to cause a nosebleed. Among the people who saw him do it was Amelia, and she came to reclaim her horse with a look that a groom described as something she hopes is never aimed at her, close quote.

"There was a party in the barn that evening, which Amelia Haydock attended. Your wife says Amelia hinted that she would make Bulward smart for what he did, which was not only hurt her horse but show her up for a foolish old woman who gets too fond of pretty boys. Also in attendance was Stoddard Eckiherne, a has-been trainer trying to make a comeback. He was sure to succeed except that Bulward had brought a horse likely to defeat the one Stoddard brought, and Stoddard seemed to think he had done it on purpose. Stoddard, in consequence, fell very hard off the wagon and managed to acquire some severe scrapes and bruises to his left hand he says he can't remember how he got. Bulward himself was at the party. Possibly to cover his embarrassment with Wellaway, he told a story about a sucker who brought a sterile mare from him. That sucker turns out to be State Senator Robert McIntyre, this show's manager. McIntyre wasn't at the party, but apparently this wasn't the first time Bulward told the story, and McIntyre was aware of its circulation and damn pissed because, he admits, it was damaging his daughter's dream of showing her Arabian horses.

"One of Bulward's grooms, Fran Obermeyer, was in Bulward's trailer around 1:20 A.M. taking a shower after having sexual intercourse with him. She reports hearing the phone ring, and that afterward, Bulward hustled her back to her cot at the barn and left her. He was not seen alive again.

"Some of the people staying in the barn didn't go to bed after the party, but sat up talking, or currycombing their horses, or whatever. So no one was surprised when they heard the horse shower running late last night, and the hay cart being moved around. But then some horses got upset enough to make their groom come and calm them down.

"The main squealer was a yearling filly named Leaves You Breathless, and the groom was Brittany Morgan.

"A little after six o'clock this morning, Brittany Morgan slid back the door of the prep stall, which is right next to the yearling filly's, and found Bulward dead of a cut throat. He was brought to that stall after being killed somewhere else. It appears the weapon was that knife on the table." Peter leaned forward for a look, but didn't touch it or say anything. Eleanor continued. "It was found down the drain of the horse shower at the south end of the barn, which same shower held traces of human blood. Further investigation turned up a hay cart which was left outside in the rain last night. It also tests positive for human blood. The first officers to the scene found Miss Morgan behaving in a suspicious manner and detained her."

Peter nodded. "And it occurred to you, I'm sure, as it obviously didn't to Cullen and his partner, that it was a very strange thing for a woman to kill a man somewhere else and then move the body to a place where suspicion would be sure to fall on her."

"You *are* good, aren't you?"

Again the sideways smile. "What I want to know is, who's missing a hoof knife?"

"The only missing knife we've learned about belonged to Morning Glory Farms—Keith Bulward's operation."

Peter frowned. "The murder weapon belongs to the victim?"

"Bulward was a little man, and every suspect I've developed was easily big enough to handle him. I'm thinking he went into his prep stall for that knife after he left Miss Obermeyer, to take it along when he went to meet whoever called him. She heard him open the door of a stall, she says."

"How about it was Fran who went into the prep stall?"

"Could be, but I don't think so." Eleanor elaborated on the sleeping arrangements.

"So who do you think did it?"

Eleanor told him. "But I want another word with Stoddard Eckiherne. Paul says Abner's Golden Hour cut Stoddard off his whiskey sours at a little after one and offered to call a cab for him, which offer he snottily refused and drove away. Stoddard must have been pretty drunk; they were relieved to discover Paul wasn't investigating a vehicular homicide."

Peter nodded. "A little after one? That's enough time to get back here. What about the injured hand?"

"No one in the bar remembers a bruised and scabby hand."

"You want me to hang around while you talk to him?"

"No, you look too much like a cop. He's not afraid to talk to me."

"Mind if I go talk to Amelia?" he asked.

"Not at all."

"What time did you get back to your motel last night?" asked Eleanor.

Stoddard took a deep breath and held it, frowning. Eleanor was reminded of her son back in the days of his potty chair. "I'm sorry, all I get is bits and pieces, nothing as helpful as remembering looking at my watch," said Stoddard, blowing and shaking his head. "Like I told you before, things got really blurred."

"How sure are you that you went right back to the motel after you left here?"

Again Stoddard shook his head. "Not sure at all. In fact . . ." His frown deepened. "I'm pretty sure I went somewhere else." The frown shifted into a wry smile. "If the bars were still open, it's damn probable I went somewhere else. But I can't remember where or for how long."

"The rest of the evening is one big blank, then," said Eleanor.

He looked at her and the smile faded. "It wasn't me! You've seen my knife! Mine wasn't the murder weapon! Oh, Christ!" He pressed both elegant hands over his face.

After a minute, "Do you remember a bar named Abner's Golden Hour?" Eleanor asked.

His hand dropped. "Should I?"

"According to witnesses, you were there and got cut off sometime around 1:00 A.M. and left in a snit."

Hope unfurled like a morning glory. "Is that good? I mean alibi-wise?"

Eleanor shook her head. "It puts you out on the road just in time to get back here and meet Mr. Bulward."

The brief bloom curled in on itself. "This can't be true, there's got to be something . . . Sure! Look, I understand that groom, Brit Morgan, was threatened by Bulward late last night, and threatened him back. Since the body was found in her part of the barn, that's got to mean something."

"When did you hear about that?"

"Just a little while ago, or I would have mentioned it earlier. But it is important, isn't it?"

"Yes, but it's a fact we've been aware of for some time. And it doesn't change the fact—"

"Wait, there's something else. It's about the show manager."

She let him go on, hoping he'd tell her something she didn't already know, but all he did was trot out the tale about the sterile mare. When he saw that didn't impress her, he added, "Well, did you know that he's up for a position on the State Finance Committee? And that some people think he doesn't deserve it because he got taken in that horse deal?"

Eleanor took a moment to absorb that, but then continued, "Right now I'm focusing on the facts that you became very angry when you heard Bulward was here at the show to

compete with you, that you were out on the road at a critical
time last night, and that you have an injury to your hand
you can't explain."

Stoddard made a fist with his good hand and thumped his
thigh. "Hell," he murmured. "Dammit to hell." He grimaced, thinking. "Wait, I do remember something else. I
think—let's see, there was a car, I almost hit it. I was angry,
talking to myself, and suddenly there was my turn, and a car
was coming out, right at me." He thought. "It was the parking lot, I was coming into the motel parking lot! Sure! And
I almost hit a car coming out. He blew his horn and I blew
mine back and it was ridiculous, because he had one of those
musical horns and my truck sounds one thin note, like a
toy. It made me mad, him in his big, rich car and honking
at *me*. I mean, I had the right of way! He was coming out of
the parking lot, so he should have been the one to stop."

"What kind of a car?" asked Eleanor.

"I don't know. Cadillac. Or Lincoln. Something big and
shiny. Dark windows, because I couldn't see who was inside."

"Yet you said 'he' and 'him,' " noted Eleanor.

"Well, of course. English hasn't got a personal pronoun
that means it could have been either she or he, does it? I
can't very well say, 'it was driving too fast,' can I?" He nodded. "He—or she—frightened me, coming out all of a sudden
like that, but it was he who first blew his horn."

"What color was the car?"

Stoddard thought, then shook his head. "Sorry."

"Dark, light?"

"Dark, I think. Or a medium shade. What I can remember
is that it had dark windows, like one of those God-awful
stretch limousines." He was relaxed now, feeling this somehow proved something in his favor.

"Do you know what time this happened?"

"No, but I must have been on my way home from Abner's
Golden Whatever, because I was still angry."

"Okay." She lifted her hands to an imaginary steering

wheel, using a memory recall technique. "Now. Relax. You must have felt something while you were yanking on the wheel to get out of his way: Did it hurt? Was your hand injured when you made that turn into the parking lot?"

Stoddard lifted his own hands, looked at the injured one. The bandage was dirty. "No," he said, and shifted focus to look her right in the eye. "It was fine." He looked at it again, gestured with it. "Yes, I remember that now, too. I fell getting out of my car. I remember now, I fell."

Amelia sat in the comfortable, extra-large folding chair in the back room of the arena office, a private retreat for judges and show officials. The chair was her own, she brought it with her to every show, whether she was there as owner, trainer, or judge.

She had turned to her favorite time-passer and tension-reliever, *The Daily Telegraph Cryptic Crossword Book*. The books were from England, sent to her by a friend via surface mail, so she knew there was always another on its way to her, that she would never be ahead of the publisher. This had been true for a long while; the book in her hand was the nineteenth edition, and number twenty was deep in the hold of an ocean freighter.

"Curtsies for shillings," read the clue. Four letters. Of course: bobs.

"Cart horse, in good shape to take the strain." "In good shape" meant in proper shape, a clue that she should shift the letters in cart horse around to spell a new word, one that had to do with strain. Heave, load—traces! No that didn't use all the letters. Strain, strain . . . as of music? She tried out syllables in the margin. *S, T, R, A*—ha!! Orchestra. Very clever. What a mind it must take to think these things up!

"Chivalrous Moslem leader gets in after a summer snack." Amelia paused. A summer snack, plus "in." Chicken? No, that already had an in. Melon, ice tea, sherbet. Abdul. Mohammed. Mohammedan! Too many letters, and anyway, there was nothing to eat in it.

Amelia heard a noise, as of a throat clearing, and looked up to see Kori Price Brichter and a slender man with piercing gray eyes looking at her.

"Yes?" she said. There was an air about the man that kept her from challenging their right to interrupt her while in sanctuary.

"Good afternoon," he said. "My name is Detective Sergeant Peter Brichter."

"Ah, you're Kori's husband."

A smile tweaked his too-thin mouth, and he suddenly looked much less threatening. "Yes."

"Do you know lots about the Middle Ages, too?"

" 'Too'?"

"Aren't both of you members of that organization that studies the Middle Ages by dressing up in costume?"

The man's crooked nod agreed while indicating there was more to it than that.

"Why, that's amazing," said Kori. "Because that's one of the reasons we're here to talk to you."

"It is?" Amelia was amazed as well, but said, "Here's the clue: 'Chivalrous Moslem leader gets in after a summer snack.' 'Chivalrous' may mean a medieval name."

"What clue?" asked Peter.

"For my crossword puzzle." She held up the book so they could read the cover.

"Oh."

Kori said, "I don't know about summer snack, but Saladin was famous for his courtesy."

"Of course! Salad, in." Amelia filled in the blank, then looked up to find them still standing there. "Yes?"

"It's about the costume contest," said Kori. "I was thinking about entering, but I wanted your advice about it."

Amelia left off frowning at Peter to frown at Kori. "What about it?"

"I wondered what the rules are about Crusaders."

"Are there rules about Crusaders?"

"What I want to know is, do they allow Crusaders in the

costume contest? I don't know because I almost never watch one. They're so"—Kori stopped short. Some people took the costume contests very seriously.

"Tacky?" suggested Amelia, smiling now.

"All those pink tassels," gestured Kori, her own cheeks pinking. "And silver lamé harem pants."

Amelia nodded. "You want to enter as a Crusader, instead of an Arab. Fine. No sword, though. Or spear."

"No, I wasn't going to wear armor. Armor's too much work. But I've been working on new thirteenth-century garb. And a friend of mine has made this wonderful saddle for me, also thirteenth century, because I want to take Blue Wind to the War this year. I've wanted to take a horse to the War for some while, but didn't want to buy a Frisian just for that, so I thought that if I said I was with my husband on Crusade, then my own Arabians would be right."

Amelia was puzzled at this explanation, but nodded gamely and waited for things to get clearer.

Kori continued. "I've been thinking it would be nice to make the saddle and garb do double duty, like at the horse show costume contests. When I saw there was one at Lafite, I brought it along in case. But it's different from the usual sort of stuff."

"Different how?"

Kori produced a photograph and handed it to Amelia. It was of a peculiar-looking saddle. Instead of leather, it was covered with gray velvet cloth, and it rose so high fore and aft that it looked like a safety seat. The velvet split into three long streamers, and each streamer was self-knotted, a decorative effect. The stirrup was plain iron, but hung toward the front rather than the center of the saddle.

"I assume your costume is as authentic as the saddle?"

"I can document the whole thing as about 1360," said Kori.

"A pity you won't win."

"No?"

"No silver lamé, no pink tassels."

"Ah." Kori took the photo back and stroked it with a thumb as if consoling it, or herself.

"But please," said Amelia, "do enter."

"Thanks."

"Um, as long as we're here," said Peter, "may I ask you something?"

The frown came back. "Judging soon," Amelia warned.

"Did they change your schedule of judging?" asked Kori.

"No."

"And performance classes don't start until halter classes finish. But don't take too long, Peter."

Thus boxed, Amelia faced him directly, a tacit consent.

"Adam Croy suggests you preferred Keith Bulward alive because there were worse things you could do to him."

"Than dying?"

Peter held up a big hand and began counting off on his fingers. "Never give him a first, no matter how good the horse. Place him fifth of five in a small class. Pull out seven horses, including his, line them up, and give the other six the ribbons. When he brings his horse to be judged, the minute he's got it set up, ask him to set it up again, and again, until he's so rattled he can't set it up at all. If someone questions your judgment, say you liked his horse but couldn't place it because he was allowing his farrier to ruin its feet."

A smile tweaked Amelia's mouth. "I hadn't thought of the setting-up trick."

"But the others?"

She sighed wearily. "There's a lot of politics in showing."

"I know. My wife says between the fads, the politics, and the stress of showing on her horses, it almost isn't worth it."

"Trophies make a horse worth more."

"And that's the catch. She has this twitch about making the farm pay."

"Not a need?"

Peter almost smiled; a few years ago he would have said no. And been wrong. "Not a monetary one," he said, looking at Kori, who smiled back, but said nothing.

Amelia nodded. "I see." She shifted as if about to turn away, then changed her mind and said, "Who killed him?"

"It could have been you," replied Peter bluntly. "You were very angry with him, you hinted that you had plans for revenge, someone with a deep voice had a quarrel with him just before the murder."

Again she leveled that look at him. "And I have no alibi," she said.

"You slept alone in your motel room?"

The flinch in her gaze was almost undetectable. "Yes," she said.

Walking back to the barn, Kori said, "Peter, about that hoof knife."

"What about it?" His tone was wary; Eleanor had not reminded him because he already knew better than to share details of a case under investigation with someone involved in it. Even his wife.

"Do you now who it belonged to?"

"Yes."

"Was it some innocent bystander?"

A pause. "No."

"Was it the murderer's?"

"*Fy'n galon*—"

"Please."

"No, it doesn't belong to the murderer."

"Thank you," she said. "Where to now?"

"I'm going to report to Sergeant Ritter."

"Does she know who did it?"

"I'd rather say an arrest may be imminent, okay?"

"I'd rather you tell me who she plans to arrest. Is it Amelia?"

"He looked away.

"Is it? Or Senator McIntyre?"

He did not look back.

"Peter, is it Stoddard? Maybe I should—"

He turned to take her by the upper arms. "I've talked to

her, and it's clear to me she knows what she's doing. There's no need for you to interfere."

Hmmmm, he thought on his way back to Eleanor's temporary office. Female companion in that motel room, he'd bet a month's pay. Because while Amelia liked pretty young men, it was for reasons other than sexual. He hoped it wouldn't come down to her needing to provide the alibi after all.

"Stoddard's lying at least about the hand," said Eleanor. "I don't know about the rest."

"I'd say the whole thing's a lie," said Peter.

Eleanor was consulting her charts. "Say, do you know who has a big green Lincoln Town Car with dark windows?"

"Who?"

"Senator McIntyre. And he's staying at the same motel Stoddard Eckiherne is."

Peter made a whistling shape with his mouth, eyebrows high. "No shit."

"Maybe he can tell me something about it."

"Okay if I go along?"

"Please do. He reacts very well to a hardnose mixing with my nice lady, and I sent Paul to talk to Missy."

"Well," said Peter, "I know my looks are against me, but if I put my mind to it, I can be a little bit of a hardnose."

When Eleanor finished laughing, she said, "Let's see if the senator remembers almost hitting someone, and please God let him remember what time it happened."

McIntyre was impatient with the Miranda warning Eleanor handed him and emphatic that he was asleep in his motel bed by eleven and did not leave until nearly seven the next morning.

"Suppose I can produce a witness who saw you leave the parking lot some hours before that?" said Peter, who could be hardnose with no effort at all.

"He's lying," said the senator, setting his chin yet more firmly and not looking Peter in the face.

"What if there's someone else to corroborate his story?" asked Eleanor, but sadly.

There was a long silence while McIntyre fumbled for his pipe and began the complex process of firing it up. But the hand that held the lighter to the bowl was trembling, so he snapped it off without drawing smoke. "Hell," he murmured.

"Tell us about it," coaxed Eleanor.

"You'd think a politician of my experience could handle anything, wouldn't you?"

"Meaning?" demanded Peter.

"Meaning barbecue! There's a little place on this side of town run by a black—excuse me, African-American—family. All of 'em, father, mother, teenaged sons and daughters, working as a team, and they smoke their own meat and have this secret family recipe. Every time I'm anywhere near Lafite, I stop in and load up. Goat, would you believe, and the best damn barbecue I ever tasted. But I'm getting old or something, because lately it backs up on me. Wakes me up with headache, heartburn, gas, the whole sad story. And that's what it did this time. And wouldn't you know it, I forgot to bring my bicarb with me. I had to pull my pants on over my pajamas and go looking for a drugstore open at that hour."

"If it was so innocent, why lie about it?" asked Peter.

"Because if I admit I went out, you'll think I came here to the fairgrounds and waylaid Keith Bulward."

"Well, if the facts fit . . ." noted Eleanor.

"Well, I didn't. I did go out, but it was just to buy some bicarbonate of soda, and I was too damn sick to do anything but get it and come right back."

"Do you remember almost hitting someone on your way out of the parking lot?" said Eleanor.

"Ah." McIntyre nodded. "No, I remember someone almost hitting me. Must've been drunk, swerving in like that at the last second."

"You honked at him?'

McIntyre grinned. "Shouted, too, but my windows were rolled up."

Peter said, "You say you weren't gone long? How long?"

"Oh, I don't know. Half an hour? All the drugstores were closed, so I found an all-night grocery store somewhere. You ever go into a grocery store in the middle of the night? You see people you'd never believe, buying cornflakes."

"What time was it when you went out?" asked Eleanor.

"I think midnight. No, later than that."

"After one? After two?" asked Peter.

McIntyre grimaced. "Hell, I don't know. I was asleep for a couple of hours, then woke up. I tried to tough it out for what seemed a hell of a long time, but finally got so miserable I had to do something, and then I drove around for some while until I saw the lights and could go in and buy some welcome relief."

"Do you remember the name of the grocery store?"

"No. But it's not too far from the motel, because I had about given up and was circling back when I saw it. Went in, bought the stuff, went straight back and took it, and went right to bed. It was a lesson I won't forget." He grinned. "At least not until the next time."

"Missy, this was your first horse show, right?"

"Oh, no; I've been to four horse shows, if you count our county fair the last three Julys." The child's eyes were alight at this opportunity to be helpful. Paul wondered if anyone at all had been fooled by her claim to be sixteen.

"Have you worked at a horse show before?"

"No, that's why I was so happy when Mr. Bulward asked if I wanted to come to this one. My mother almost had a cow, but I told her Fran would be here with me and nothing bad could happen." She sobered and grimaced. "I was wrong, but who would've thought? I mean, it makes you wonder. Who would do something so evil?"

"You don't have any idea who it might be?"

"Uh-uh." Missy shook her head.

"Tell me about the sleeping arrangements between you and Fran."

"We both slept in here. We'd move stuff around, stack it up, and we each had a little camp cot that unfolded. Fran said to bring my sleeping bag, which I'm glad she did, because it got really cold last night."

"But you slept all night?"

"Oh, gee no! There was a lot of strange noises that kept waking me up."

"Like what?"

"Well, people walking horses around and talking and laughing and stuff. And then when Fran came back, her coming in woke me up, and it took me a long while to get back to sleep, and I was just getting there when a horse had some kind of screaming fit. It made some of the other horses over there start in, too; and I was gonna wake Fran up to see if maybe we should do something when I heard it start to settle down, like someone else was with it, and so I laid back down and went to sleep again."

"Do you know what time this was?"

"No. Pretty late, I think. And I woke up again when two people right across the way started making sounds like . . ." Missy ducked her head and covered her mouth with her cupped hand.

"You mean like making love?"

Missy nodded without looking up. "I didn't know whether to make a noise myself to let them know I was awake or just keep still and hope they stopped soon."

"Do you know what time this happened?"

"No. But not too long before we had to get up and get started for the day, because I was still awake when the alarm went off."

"Do you remember hearing a stall door sliding open *after* Fran came in?"

Missy frowned, then her brow cleared. "Yes, it was a stall close to us, maybe the people behind us."

"What about before?"

". . . No. I mean, not right before. Those doors sliding open sound like shingles sliding off a house, so at first I was having trouble getting to sleep because people kept going in and out all around me. And Fran wasn't here when I went to bed, so I was kind of nervous. But I got used to it. Unless it was real close, like the one after she came in."

"How sure are you that Fran didn't slip out while you were sleeping?"

Missy's look was direct, even a little surprised. "Very sure. I mean, when the alarm clock started in and she got up to shut it off, her cot jiggled against mine; and if she had got up before, that would've woke me up. And sliding that door open. No way I could have slept through our own door opening. No, once she came in, she was there the rest of the night."

$\triangledown$

13

"Y OU GOING TO BE there?" asked Peter.

"No," said Eleanor, "I find it's easier to get a subject to talk to me if someone else makes the arrest and takes them through the booking process. See, that way they don't blame me for what they've just been through."

Peter nodded, storing that helpful fact away for future use. "Unmarked car?"

"Oh, yes. And no cuffs unless he needs them. I want as little fuss as possible taking him out of here."

"When did you know?"

"Early on, actually. He was far more scared than he needed to be. And he's a surprisingly bad liar. You know, if he'd only raised the alarm as soon as it happened"—she stopped, shrugged.

"Stupid," agreed Peter. "I can't think he meant to kill him."

"Well . . . it wasn't an accident, either. He was mad, probably. And scared. He grabbed for the knife, and then swung once he had it."

"A good lawyer will argue that Bulward charged him and he swung without thinking."

"That might even be the truth. But hiding the knife and moving the body, that was very bad. It strongly indicates something more serious than an accident. You want to go along when I send Paul and Al to get him?"

"Sure."

"Mrs. Brichter! How may I help you?" Senator McIntyre rose from his chair and gestured at Kori that she should come in.

"Good afternoon, Senator. Does it look as if we'll get back on schedule by the end of the day?"

McIntyre gestured at the window to the office, outside of which was the busy clatter and talk of a show barn when the show is finally under way. "Yes, if everyone continues to cooperate. We'll run today's schedule until midnight, and by then we should be all caught up. Makes for an early Sunday, I'm afraid, but the show will finish on time. Are you going from here to another show?"

"No, I'm going home from here, thank goodness. It's going to take some time to get over this."

"Yes, of course it will. All of us will be glad when it's over."

"Except the person who did it, of course," said Kori. "He won't be going home."

"Er, no. Or she, of course."

"She? Who do you think did it?"

"Why . . ." McIntyre hesitated. "I don't know, I'm sure. And thank God it isn't my job to find out."

"You told Sergeant Ritter that you think it was Brit, didn't you?"

This was not said accusingly, and McIntyre reluctantly nodded. "She came to me and asked me to send him away. I only wish I could have; he'd be alive today."

"Then you knew about the quarrel."

"Oh, it was more than a quarrel. Miss Morgan said Keith Bulward had tried to assault her. Now he was unexpectedly at this show, and she was afraid there would be trouble if he stayed. She indicated the trouble began with him, so that he should be the one to leave. But that if he didn't, she might have to do something herself. I'm afraid I think she did."

"Good afternoon, ladies and gentlemen," said a cheerful mechanical voice. *"This is first call, first call for two-year-old colts. Two-year-old colts, Amateur Owner to Show. Please bring your colts to the arena as promptly as possible. First call, two-year-old colts, AOTS."*

McIntyre had turned his head to listen to the announcement, and the muted cheers that accompanied it. He turned back and Kori said, "Stoddard didn't know about the quarrel."

"Stoddard? Oh, you mean Eckiherne."

"Yes. He also was upset that Bulward was here, and he turned up this morning with an injured hand. He says he had an alcoholic blackout about last night."

"Does he now? That's very interesting. Do you think he's the guilty one?"

"Sergeant Ritter does. But I think you are."

This was said so casually that McIntyre nearly missed it. "Perhaps we shouldn't speculate—wait, you think *I*—?"

"Yes. Because the body was moved, you know. Bulward wasn't killed in that prep stall, he was brought there from somewhere else. Someone brought the body there to make us think Brit did it."

"And you think that someone was *me*?"

"Yes."

"In heaven's name, why choose me?"

"Two reasons. One is the murder weapon. The murderer hid it, you know."

"But the police found it. They showed it to me. It was a very peculiar thing, with a damaged blade."

"No, sir, it was a very common thing, and there was nothing wrong with the blade. There are dozens of them here at the show, most looking exactly like that one."

"No, the blade on this one was bent."

"All hoof knives have a bent blade. Brit knows that. If Brit had done it, she wouldn't have felt any need to hide the knife; she would have cleaned it off and left it on the floor somewhere. They're so common anyone seeing it would have picked it up, or even taken it away, thinking it was his."

"Very well, then, Mr. Eckiherne—"

"Stoddard would have substituted it for the one in my carpenter's box when he brought the body to the prep stall. The Tretower hoof knife looks exactly like the murder weapon, except for the small Tretower mark on the handle, which is easily missed in poor light. But which Brit knew about."

"But since she did—" began McIntyre, but Kori interrupted him.

"No, Brit is out of it. Don't you see? Brit wouldn't have moved the body from wherever he was killed to her own prep stall."

That stopped him cold for an embarrassing while. "What about Miss Haydock?" he asked at last. "She was very angry with him."

"Yes, but Amelia wanted him alive. She had some very nasty plans for revenge, and they could only be done to an alive and deeply unhappy Keith Bulward."

"Now wait, now wait. You must be missing something. You just said the police are going to arrest Stoddard Eckiherne."

"I think they are, true. But they're wrong, because Stoddard didn't know about Brit and Keith. Stoddard might have moved the body, but it wouldn't have been to our prep stall, because he didn't know that Brit had exchanged threats with Bulward. That's why you put it in, because you want to put the blame on her."

"That isn't true!"

"And, you didn't know about hoof knives. The murderer hid the hoof knife down the shower drain because he thought it was a unique weapon. You thought it was a unique weapon."

"That doesn't make me the murderer! I had no reason to wish Keith Bulward dead!"

"Yes you did. That tricky deal he pulled on you over that sterile mare left you very upset."

"If every man who thought he got taken on a horse trade killed the seller, there'd be no horses sold, ever."

"That isn't true. But that isn't the point, either. You have been nominated to the State Finance Committee, which oversees all spending. That's an appointment of enormous power and prestige, one that can help you when you make your run for governor. And Keith was taking great delight in spreading the tale that when it comes to finance, you are an idiot."

He gaped at her while fumbling futilely for his pipe. "No, no, no," he said at last, flinging his hand out of the pocket empty. "I was angry with him because his spreading that story might prevent Birdie from following her dream of showing Arabian horses."

"That, too." Kori nodded. "But the real reason is that Keith was endangering your political career. You sold your partnership in your law firm to be a full-time politician, didn't you? Because you had enough money at last to start a run for the governor's chair. But first you had to make a good showing on that Finance Committee. And it simply wouldn't do to have it all spoiled by a horse dealer who suckered you on an unimportant sale."

Senator McIntyre had gone gray. "Not true, not true," he murmured, with no conviction at all. Then he asked, "Have you shared this ridiculous theory with your husband?"

"Yes, of course she has," said a low voice. "She's not a fool."

Kori turned and there was Peter in the doorway with Al and Paul. "Very good, *fy'n galon*. But you should have a little more faith in police methods."

"You should have told me whom Eleanor suspected. I was afraid it was Stoddard. I thought if I could get the senator to say something incriminating, then you'd have to arrest the real murderer." She gestured at McIntyre. "Him."

Paul said, "I hope you agree, Senator, that we don't want a scene." He started toward the man, who was frozen in place, one hand fumbling in a pocket. "Will you be careful what you have in your hand when you take it out of your pocket?"

McIntyre snorted faintly, then seemed to realize where his right hand was. He slowly pulled it out and showed his pipe to Paul. "This is a terrible mistake you are making," he said, putting the pipe on the desk in front of him.

"In that case, let's just go quietly away and straighten it out."

"Yes. Yes, of course. Mrs. Brichter"—he made a little bow in her direction—"will you instruct my staff to continue the show until I return? They are competent to do so, I assure you."

"Yes, sir, I'll do that."

"Tell them I hope to return in time to hand out the championship trophy tomorrow evening." His eyes begged her to join in his pretense.

"All right."

"Thank you, you are very kind. Now, sir, if you will lead the way." And he followed Paul as if Paul were the sergeant at arms leading him to his place in the State Senate. Al, turning to bring up the rear, winked approval at Kori and shook his head at Peter.

"What made you decide to play sleuth?" asked Peter.

"It was you who told me the first twenty-four hours of a case are the most important. I was afraid they'd arrest Brit and stop investigating, and clues would get lost. I guess I should have trusted Sergeant Ritter, but she was so standoffish, I couldn't get close enough to see how competent she was." She looked at the investigator, who was sipping a farewell cup of decaf coffee. "I apologize."

Eleanor shrugged. "I can understand your apprehensions, I suppose. On the other hand, I wasn't about to make friends with someone who had a stake in this investigation. I figured you wouldn't be interested in anything that didn't go toward proving Brit was innocent, and might even hide evidence to the contrary."

"If she'd known you thought that poorly of her," said Peter, smiling behind his Styrofoam cup, "she'd have come and called you some interesting names."

"Interesting . . . ? Oh, you mean in Latin."

Kori bit her lip but couldn't help asking, "Was it Stoddard who told you?"

Eleanor nodded. "I'm not exactly sure what his point was, but he told me you could insult people in Latin."

"She doesn't do it too often," said Peter, still smiling. "It's too complicated a language. By the time she recalls which of the five declensions the word belongs to, and runs down the list to find the right case and number, she's usually not mad anymore."

Kori agreed. "It's better than counting to ten." And to Eleanor, "Stoddard told me he was using everything he could find or think of to make you think it was someone else."

"So did Senator McIntyre," said Brit. "He was telling everyone about how he got the deal of the year when he got you to agree to sell Breathless to him."

"Poor man," said Kori, and meant it.

Danny said, "Did he confess? The senator?"

Eleanor shook her head, smiling. "Lawyers don't confess."

"Not until they've made some kind of deal," amended Peter.

Brit said shyly, "I'm glad both of you found out it wasn't me."

"Yes, but the next time a groom says she wants to go home she goes," said Kori. "It may save her—and me—a lot of grief."

"What made you decide it was Senator McIntyre?" Danny asked Eleanor.

"First, he was so nervous. Politicians are used to being in difficult situations. Senator McIntyre has been in the State Senate for almost fifteen years, and yet he was nervous as a snake at a mongoose convention—"

Kori, surprised, chortled.

"Don't blame me for that, blame the other sergeant over

there. And the hoof knife business; he was the only one with a motive who didn't know what a hoof knife was.

"But the thing that put us over the edge was that we found out he left the motel at about the right time to get him here in time to murder Bulward. He said he went to a twenty-four-hour grocery store to buy a stomach aid, but there isn't one in Lafite."

Kori frowned. "Yes, there is. It's not too far from the motel; I saw it when I was looking for a place to have breakfast—was it only this morning?"

Eleanor smirked. "You made the same mistake everyone does. There's a big paper sign in their window saying Open Twenty-Four Hours, but if you get closer, it says in smaller letters, Starting June 1. He saw the sign, but there's no way he could have bought antacid in there after eleven last night."

"Maybe some other grocery store?"

"Nope, they're all closed by eleven; only this one plans to start operating twenty-four hours a day." She sighed, sipped her coffee, and looked around. There was a short row of ribbons gleaming over the tack stall behind them—Kori had come in third showing Storm Wind at halter in the Aged Mare class and gotten her blue on Blue Wind in Country English Pleasure.

Eleanor continued, "This is the first time I've been at one of these things. It might have been interesting, if I'd had the time to get into it. My kids are after me to buy a horse. I suppose a horse show is a good place to have a look at what's involved. Not to buy, of course; I couldn't begin to afford an Arabian, much less a show-quality one."

"Oh, I don't know," said Kori. "I know someone who's selling an Arab gelding, three years old, very sweet disposition, for a thousand dollars."

Eleanor snorted. "What, one of your cow-hocked, ewe-necked specials?"

Peter laughed and Kori looked shocked. "Oh, no, no! He's got excellent conformation, he'd be a candidate for endurance riding. He's a little on the small side, and his topline isn't flat—which you don't want in an endurance horse, anyway."

"Is he by some chance a bay?"

"Yes." She saw the look in Eleanor's eye and burst out laughing herself. "No, no, he's not one of mine. Amelia Haydock has him and a half-brother of his. She rescued them from a bankrupt farm last winter. They and a half dozen others were almost dead of starvation. She wants a thousand because that's what it cost her in vet bills to bring him back to health. The other is only six hundred, but he's just two, and you can't ride a two-year-old Arab."

Eleanor shook her head. "What a screwy business you're in. Thousand-dollar Arabians, million-dollar Arabians, and us ordinary folk probably couldn't tell the difference if one of each were standing side by side looking back at us."

"It's worse than you know. You can pay two thousand dollars to breed your best mare to that million-dollar stallion and get a foal you couldn't give away. Or you could buy the stallion, take him home, have him fall down getting out of the trailer, and he's four hundred dollars' worth of dog food. Or you could buy that thousand-dollar gelding and win performance ribbons with him for the next twenty years. Not all the people who gamble on horses are at the race track."

"But you're not quitting, I guess."

"I may quit showing, but I won't sell my horses as long as I can at least get down to the paddock so I can look at them."

The lights went out, except for the dim row down the center. The barn was quieting for a short night's rest. At eight tomorrow Danny would have Breathless ready for her professional debut in the show ring. He had slipped away, and could be heard communing softly with the filly now, and she grumbling softly back. Brit stood, stretched, yawned. "I better see if everyone else is all right for tonight," she said, and walked away.

"What about Brit?" asked Peter. "Are you going to keep her?"

"I can't. She says she's quitting after this show. She wants to think about things. She says she may get out of the horse business altogether."

"But you don't think so?"

"No." Kori yawned hugely. "There are two kinds of people in the world: Those who smell horse and go 'pee-yew,' and those who smell horse and go 'mmmmm.'"

Eleanor stood and put her coffee cup into the wastebasket beside the table. "I'll have to think about things myself before I decide which I am. Thanks for this," she added.

"Come down and see us sometime," invited Kori.

"Maybe. Do you give riding lessons?"

"For you, free. But it's a long haul from here to Charter."

"Maybe not, then. Good night."

"Good night."

Peter stood and leaned forward to inhale deeply in the region of his wife's left ear. "They aren't expecting me back in the squad room until Monday," he murmured. "Let's go to the motel and I'll show you which kind of person I am."